THE SKIPPER'S
DOG'S CALLED
STALIN

ALSO BY DAVID BLACK

Gone to Sea in a Bucket

DAVID BLACK

THE SKIPPER'S DOG'S CALLED STALIN

f THOMAS & MERCER

This is a work of fiction. Names, characters, organizations, places, events, and incidents are either products of the author's imagination or are used fictitiously.

Published by Thomas & Mercer, Seattle

www.apub.com

Amazon, the Amazon logo, and Thomas & Mercer are trademarks of Amazon.com, Inc., or its affiliates.

ISBN-13: 9781612184517
ISBN-10: 1612184510

Cover design by Stuart Bache

Printed in the United States of America

To Mark.

I wouldn't have got the show on the road without you.

Chapter One

Gil Syvret was lounging in a high-backed chair, still astounded by the sheer grandeur of *Durandal*'s wardroom, when the first shot was fired. He'd been in there for most of the evening, at this interminable summit of senior officers gathered from over a dozen or more French warships currently holed up in ports around the English coast. He was sitting at a proper table; behind him, hanging on a wallpapered wall complete with wall lights, was a portrait of the French Navy's Commander-in-Chief. There was also a drinks cabinet in the space, and the table had a tablecloth and something that should never have been there – ashtrays. He just couldn't get his mind round it. *Durandal* was a submarine.

Gil wasn't a senior officer himself, but a mere Lieutenant de Vaisseau. However, his Captain was away, detained on staff duties Gil could only wonder about. But they all lived in troubled times, so Gil was now acting Captain of his submarine, and that was why he was here, in *Durandal*'s wardroom. Aboard his own submarine, all the officers had for a wardroom was a C-shaped cubby off the main passageway; with a banquette and a table top with hollow plinth, which stored a gramophone and other assorted fripperies. And they thought that was luxury, even though the five of them could not all fit in at once. But here . . . here there was enough room for a dozen. More if you squeezed.

There was even room for them all to leap to their feet and push back their chairs, when the shot went off, and then push for the door; for yes, Gil had to remind himself, *this* submarine's wardroom even had a door. And there was shouting coming from beyond it, and not all of it French; a lot of shouting. Gil thought he'd better get up too, although the idea of rushing towards even more bad news tonight was the last thing he felt like doing. He banged his head on one of the deckhead fans as he moved towards the door – a deckhead fan, for Christ's sake! On a submarine!

There was a scrum in the passageway and lots of jostling heads. But, being a particularly tall chap, Gil could just see over the throng, enough to observe the distinctive British tin hats in the control room, and the flash of a bayonet. Two bayonets, no, more, and the instantly recognisable harsh Anglo-Saxon profanities of Royal Marines. The British were in the control room, presumably uninvited.

It had to happen, he thought, sooner or later. That was why that podgy, heavy-lidded Vice Admiral had been here all evening, lecturing them on the *honneur* of the Marine Nationale, and the course they must now all follow if it were to be maintained. A *retired* Vice Admiral, to be precise, so just what he imagined his authority was had been left unsaid. Muselier had been his name. Just off the plane from France, he'd said. Managing to be effusive and jovial as he told them France was throwing in the towel; positively crackling with bonhomie as he insisted that it was now up to them to uphold the honour not only of their service, but of the nation too. Wouldn't shut up, not that Gil had been listening to him. Gil and the boys on his boat – cross-grained, bloody-minded Bretons, poor farm boys from the Charente and the Loire, boys who hadn't wanted to end up down the mines around Lille and had gone to sea instead – had already made up their mind what they were going to do. None of them intended to hang about while Germans marched into their country and made themselves at home.

Gil could speak English and was shoving his way through the press of men before he realised what he was doing. Oh, well, heading for trouble again. One day he'd learn to just stand back. He took in the tableau in an instant. Lying sprawled on the control room deckplates was a Royal Navy Lieutenant, with two RN sailors in their distinctive round caps, wearing webbing belts and revolvers, leaning over their wounded officer.

The officer's face was fish-belly white, apart from the blood spatter on his left cheek; his mouth opening and closing like a fish too, and his eyes rolling. The two sailors were busy trying to pack a wound deep on his shoulder. Back against the chartroom – yes this infernal affront to submarine design had a chartroom too – stood one of *Durandal*'s officers, pinned by a Royal Marine's bayonet pressed against his throat, with another RN officer, a Lieutenant Commander, wrestling and grunting with the Frenchman's right arm, at the end of which was a pistol.

'Let . . . the . . . fucking . . . gun . . . go!' the Lieutenant Commander was incanting slowly in the Frenchman's ear. 'Or I swear to God I'll saw your fucking hand off with this bayonet!' And he brandished it for effect.

Gil translated, sans the Anglo-Saxon. He had to shout above the din of the general bellowing in the compartment, where four other Royal Marines were holding a crush of French sailors at bay with their levelled bayonets. That they could actually level their Lee-Enfield .303s and fixed bayonets in what, in any normal submarine, would have been a very confined space was yet another affront to submarine design.

Gil saw by the panicked swivel of the French officer's eyes that he now understood. After what seemed like an age, he slowly

3

released his grip on the revolver. His RN dance partner took it and released his arm.

'What did you do that for?' The British officer yelled at him, not looking at the Frenchman, but back at his maimed colleague. But the French officer couldn't reply because the Royal Marine's bayonet did not move one fraction from his throat. Gil stepped forward and introduced himself.

'I am Lieutenant de Vaisseau Gil Syvret, of the French Navy submarine *Radegonde*. I speak English. Whom do I have the honour of addressing?'

'By order of His Majesty's government and the Port Admiral, Plymouth, I am now in control of this boat,' said the Lieutenant Commander, staring wildly around him, his statement shouted at no one in particular. He was breathing heavily and clearly quite distressed, thought Gil. Not surprising really, with a badly wounded friend on the deck.

'My dear Lieutenant Commander, if you forgive that I am pointing out the obvious, you have not control over very much of this boat at the moment. Your colleague, however, is disporting himself in wounds on the deck . . .'

'Disporting!' The RN officer turned on him with rage in his eyes.

'Ah,' said Gil, stepping back, hands held open. 'My English. I know perhaps too many words, and not always the right ones for the moment. But I still suggest we all do something to get this young man to medical help proper. Quickly.'

The British officer seemed to gather himself, fixing on Gil: 'My orders are to prevent this boat from sailing back to France, and to secure her. Your crew will be offered repatriation should they choose. But your boat is going nowhere.'

'My dear Sir—' said Gil. But he didn't get any further.

Raising his head and voice the RN officer began bellowing in excruciatingly accented French to the rest of the control room:

'*Nous sommes la marine Britannique! Nous sommes vos camarades!*' We are the British Navy! We are your friends! Which was nice of him to say, thought Gil. Indeed, the words appeared to be instantly greeted with a defusing merriment by *Durandal*'s crew, until the RN officer's tone changed: '*Levez vos mains!*' Hands up! '*Montez! Montez!*' Get up on deck.

Gil only had an instant to think to himself, *stupid rosbif!* before, out of the corner of his eye, he caught one of *Durandal*'s ratings turning to the main electrical board; a flash of white wrist, and the entire control room was in darkness; the sailor had pulled a circuit breaker. One of the Royal Marines had seen him too, and from the sickening meat-thump that followed, a rifle butt must have travelled through the dark to where the sailor had been standing, and connected.

What had been all that rubbish about sailing back to France? No one was going back to France. The Germans were not to have France's Navy. The French Commander-in-Chief, Admiral Darlan, had made that clear. Well, perhaps not *that* clear given the signal that had been received this evening, and which that chatterbox Vice Admiral had been trying to persuade them to ignore.

The Vice Admiral might have got somewhere had he not kept going on about giving their allegiance to that upstart from the army, that ex-Colonel, just promoted to General, called de Gaulle, whom nobody had ever heard of and who kept being allowed on the BBC. If France's Navy hadn't exactly covered itself in glory in this war so far, that could be put down to lack of opportunity. But the army; the army had been humiliated. And now this de Gaulle Johnnie was telling them about saving the honour of France!

The lights came back on and broke Gil's train of thought. There, for all to see, was an RN rating standing at the switchboard now; also, for all to see, were the backs of several French sailors disappearing down the passage, heading aft towards the engine rooms. Everyone was shouting to be heard. The RN Lieutenant Commander turned to Gil, mouthing something. Gil leaned closer.

'We need to . . .' he said.

Gil nodded and turned to grab one of the French Petty Officers out of the press of sailors, shoving him towards the wounded British officer, and gesturing up the hatch. With his other hand he was waving the rest of *Durandal*'s crew back up the passageway leading for'ard.

Where in God's name was *Durandal*'s Captain? Gil had thought it strange he wasn't around when the officers from all the other French warships in Plymouth and elsewhere along the south coast had begun arriving, but assumed he would turn up later. He hadn't and now Gil was cursing him. He should be here to take command of his vessel, because everything was starting to happen very fast.

The yelling RN Lieutenant Commander – gun in hand – was disappearing after the French sailors who were heading for the engine rooms; the matelots still in the control room were struggling to get the wounded British officer to the bridge ladder, on which two blue-serge legs shod in wellingtons had just appeared, coming down.

The French Navy's order of battle described *Durandal* as a 'Submarine Battlecruiser' – over 90 metres long, almost 9 metres in beam and nearly 3,000 tons, with a 305mm gun sunk for'ard into her commodious bridge, and at the back, a hangar for a tiny Besson MB411 floatplane. She was a big boat by anyone's standards. Every compartment was roomy, and there were passageways where sailors could actually pass. She was the most ridiculous thing Gil had ever seen, especially when compared to his 65-metre-long *Radegonde*, with her mere four main torpedo tubes and two piddlers on the stern and a single 75mm deck gun; altogether weighing in at a puny 780 tons.

The two legs shod in wellingtons turned out to be a new RN officer, a Commander this time. Armed RN ratings were following him. Gil faced up to the bewhiskered new arrival; an older man who was obviously angry, rather than alarmed.

'We need to calm this down, Sir. Now,' Gil said.

'Unimprovably put, M'sieur. Couldn't agree more,' said the RN Commander as he took in the scene. 'Are you in command here?'

But before Gil could answer, more shots rang out. Gil's eyes rolled; what in God's name were these idiots doing? There was rapid fire and a lot of pinging as rounds rattled off steel bulkheads and fittings. A deckhead lamp disintegrated; glass tinkled and then there was a scream. Gil was at the aft passageway door when another round whistled past his face. He felt the draught of it. He leaned out again and could see the RN Lieutenant Commander; the one who'd run down the passage a moment earlier. Except now he was kneeling on the deck, swaying, with one leg bent under him and blood beginning to puddle; another body lay further on – a French sailor, trying to rise on all fours as if to crawl. And further beyond, a watertight door was shutting and being dogged.

Gil spun round, and ran back into the control room, his arms outstretched . . . *Outstretched? On a submarine?* . . . to corral the remaining French crew there.

'Enough!' he shouted. 'Enough! That's an order. Stop!'

And as if they'd just been waiting for someone to tell them so, they did. The calm, like the snap of a finger, was followed by the RN Commander gesturing to his sailors and the Marines to lower their weapons. In the swift silence, the distant gurgling of water and the trilling of a sound-powered telephone on the control room bulkhead came all at once. Gil stepped to pick up the handset, his eyes seeking out several of *Durandal's* own officers as he moved. Despite the conspicuous absence of their Captain, none of them showed any inclination to step in.

'Control room,' he snapped.

'Engine room,' came the clipped reply. Gil listened then answered, purposefully not looking at the RN Commander. 'He doesn't speak French,' Gil said in French.

But the arch of the Commander's eyebrows showed that he did. Gil continued to listen, his heart sinking; then he held the handset to his chest.

'The crew aft say they cannot allow you to take over the boat,' he told the Commander. 'For the honour of France. Etcetera. They've . . . how do you say? . . . "Opened the sea-cocks". They're flooding the boat from the engine room pumps . . .'

The Commander heard Gil out, then began issuing orders to his men. The injured RN officer had already been lifted out, the other wounded were to go next, then the French crew should be invited to follow. Those latter orders the Commander addressed directly in clipped French that did not actually murder the language like most rosbifs. Then he instructed another newly arrived junior RN officer to shut the aft control room watertight door and secure it. The order effectively sealed the boat aft, isolating everyone in there. It could not be opened again from the other side. Only when all was in movement, did the Commander turn back to Gil.

'Tell your chap in the engine room, the Royal Navy says, "suit yourself".' And he leaned under the tower hatch and called up, 'Secure the aft escape hatch!' Then, pointing to the upper deck, he gestured to Gil. 'After you.'

Gil understood now what the Commander intended. If the *Durandal*'s crew were going to sink her, this Royal Navy officer was going to make sure they sank along with her. Well, at least that was the Royal Navy he knew; simple solutions to even the most complex problems. But Gil couldn't just stand by and let his fellow country-men drown because of their own stubbornness.

The Commander was gazing around the vast control room, with its space enough for spit and polish, and room for everything to be installed with the luxury of fine lines and neatness. Then, as if he'd just noticed Gil, and that they were the only ones left, he turned and smiled. In the silence you could hear the harbour water rushing in; rising steadily up from the bilges to flood the boat.

'Where's her Skipper?' asked the Commander, in French.

'Conspicuous by his absence,' replied Gil tartly, digging out a packet of cigarettes and offering one to the Commander. The Commander scowled with a mixture of amazement and concern.

'I thought French submarines were . . .' he said.

Syvret interrupted, '. . . were no smoking. Because, unlike Royal Navy submarines, we have open battery cells, that might leak hydrogen; and naked flame and hydrogen do not mix . . . or rather, mix too well.'

'Well, yes,' said the Commander.

'Oh, it's all innovation here on *Durandal*, Commander. Battery tops and everything.'

The Commander smiled. 'We'll give the crew to the last possible moment,' he said, eyeing a tiny lip of water creeping over the edge of the deckplates. Someone must have opened up the watertight bulkhead's bilge valves. 'Even if it means I end up ruining my shoes,' he added before pausing to look around *Durandal*'s control room again: 'We've had a few fanciful death traps like this 'un in the trade too, you know.'

The trade; the name the Royal Navy's submarine service gave itself. So this man really was a submariner, just like him.

'Who thinks them up, Lieutenant, eh?' the RN Commander continued. 'Not chaps like us.'

While they waited for the engine room crew to come to their senses, Gil didn't need to wonder how his new friend would have reacted to meeting *Durandal*'s Skipper. Capitaine de Vaisseau

Antoine Boudron de Vatry was a high flyer in the Marine Nationale, and Gil knew him by reputation. He might have been about the same age as Gil, but his light shone far more brightly; indeed, he had already acquired a certain notoriety within the fleet, as even young men can achieve if they attach themselves to the right faction. Which made it easy for Gil to guess why Capitaine de Vatry wouldn't have wanted to be around, if he knew, or even suspected, his command was about to be taken over by the British. He wouldn't want such a taint on his reputation. It wouldn't look good for a man who intended to continue his self-advancement under the new Vichy order, to have surrendered his command to the British. But there was another reason why the RN Commander wouldn't like the Skipper very much. Boudron de Vatry, as anyone in the Marine Nationale could have told you, was perfectly content with who had just won the Battle of France.

Leaning by the chart table, Gil registered the time and date. He wanted to remember this night; not realising then that this date would be burned into his memory forever, not by what was happening here, but by other events, far away.

It was the early hours of 3 July, 1940, and 2,500 kilometres to the south, a Royal Navy squadron was steaming off the Algerian coast outside the French naval base of Mers el-Kebir, preparing to decide the future of the French fleet in a far less merciful fashion than this RN Commander.

Chapter Two

Lieutenant Commander Purkiss's desk was at the bay window end of a drawing room in a converted Victorian mansion overlooking the River Tay above Dundee's bustling docks. Sleet slathered the window in sluggish wind-streaked rivers so that as he stood looking out, he could see nothing of the Fife coast across the slate-grey Tay, and barely the Eastern Wharf below, where the dockyard part of HMS *Ambrose* nestled.

HMS *Ambrose*, the Royal Navy's shore establishment in Dundee, served the nation's war effort through a variety of functions, one of them being home to an ad hoc, scraped-together collection of refugee submarines from several now-defeated Allies, now known as the Ninth Flotilla. Lieutenant Commander Purkiss was the base's second-in-command, and usually he saw to it that he had as little as possible to do with those wretched submariners. Today, unfortunately, events had conspired against him. He struck a heroic pose in an attempt to shrug off his gathering gloom, while the two Wrens who typed and 'did' for him, looked up from their adjoining desks at his unimpressive back and shiny pate, and sniggered to each other. For Lieutenant Commander Purkiss was not heroic; he was, at heart, exactly what he looked like – 'something in insurance'.

The only reason he was here now, in his blue suit and two and a half rings, was because of his earlier, largely failed, career in an earlier Royal Navy. As a boy, as the war clouds had gathered over Europe in 1914, he had emerged from the Royal Naval College, Osborne, a fully fledged 'snotty', or as known more formally, a Midshipman. Along with nearly all his classmates, he went straight into the gunroom of a dreadnought battleship and remained there for the entire Great War; part of the Grand Fleet, anchored between the gale-swept, treeless islands of the Orkney Islands' Scapa Flow.

Four long years – the finest of his youth – marooned in a base that had begun life with one landing jetty and one peat-rutted football pitch to entertain over 40,000 sailors. The war had done little to improve its aspect and the battleship remained a universe away from any city street, bar or dance hall. Aberdeen was over 200 miles south and all the young Purkiss had had to look out over was a land and seascape where it was either raining or about to rain; a place where the only break with tedium was coaling the giant warships, or the very rare sorties to sea. Even when his ship had taken part in the Battle of Jutland in 1916, so far had been his battle squadron from the van of the fleet, he only discovered he'd been in a battle after they'd returned to the anchorage and the crew of a passing pinnace shouted it through the gunroom scuttle. The only time he ever saw a German warship was when the High Seas Fleet sailed into Scapa to be interned in 1919, long after the armistice had been signed.

A year later, Purkiss was retired from the Fleet, no longer required by an ungrateful nation. So he'd boarded a train to Cheltenham where he took to clerking like a natural, married a nice girl and settled down to cultivate his narrow view of a hostile world and nurture his permanent state of irritation. Indeed, no one could have been more irritated by the fact that the Great War, the so-called war to end all wars, hadn't at all lived up to its claim. And now here he was, dragged into another one; dragged from his comfortable Cheltenham fireside, his wife and compliant, near grown-up children, and with only an extra one and a half rings for his trouble. And that was why, in these, the closing days of February 1941, the only comfort he felt left to him was to wallow energetically in self-pity and a relentless mealy-mouthed gloom, the comic bathos of which provided the only entertainment for his two Wrens in their otherwise tedious tasks.

And on top of it all, there was the bloody knock on his door that he'd been expecting.

'Come!' he barked, causing the girls to simper once more.

The door opened and in stepped an RNVR Sub-Lieutenant, cap on, and gas-mask bag and tin hat slung shoulder to hip over his No. 1 jacket. He was a tallish lad, neatly turned out, still full of the blandness of youth, thought Purkiss. Another child sent to try me. And he didn't half look a bit pale. Surely not a sickly child to boot! The two young Wrens, on the other hand, saw nothing bland about him at all. Their eyebrows shot up in choreographed appreciation of this rather fetching young Turk who, even before he'd opened his mouth, had managed to brighten their day.

'Gilmour, Sir,' he said, coming to attention, but not, thankfully, trying to salute him. At least he knows that much, thought Purkiss, who would have been unable to return the salute as he wasn't wearing his cap. 'I was told to report to you by the dock office, Sir,' continued the young man. 'To present my papers. I am appointed Liaison Officer to the Free French submarine *Radegonde*.'

A cloud of deeper gloom descended on Purkiss at the mention of the submarine's name. He walked over to his desk and sat down, then, almost as an afterthought, gestured to Harry Gilmour to sit also.

'Well, your submarine is here all right, Mr Gilmour,' said Purkiss, hands splayed over his empty desk. 'We've been expecting you. Well, someone at least', and then he changed his tone to something more imperious. '*Radegonde*'s books!' he said.

It took a moment for Harry to realise Purkiss was talking to the Wrens. At the edge of his vision Harry was aware that one of the trim girls in uniform had shot up and was retrieving something from a metal filing cabinet. The entire room seemed in thrall to the timeless clack and silence of eternal bureaucracy. Purkiss's fingers drummed lightly. When Harry managed to raise his eyes from them he was suddenly aware that Purkiss had been staring at him, his eyebrows in a questioning arch. In a fluster, Harry reached into his gas-mask bag.

'Ah, yes, sorry, Sir. My, ah, orders, ah. Mmm . . .' – rummage, rummage – '. . . here they are!' And Harry produced an envelope.

The Wren arrived with documents, and Harry handed over his. Purkiss began his perusals. Slips of paper were passed to Harry, with a 'sign these'. Finally his orders were returned for handing on to *Radegonde*'s Captain. Purkiss sat back with the air of a man who'd just completed a job well done. But it didn't last. His face clouded over again. There was something on his mind. Something, Purkiss reflected to himself, very serious indeed. He began.

'Your submarine is in dockyard hands at the moment,' he said. 'She's having some new boffin-box fitted . . . you'll still have to join her right away, though. Regardless of what mess she's in. It's all very inconvenient. Meanwhile, there's a matter of some urgency for you to sort out. I have no idea how you are supposed to do it, but sort it out you will. Do I make myself clear?'

Not in the slightest, thought Harry. But Harry these days was too weary, too dazed, to fight back. He smiled a compliant smile. Purkiss's frown deepened.

'There is no one to do a handover with you,' said Purkiss in a tone that said this was entirely someone else's fault. 'Your predecessor' – the latter word sneered – 'did not see fit to remain with the submarine until you arrived. They docked and he was down the gangway and off to Dundee West railway station. Neither us, nor his Commander (S), received his personal report. He also left outstanding a matter of even greater gravity. He has not returned *Radegonde*'s Confidential Books. I want them back in my safe this afternoon!'

'Where are they, Sir?' asked Harry, affecting keenness.

Purkiss eyed him, as if assessing whether he was being made sport of.

'You do know what Confidential Books are?'

Of course Harry did. But Purkiss was going to tell him anyway.

'They contain all the codes and ciphers and call-signs, recognition signals of the day, emergency procedures in case of emergency events . . . for the entire fleet . . . everything a German agent or Fifth Columnist could ever dream of . . . They can only ever be in one of two places. In the custody of a duly appointed and read-in Liaison Officer, or in that locked cupboard over there.' Purkiss gestured, irritated, to an ungainly dark-wood, wardrobe-like edifice against the back wall. 'They're in neither,' he said.

'They've been lost, Sir?' asked Harry, wondering what he was expected to do about it. This was a goad too far for Purkiss. And when he got angry, his voice became squeaky. He knew it, and that *really* irritated him even more.

'Confidential Books are not *allowed* to be *lost*, Sub-Lieutenant!' he squeaked. The Wrens simpered behind their typewriters. Harry looked shocked. 'They are in a place where they are not permitted to be,' Purkiss continued. 'You are ordered to ascertain that place, retrieve them and return them to me for safekeeping until *Radegonde* is ready to return to sea. Do I make myself clear?'

'Aye aye, Sir!' said Harry.

'Well . . .?'

'Yessir. Sir. If you could tell me where . . .?

'I don't keep little drawings of where every ship in the dockyard is located, Sub-Lieutenant. Ask at the dock office.'

'Who should I ask for? Her Captain? First Lieutenant? Do you have a name?'

Purkiss glared at this impertinence, unable to speak. Even through his fatigue, Harry, a sea-going, fighting officer, was getting a bit pissed off with this desk-bound oaf, even if he was a Lieutenant Commander.

'And the boat, Sir? What about the boat?' he persisted, goading him now. 'What do I need to know?'

'Need to know, Sub-Lieutenant?' A pause, to let the sneer in his voice sink in. 'Her CO is called Syvret. He keeps a pet dog on board. And he calls it Stalin. That should tell you all you need to *know* about *Radegonde*. You are dismissed, Sub-Lieutenant. And remember: this afternoon!'

Sub-Lieutenant Harry Gilmour RNVR – Royal Naval Volunteer Reserve – was still a bit of a rare beast even in the early months of 1941. A Royal Navy officer, who wasn't entirely Royal Navy; not quite your proper Andrew – which was, as Harry had learned, service slang for the service. The fact that you were 'Volunteer Reserve', and your officer's gold braid rings on the ends of your sleeves were wavy and not solid; it all meant you weren't proper RN, you were RNVR; a wartime expedient, an experiment. Officers recruited for hostilities only. No career path through Britannia Royal Naval College at Dartmouth; no steeping in all its attendant arcane traditions and lore.

The RNVR boys were the sausage meat in a sausage machine; a naval production line that fed civvy landlubbers into a converted Leisure Centre on the promenade at Hove, now miraculously transformed into an officer factory by the simple act of changing its name to HMS *King Alfred*; a place for manufacturing fighting sailors to feed a Fleet greedy for manpower as it hastily made up its numbers to meet the Hun.

They hadn't actually swamped the senior service yet, but more and more were coming through. Bit of a bloody shower actually, if you'd asked any of the proper chaps. But, most of the more intelligent ones would have conceded, a necessary evil. If you were going to man a fleet expanding at a rate never before seen in its history, then you were going to have to get the blokes to man it, and not be too particular about it. The new boys would learn in time. They'd have to! But nobody should kid themselves they'd ever be proper Andrew.

So that was Harry. In, but not in; neither fish nor fowl. And as long as he sported those wavy rings, there would always be someone there to remind him.

But the wavy rings were out of sight, beneath a tightly buckled navy blue trench coat, when Lieutenant de Vaisseau Gil Syvret first set eyes on Harry, striding out down that miserable Dundee quayside in the slanting sleet, his gas-mask bag slung athwartships, lugging a not particularly bulky kit bag, and with a pair of what looked like Eskimo boots dangling down from around his neck.

Syvret was leaning over the bridge of his command, the Free French submarine *Radegonde,* scanning through the grey murk, up and down the bustle of the dock looking for that laggard, flat-capped worker they'd sent to hunt down the latest forgotten component for the new box of tricks that was currently being bolted into his control room.

And there was Harry, coming round the crane, weaving past a mound of scrap cable being added to by a gang of labourers with a rusty wheelbarrow who had hauled it off a rusted, ancient-looking minesweeper undergoing her refit on the adjacent berth. Harry was making a beeline through all that chaos of industry, directly for him. His new LO – Liaison Officer.

Oh god, oh god, thought Syvret, *not like the last one, please.*

17

His contemplation was disturbed by a discordant and screaming roar of aero engines. He looked west up the Tay and, coming over the rail bridge, he saw a twin-engined job – obviously a Jerry – and a smaller, single-engine fighter chasing it. They were out over the river, and the Jerry was jinking, engines racing.

Everyone on the dock stopped to look. There had been no air-raid warning, so bizarrely, no one was taking cover. The two aircraft looked joined, as if one was towing the other, as they swept low down the river, at less than 100 feet, Syvret estimated, over the coast heading for Claypotts Castle and were lost. Seconds passed. And then the distinctive *tacka-tacka-tacka* of machine guns echoed back. *The fighter pilot; he's waited until they've cleared the town before he's opened up*, thought Syvret. *They are such gentlemen, the British.*

When he looked down, the new LO was standing at *Radegonde*'s gangway, looking up, obviously waiting for permission to come aboard. *See, I told you so!* Syvret said to himself with a smile. 'You are my new Liaison Officer, I must take it. Come aboard, please,' he shouted down to Harry.

Introductions made, kit stowed, Harry sat with his new Skipper, each with a glass of red wine before them, in the submarine's wardroom. The layout was similar to Harry's last boat; an alcove set off the main passageway, but smaller and more homely. Harry didn't realise at this point that there was more room for fripperies because *Radegonde*'s officers had their own tiny cabins, two to a berth for the junior ones and a single for their Captain – a luxury unheard of on a Royal Navy submarine. Other luxuries included a secure rack for wine glasses, a small wooden keg that held brandy, several crudely framed sketches that were neither fine art nor cartoon, and other souvenirs of foreign ports, including a Reichsmarine sailor's cap, with a cap band that read *Emden*, hanging from a light fitting. The other thing Harry noted was that, on first appraisal, the entire boat appeared less cluttered, less of a cat's cradle of pipework and cable-runs, than British boats; and cleaner too.

Harry's musings were interrupted.

'So it was a Junkers 88 being chased by a Spitfire,' said Syvret. 'You know these things.'

'I'm a walking recognition chart, Sir,' Harry replied with that lopsided smile Syvret was already coming to recognise even on such a short acquaintance. 'Can't help it. Some chaps had a misspent youth, me; I . . . well, you know. I was never any good at cards.'

Shy, thought Syvret, *which is already a head start on the last one, hence all the facial contortions. And I particularly like the 'had', as in his relative youth. It shows you're optimistic. Christ! You're still just a teenager. And if you're not, it's only by a matter of days.*

In the pause, Harry added, 'Anyone would think there was a war on, Skipper.'

'Captain,' said Syvret. 'I am the Captain, not the Skipper.'

But Syvret's thoughts weren't so severe; he was just making sure his new LO knew his place, remembering the last one.

'Sorry, Sir,' said Harry, a little mortified and showing it.

Definitely shy, thought Syvret, smiling to himself. *And the grin; am I going to get used to it or is it going to make me want to kill him?* But there were other things Syvret was seeing. This Harry Gilmour might be a boy, but he was a boy who'd been in a fight. Syvret could tell. You always could with the ones who'd actually been to war. There was something a bit knocked sideways about them. They'd been somewhere others hadn't, and to greater or lesser extents, were still on their way back; as if they'd been knocked off course and had still to apply a touch of corrective helm, and maybe rebox their compass.

And what did Harry see? Certainly, a more mature man than himself; and one as handsome as his own father, but with a more hawk-like, European mien to him. Harry could imagine him a knight in the host of Charlemagne. Dark, with tight curls, and a skin pale, not olive, yet still exotic. And the eyes. Young men Harry's age don't recognise the colour of other men's eyes, but if they are observant, they sense what's behind them. But with this one, Harry saw nothing but a surface calm, flat as flat can be. Instinctively, Harry found himself liking him for no reason he could fathom. It was disconcerting.

'And you are an experienced submariner . . . who speaks French?' asked Syvret, raising his glass to Harry, with a smile, and taking another sip.

'Yes, Sir,' Harry replied, reluctant to expand on that. If asked, he'd have to stop and think about the number of war patrols he'd completed, and he was too tired to contemplate trying to explain that his first boat had been sunk with him it; or that his last had been battered into a crumpled, limping wreck by German depth charges, and that she was in a dry dock somewhere, with someone probably still trying to decide whether to repair her or just break her up for spares.

'We don't get many experienced submariners,' said Syvret. 'Linguists, yes, but they tend to be a rag-bag. Your detritus? Is that the word? Your experienced officers, they tend to go into your own boats.'

Harry affected a look of distraction, as if thinking hard, then smiled the smile: '*Radegonde*,' he said, 'as in Radegonde of Poitiers, the sixth century Frankish Queen and later nun. St Radegonde even. Did you know she has a connection to England?'

Syvret quietly admired the way the youth had dodged the subject. 'Really,' he said with all the insouciance he could muster – which was considerable.

'Indeed,' said Harry, smiling, 'she is a patron saint of Jesus College, Cambridge. Cambridge University, you'll have heard of it?'

'*Oui*. One of your arriviste seats of learning,' said Syvret, squint-ing at Harry. 'Why do you carry an Eskimo's boots?'

'They're flying boots, Sir. RAF. To keep my feet warm on watch.'

Syvret's eyes arched involuntarily. *No mere Liaison Officer is ever going to stand a watch on my boat*, Syvret said to himself. But to Harry he said, 'You look very tired, Mr Gilmour. Have you travelled far today?'

'No, not far,' said Harry.

Only from Inverness, where he had spent the last few weeks at the new Raigmore Hospital, recovering from wounds. But Harry didn't say that. Nor did he say that he had arrived in Dundee into mayhem.

When he had first reported to the HMS *Ambrose* staff office that morning, he had been assigned shore accommodation at an evacuated orphanage in the town called Carolina House, but when he'd turned up at the rambling Victorian pile, he wasn't allowed to 'take possession' of his cabin – which was the navy way of saying room, because in the navy everything is on a ship, even if the ship is bricks and mortar. The floor is the deck; the toilet, the heads; and the rooms, cabins. It wasn't that his cabin wasn't ready; it was free all right, but in his rush to the station, Harry's predecessor hadn't signed out, so the room was still technically occupied. When Harry had tried again, after his interview with Lieutenant Commander Purkiss, they still wouldn't let him in. He was truculently informed by a Regulating Petty Officer, with a pinched nose, razor rash and a cap skip bent to all but cover his eyes, that his predecessor '. . . hesn't ach-elly, offish-ly, *left* . . . Suh!'

Harry had reached in the Petty Officer's little cubby for the cabin's numbered key, which had been very obviously left hanging on the Petty Officer's very regular numbered key rack, and snatched it up before the Petty Officer could stop him. Harry then stamped up the stairs with the Petty Officer, who looked twice Harry's age, stumbling after him, yelling in as respectful a fashion as possible while still managing to include swear words and threats.

When Harry reached the cabin door, he paused and turned to look directly into the Petty Officer's now puce face, which was insubordinately close to his own and said softly, 'Petty Officer, you have no idea how much I hope you are actually going to lay a hand on me . . .' Because as they both knew, actually striking an officer would take this little farce to a new level.

The Petty Officer had leapt back as if he had been struck and Harry had opened the door and let himself in. Before he'd unpacked, he'd searched the room. There was not even a hint of a Confidential Book to be found. Bugger!

So he had returned to the HMS *Ambrose* offices, managed to buttonhole one of Purkiss's Wrens and got her to point out any nook or cranny where that last bloody Liaison Officer might have dallied, frequented or skulked in, and he searched some more. Still nothing.

When he had returned to Carolina House, the Petty Officer had summoned the Shore Patrol. By then, Harry was too tired to fight his eviction. And so now he was aboard *Radegonde*, with all he possessed and nowhere else to go and time on his hands to contemplate his impending reprimand – or even Court Martial – over the loss of the Confidential Papers. Papers, according to Purkiss, that were so secret that even the fact they were secret was a secret; and so vital to the war effort, that if they were not accounted for, the war would be lost. The residue of civilian logic still left to Harry, led him to wonder why such critical documentation should have been allowed to become the responsibility of a mere LO, especially an LO who'd never even clapped eyes on them in the first place, let alone had them in his possession. But then that was life in a blue suit, wasn't it?

He was now officially at a loss as to what to do. He could always ask his new Skipper, but for all that Harry found him likable, the last thing he wanted to do was to inquire as to the whereabouts of the boat's most top-secret documentation, especially as Harry was supposed to be the man in charge of it. It wasn't the way you went about making a good impression on your new CO.

Syvret was still looking at him. Then in a sudden movement, he poured Harry another glass and swept his own away.

'We are at twelve hours' notice to sail,' said Syvret, 'even though your dockyard Johnnies are still wiring up that new jukebox for our entertainment. There are things I have to attend to. So I will leave it until later to introduce you to the boat and her crew, and your two Royal Navy signallers who you will work with.' Then gesturing to the wine, he added, 'Drink that and then get your head down on the bunk.' This time the gesture was to the banquette where Harry was sitting. 'I'm afraid it will be where you will be sleeping anyway. It's all the room we have for you. Don't worry if it is too short. See that little panel at the end . . . take it out, that is where your feet will go.'

Harry turned round. It looked bloody comfortable compared to the fold-down shelf he had on *Trebuchet*. The *condemned man had a good night's sleep*, he thought, and reached to remove the panel. 'What do you keep in here?' he asked.

'Your predecessor used it for his kit,' said Syvret. '*À bientôt*. I'll see you later, for dinner.' And he was gone.

Harry looked in the little cupboard. And there were the Confidential Books.

Chapter Three

Harry was leaning in the lee of *Radegonde*'s periscope stands, staring into a pitch black night, seeded with sleet. Beneath his feet, Harry could feel her punch and buffet into a sea running from the northeast. The periscope stands shielded him from the worst of the wind, and hid him from the hunched figures of Syvret and the two lookouts. One of the first things Harry had noticed about *Radegonde* was how big her conning tower arrangement was, and right now he was taking advantage of that size for a last intake of privacy.

Somewhere out there to port in the black, wet murk was Montrose, or so Harry calculated from his last look at the chart, and the time they'd been running. It was almost 21:00 hours and *Radegonde* had sailed some two hours previously, on a patrol to Norwegian waters that would last three weeks. They would lay a new minefield on the approaches to Bergen, then engage in what Syvret referred to as a spot of *vandalisme* – and what his orders described as attacks on 'targets of opportunity' among Norwegian coastal traffic.

The final loading of stores before they sailed had resembled a medieval fayre, despite the sleet and rain and wind. Sodden boxes spilling tins, bread panniers shielded by rubber macs, vegetables of all descriptions, and entire hams – a sight no longer seen in British butchers – and spares for the engineers and electricians to squirrel away. All of it being wrestled by scrums of sailors, both British and French, who had swapped caps: *les matelots* wearing flat black pill boxes, and Jacks (the name the British lower decks gave themselves) sporting red pom-poms – all done more in a spirit of anarchy than fraternity; to confuse the officers, rather than because they loved each other. And because wild anarchy seemed to follow the French sailors at times like this in a way their Royal Navy comrades seemed to envy.

The air was blue with bilingual obscenities, as they had man-handled *Radegonde's* stores down a single plank and into the bowels of the boat through the forward torpedo hatch. It had been like a scene from Hieronymus Bosch. In Harry's experience, storing a British boat had always been a bit like organised chaos, but this had been an affront. You weren't meant to *enjoy* it! But they did things differently in la Marine Nationale, apparently.

Less than three days ago, Harry had been sitting in a wicker chair in Raigmore Hospital, looking out through rain-streaked windows at the endless ranks of huts, listening to the wild tales of Hank the Yank – an American ferry pilot. Hank had flown a Lockheed Hudson destined for the RAF all the way from Gander, but his last leg from the Faroes to Dyce had ended up crumpled at the end of the runway.

Hank the Yank, whose femur was healing nicely, as were the sundry gashes on his head, entertained the recovering wounded with his wild tales of 'over there'. The United States of America; a place at peace, where you could still buy bananas and nylons and chocolate, and could walk home at night without fear of falling in a hole because the street lights were still on. Hank the Yank, hot-foot from the land of plenty, flying in the weapons the Brits needed to keep fighting the war. Nobody believed half of what Hank the

25

Yank told them, of course. But he was larger than life, and nobody had ever met a Yank before, and his good fun was infectious. He stopped the men from dwelling on how they'd ended up in hospital, or on their mates who hadn't.

Hank would be home by now, and Harry was back in the war. Not that Harry was complaining. He'd volunteered after all.

At night in the hospital, when the nurse closed the blackout curtains, and Harry looked into the dark, he could still see his nineteen-year-old self walking into that recruiting office in Glasgow, his head full of dreams of adventure. Just seventeen months ago.

The navigating officer on his first boat had once told Harry, 'A lot can happen in a submarine in six minutes.' Lieutenant McVeigh had been his name and Harry wanted to ask him now, 'If a lot can happen in six minutes, what can happen in seventeen months?' But he couldn't. No one would be asking Lieutenant McVeigh anything anymore.

And now here was Harry on a French submarine, three months short of his twenty-first birthday, coming to terms with the fact that he might not live to see it. 'A lot can happen . . .' as Lieutenant McVeigh said. He wondered what life aboard *Radegonde* was going to be like.

⌣

At the change of watch, Syvret called Harry down to dinner in *Radegonde*'s tiny wardroom. This was going to be Harry's first meal aboard. He'd now met all the officers separately, but never en masse. He'd even met Stalin, a terrier of some indeterminate breed with a disturbingly taciturn nature, except when, as Harry had discovered, he came within scenting distance of the dockyard cat. Then he had displayed the most alarming turn of speed. Another unusual thing Harry noticed about the little black, brown and white beast was that so far he had not heard him bark. Harry was settling in on the banquette when he noticed that Stalin was joining them for dinner.

Syvret sat at the aft end of the banquette, and Harry sat on what was his bed, to Syvret's right, Stalin perched on the corner between them. Next to Harry was Enseigne de Vaisseau Claude Le Breuil, the gunnery and torpedo officer, the equivalent to an RN Sub-Lieutenant, the same rank as Harry. Next to him, facing back towards the Skipper, Enseigne de Vaisseau Henri Bassano, the navigator. Opposite Harry and Le Breuil was Philippe Faujanet, the Aspirant, or as the RN would've had it, the Midshipman, sitting on a tiny three-legged stool because there was no more room for him on the banquette. The First Lieutenant, Armand Poulenc, was on the bridge, on watch.

If anything, the wardroom was even cosier than the one Harry remembered on his last boat. He was particularly taken by the deck-head lights with their little etched glass shades instead of the regulation cages. The other thing that struck Harry was that the lamps were ordinary and not red. This was a war patrol. On a Royal Navy boat, proceeding on the surface at night, they would have been sitting in red light to preserve their night vision in case they were needed on the bridge. Urgently. Instead, everything was as warm and intimate as a Paris bistro. But nobody, least of all the Skipper, seemed particularly worried.

So Harry decided not to worry either. After all, he had a full glass of red wine, like everyone else, and a very nice wine too, Harry concluded. Not like the vinegar served by his university tutors at their obligatory bohemian at-homes, along with hacked lumps of crumbly cheddar just to round off the salon effect. But Harry didn't comment, in case he revealed himself for the ingénue he was, at this worldly soirée.

The food, when it arrived, was served by a matelot of indeterminate rank in an immaculate blue-and-white-striped singlet,

27

with more grease on his slicked-back hair than was in the dish, and whose olive skin seemed to glisten.

A seamless babble of French fired back and forth across the table. Bassano, who was of an age with the Captain, reminded Harry of that American actor in that fish-out-of-water Hollywood comedy from a couple of years ago; what had it been called? *A Yank at Oxford*. And Robert Taylor had been his name. Like him, Bassano was dark and Mediterranean, and his features all Vs and points: his pointy jet-black widow's peak, the angular nose and the way his mouth came together. And his voice, which seemed to come from way down inside. Not that he said that much, but when he did, he was more considered. His words meant something, unlike the other two junior officers, who were but youths.

Le Breuil, although he must have been about the same age as Harry, struck Harry as being much younger. He was a dapper, dandyish sort of boy, who had not as yet troubled a razor. And there was something else Harry couldn't help but notice since setting foot aboard *Radegonde*: Le Breuil insisted every second day that the matelot who served as wardroom steward trim his rich golden locks, snip by tiny snip, on the banquette where Harry had to sleep. And he could be quite petulant when criticised, or wasn't getting his way.

The other youth, Faujanet, the Aspirant, should still have been in school. He reminded Harry of the Tigger, the junior torpedo and gunnery officer from Harry's last boat; last heard of still in the hospital at Haslar recovering from the wounds he'd received in that Russian fjord, when their Skipper had decided to take on an entire Jerry invasion force. That lifetime ago. The French youth had the same unformed face, and a shock of hair Harry's grandmother would have described as 'straw hanging out a midden', and the same untroubled countenance. He also had a barely tenuous grasp on what Harry would have described as naval discipline. If he ever needed to amuse himself, Harry only had to wonder what the battleship officers he'd served under, and who'd found him such an affront, would have made of M. Faujanet. But Harry wasn't on a battleship anymore; nor even on a Royal Navy warship. He was here, on a French submarine.

His appointment to *Radegonde* had been based on his claim to be able to converse in French, and right now that skill could just about allow him to discern the talk was nearly all shop, but he was buggered if he could keep up with the staccato barrage of words that ran together too fast for him to follow.

The matelot in the striped jersey flourished an enamel basin that looked knocked off from a barbers' shop, like he was a George Cinq maître d'.

Syvret turned to Harry. 'Our chef,' he said in English. 'You are in for a treat.'

The basin was full of a dizzyingly aromatic lamb shank cooked à la Lyonnaise. Two army mess tins of potato dauphinoise followed. The officers barely stopped talking as they began shovelling the food on to their plates and then into their mouths. There was no ceremony or etiquette. This was like no wardroom table Harry had ever sat at. They only stopped talking to gulp the wine, which, admittedly, was very gulpable.

Only Faujanet was ever interrupted – by sailors needing to squeeze past along the passageway. But if he minded repeatedly having to get up, grab his stool and go back into his own cabin space, he didn't show it.

Syvret fed Stalin the occasional morsel, and Stalin stared, almost without blinking at Harry. The food was sublime.

When it was finished – and the plates and basin had been cleared with bistro deftness by the chef – the Captain and Bassano, in one practised movement, lifted their table up and Le Breuil leaned into a space in its plinth and produced a wind-up gramophone. The table was replaced and the Skipper leaned behind him to produce a clutch of acetate 78s. More wine was poured and then everybody stared at Harry as if to say, *Well, what are you doing here?*

'You won't have much to do aboard *Radegonde*,' a distracted Captain (S) had told Harry a few hours before they'd sailed. The (S) stood for 'submarines', indicating that the sprightly, well-laundered fifty-something was in command of the joint Allied Submarine Flotilla. He'd lost no time in guiding Harry back to the door of his office after he'd handed over his orders.

'The job's simple. Look after all the charts, monitor all the radio traffic, do all the encoding and decoding, and make sure their Skipper only goes where he's supposed to . . . keep him out of the way of the RAF . . . and generally get on with our French allies and reassure them they're doing a splendid job for the war effort.' In other words, he was telling Harry, *I'm busy, get on with it.*

Despite the sleet the Captain (S) had come down to the quay-side to see *Radegonde* off. But then, as Harry already knew, that was what a Captain (S) was supposed to do. Harry wasn't impressed, but he didn't mention any of that to his new shipmates who were look-ing expectantly at him now.

'I didn't realise *Radegonde* was a minelaying submarine when I was appointed,' Harry said, in French, to break the impasse. 'A tricky job, is it? Laying mines?'

The Skipper pouted noncommittally. Le Breuil nodded sagely, and said in English, 'Of course.' Faujanet's face scrunched a little and his shoulders rocked. Stalin kept staring at Harry.

'I'll be staying out of your way when you're doing it, of course,' added Harry.

Faujanet's eyes positively glittered with something, so that he had to look away.

Le Breuil said, 'Of course', again. In English. Sonorously.

There was a pause while everyone considered this. Then the Skipper said, smiling warmly all the while at Harry: 'We used to have a very efficient laying system and very good mines. But we ran out of French mines, and now we have to use Royal Navy mines, and for that we have to have a Royal Navy laying system. It was fitted at our last refit. Royal Navy mines are shit and so is the Royal Navy laying system. Can you take it back and get us French ones again, please?'

'Of course,' repeated Le Breuil. In English. Sonorously. And this time Faujanet couldn't help himself and burst out laughing; big belly whoops and in between them repeating, 'Of course . . . of course!'

The Captain and Bassano grinned indulgently. And so the pattern was set. It would become their little joke, Harry could tell.

Wonderful.

Le Breuil cranked up the gramophone and placed a record on the turntable. Artie Shaw and his Orchestra doing 'Begin the Beguine' started crackling out of the speaker.

Radegonde settled down to patrol routine, and Harry sat with the two Royal Navy ratings he had on board to assist him. He hadn't had a chance to talk to them properly before they'd sailed. Too many things had got in the way, and, although he'd twice bumped into the younger one – once as they passed at the gangway going in different directions, and again when he'd had to confirm both were aboard for the final muster – the other one had been conspicuous by his absence.

Well, they were both here now. Leading Signalman George Lucie and Leading Telegraphist Lionel Cantor. Lucie was the older; early forties, with thinning, mousy hair, and a vacant, indifferent look about him. Cantor, on the other hand, was a youth; bright, eager, intelligent with corn-coloured hair – strict short back and sides – and sticky-out ears. Both were in French Navy striped singlets and blue overalls, but were still loyally sporting their RN ratings' caps.

Their conversation dealt swiftly with Harry's main concern; he really would have very little to do on board. But there were, he was informed, two distinctly positive aspects to the posting: the first good news was *Radegonde*'s chef was without doubt the best in the Fleet; and the second was that whatever items the boat might run short of while on patrol, red wine was never one of them.

'But ya never see them drunk,' explained Lucie, with admiration. 'Not at sea anyroads. Tipplin' all day and never a wobble, Sir!' His words drew a quick sideways glance from his younger sidekick, one that Harry couldn't quite read. All three were sitting in the wardroom – the British ratings were allowed to sit there by the Captain, to keep them out of the way when the crew was busy and they were not asleep or attending to their own rare duties.

'They're a grand bunch,' said Cantor, composing himself with a cheery smile on his improbably youthful face. 'And she's a happy boat, Sir.' But Harry was looking at Lucie and thought he could detect a light sheen on his forehead, and a watery look to his eyes. It set him wondering . . . 'And a tight one too,' continued Cantor. 'They might look a rum bunch, Sir, but when things get goin', well, they're all right, whatever Mr Roper might've said to you.'

'Mr Roper?' said Harry.

'The previous LO, Sir,' said Cantor. 'He didn't quite hit it off with Captain Syvret or the rest of the officers. Or the men, come to that. Or even little Stalin, Sir. An' he'll chat to anyone!'

Roper. So that had been his predecessor's name. Never having actually deigned to meet Harry, Mr Roper had said nothing to him. But Harry didn't say that. What he did say was, 'Stalin? The dog? Chat?'

'Oh, aye, Sir,' said Cantor, his smile even broader. 'He's a chatty one, is Stalin.'

'I can't say I've heard much chat from the dog, Cantor. Not even a bark.'

'Oh, he wouldn't bark, Sir. Not on a submarine. Jerry might hear. But he does this, *gurr-urr-rurr*-ing thing when he's sittin' in with you. It's really funny. Captain Syvret says that's him bein' philosophical.'

Dear God, thought Harry.

⁓

Radegonde had dived now and was proceeding at three knots, on an east-north-east heading, having cleared the British coastal mine-fields through a gap just north of Peterhead. Harry decided now was as good a time as any to explore the boat and learn a bit about her idiosyncrasies. He stepped out of the wardroom space and before he could go either way, he was intercepted by the boat's Maître principal – in Royal Navy ranks, her senior Petty Officer – and a very tough-looking individual he was; out of the same mould as RN senior rates, Harry thought. He later learned the man's name was Robert de Maligou; but what he saw first was a man with a boxer's face, upholstered in wind-dried hide and with eye-slits narrow enough to peer into a hurricane. Harry immediately assumed he was going to be spun around and sent back whence he came. He couldn't have been more wrong.

'You want to learn about my boat.' It was a statement from the Frenchman, in French.

'Yes,' said Harry, in French. And in French, they continued.

'Good. Very professional, Sir, if you don't mind me saying so. We'll start aft.'

Chapter Four

Radegonde was at Action Stations.

'Mr Gilmour!' shouted Captain Syvret in French. 'I am looking through my periscope at Norway. How would you like to look at Norway?'

Syvret was upstairs in a compartment inside *Radegonde*'s preposterously large conning tower arrangement, which de Maligou had already shown Harry around. It contained a small attack periscope that could only be used from the compartment itself; it also accommodated the chef's galley, and the control board for *Radegonde*'s minelaying device. All very unusual for Harry to find so much vital equipment in a compartment not actually inside the boat's pressure hull. But then there was a lot different about French boats, he thought, compared to proper ones.

Meanwhile, he was down in the control room, sitting at *Radegonde*'s very own, spanking new device for sinking ships. Harry had always known it as a 'fruit machine', but *Radegonde*'s crew had come to refer to it as the 'boffin box', or sometimes it was the 'jukebox'. Everyone had been talking about it: the latest technical failure waiting to happen – the most recent of many to be foisted on the Free French's finest.

'I've seen Norway,' Harry shouted back.

'I'll do you a cut-price rate! Ten of your English bob a second!'

They were at Action Stations because they were preparing to lay mines, not because there was an enemy in sight. Because minelaying, as Syvret was never done telling Harry, was a tricky operation. Not so tricky, however, that it would deter Syvret from his endless mickey-taking.

'No need, Sir. It just looks like Scotland, except with lots of Jerries.'

Radegonde was about three miles off the Hellisøy lighthouse on Fedje Island, at one of the main entrances to Bergen harbour. To the south of Fedje was the islet of Nordøyna and a confused jumble of smaller outcrops and islets that made inshore navigation in these waters tricky. Somewhere around here, *Radegonde* would lay her first mines. It was just after three p.m. and getting dark. Harry listened to the conversation between Syvret and Poulenc, who was on the trim board.

In most ways, *Radegonde* was familiar. There was little in the control room layout Harry didn't recognise; the big navigation periscope extended down to this deck, and the trim board was here too, where all the pipes and valves that controlled the boat's ballast converged against the hull – a spaghetti tangle that allowed the officer and senior rate manning the board to dive and submerge the boat.

Diving and submerging was the same too. Each of *Radegonde's* main ballast tanks was open to the sea along its bottom. To dive, the men on the trim board opened the main vent valves at the top of her ballast tanks, allowing the air out, and the sea to flood in, sending her down.

Underwater, to keep her on an even keel, the men had a set of valves that allowed them to pump water in and out of the internal trim tanks; making her bow-heavy to dive faster, or to compensate for the sudden loss of weight forward after they'd fired a 1,360kg torpedo. Two big wheels against the other side of the hull controlled the hydroplanes – one set forward, one set aft – that acted like an aircraft's flaps, working with the boat's two electric motors to help dive or raise the boat as she moved through the water. To surface, they simply ensured the main vent valves were shut and then vented compressed air from a series of compressed air bottles into the tanks, forcing the water out and making *Radegonde* buoyant again, so up she would go.

One big difference, Harry noticed, was that *Radegonde* was beamier than his other boats, and roomier too. It meant she looked less cluttered in her control spaces; the pipes and cable runs and controls seemed more designed instead of the flung-in-together appearance of a British boat. But then she carried a smaller crew, so perhaps that helped.

The only other difference he'd noticed was that unlike British boats, *Radegonde* had a wooden-planked deck, instead of a plain steel casing. And then, of course, there was her vin rouge tank. The French didn't clutter their boats with bottles of booze; they stored it in a huge steel vat with a tap and a slop bucket that seldom ever filled.

Harry looked at his watch; it would soon be time to surface. They would wait until full night, then come up to lay the mines. Twelve mines here then two more *paquets* of ten; the first across the narrow channel between Lyngoksen and Fedje. Then they would dive during the day and go further south to Korsfjorden to lay the last ten the following night between Storekalsøy and Toftarøyna across the other entrance to Bergen.

Their deliberations around the finer points of the plan were cut short by a shout from the rating in the Asdic cubby. HE – hydrophone effects – sounds of another ship. Was that what was being yelled?

Harry listened hard to the staccato conversations all around him, the French Navy's very own jargon. He only caught the odd word, the rest was gobbledegook to him; not good if you were required to understand and obey orders instantly, as you most certainly were aboard a submarine.

Harry fretted about this for some time, trying to decide whether to alert Captain Syvret to his singular lack of colloquial French, and the threat it might pose to the boat's operation; but equally not wanting to burden the Captain with his own uselessness. Until it eventually dawned on him that since he was not on watch, nor did he have an Action Station, then none of the orders would actually apply to him. So there was no point in trying to understand every operational command and response.

Well, what do you know, Harry? he said to himself. *You're getting quite good at knowing when to keep your mouth shut.*

A bored Petty Officer was sitting next to him, with a hangdog look and over-long, flat brown hair that dangled in straggly little rats' tails from beneath a cap that was too big. An unfamiliar look of animation came over his face – it must be a ship.

Harry caught a '*trois-deux-zero!*' being called from the Asdic cubby – 320 degrees – it meant the ship must be approaching from nor'-nor'-east; in other words, it was hugging the coast.

He waited for the klaxon to sound Action Stations. It didn't come. A few more orders were exchanged; course alterations. Then, after a while, Syvret dropped down into the control room and issued instructions for *Radegonde* to go deeper.

The crew was sent to dinner, and Syvret stood by the watertight door leading aft to the wardroom, and elegantly bowed to Harry to pass through. They weren't going to do anything about the contact. Harry couldn't believe it; but again, to be on the safe side, he kept his mouth shut.

That night's discussion round the table – for as Harry had now learned, there was always a debate at mealtimes – started with Voltaire, and whether he was really any good as an enlightenment thinker? It quickly moved on to his relationship with Frederick the Great of Prussia, given that it took place during a previous era of war between France and Prussia, was it treason? Or did the concept of enlightenment transcend mere national interests in the eighteenth century? And could art do the same, now?

Everyone talked at once, loudly. No one talked about the ship that had just passed or why they hadn't attacked it. Harry's first Skipper had done that; failed to attack a potential target. Not as a result of a philosophical debate, admittedly, but because he was drunk. Harry remembered it well, and how it wasn't the drunkenness, but the lack of aggression that had subdued and unsettled the crew; the dread unease aboard at their Skipper's lack of fighting spirit. Except there had been another word on everyone's mind then. Cowardice. Not here, though; no one appeared uneasy aboard *Radegonde*.

Syvret noticed Harry and interrupted the flow of talk. 'Mr Gilmour is not happy.'

Oh, what the hell, thought Harry, *just say it.*

'The ship,' he said. 'What was she? Why didn't we attack?'

The other officers did everything but 'tut!' and Captain Syvret rolled his eyes to the deckhead. 'We are a minelayer, Mr Gilmour,' said Syvret eventually. 'We carry thirty-two British Mark Seventeen mines, designed in the 1920s . . . and they are shit. Each contains 350 pounds of explosives and they are detonated by the enemy ship hitting, and snapping off, one of the metal horns that adorn them. There are numerous fail-safes designed to prevent the mine going off before it is deployed. But they are shit too. So I have made the tactical decision not to waltz around the North Sea loosing off torpedoes while I am still carrying these pieces of shit, on their shit racks. I will lay them; then we shall attend to our *vandalisme*.

'As for the ship? I have no idea what ship she was. I saw a masthead and made another tactical decision not to hang about. Because

I have no intention of attracting German anti-submarine patrols, or German minesweepers, before I have laid my mines. And right now, after what I'm sure you'll agree has been a positive frenzy of tactical decision-making, I need a dinner to revive me.'

Harry could feel his face burning. He shut up, like he should have done earlier; he wasn't so good at keeping his mouth shut after all. There had been things he'd wanted to say about Voltaire and his work compared to David Hume, but now he'd gone and spoiled everything. And it had been warming up to be a bloody good debate too; he had experienced nothing like it since dropping out of his romance languages MA at Glasgow University, on the eve of his third year, to volunteer for this bloody shambles. He took another glug of his red wine and studied the table top.

Syvret, watching him, smiled to himself. *Definitely not as bad as the last one*, he decided.

⌣

Two hours later, they were on the surface, and Harry was back at the 'fruit machine' with the bored Petty Officer with his long spaniel face. Harry was supposed to be tutoring him on how to work the device. There was an instruction manual, but it was in English, and the fact that Syvret had assigned a senior rate and not an officer to operate it told Harry how much Syvret was going to rely on it.

Syvret, meanwhile, was on the bridge and they were about to commence their lay. Up inside the conning tower, Le Breuil, the torpedo and gunnery officer, and obviously now the minelaying officer too, was sitting over the chart Harry had provided from his little stash, showing where the mines should be laid.

They were running on diesels, so Harry couldn't really hear the barked orders between Syvret and Le Breuil, but he could hear the mines departing like trains on a miniature goods sidings going full pelt; the mechanical trundle of the mines on their ballast boxes as they rolled down the rack, and then a loud ting, like a bus conductor's ticket machine, to announce the mine had dropped off the end and was now plummeting to the sea bed, where the whole affair would sit for several hours while the securing pin corroded in the salt water. When that happened the mine would be released, trailing a tether just long enough to hold it floating at a set depth beneath the low-tide surface. The mine would then be 'live'; and there it would lurk, hopefully in the path of an unsuspecting enemy ship. It was all very simple really. Bit of a cheek to call it war.

The following night, *Radegonde* had finished her lay early, and now, with all mines gone and many long hours of darkness still ahead, she had headed down the coast where she was now hove-to, riding on the surface between Utsira Island and Haugesund.

The Skipper had become bored with having Harry hanging about his control room trying to instruct him on the intricacies of operating the latest magic box they had inflicted on him, so he had allowed him to go and sit in his own cabin out of the way.

Harry was in there reading when he heard, and felt, *Radegonde*'s diesels burble to life. The boat, with a full charge on her batteries, had had her diesels shut down and had been lolling, stopped in the long swell of a windless night, completely silent in the pitch darkness. Harry guessed what Syvret had been up to; he had been listening for other ships' engine noises carrying over the water. He must have heard something. Then the Action Stations klaxon went off, and the boat reverberated to the stamp of feet.

Harry fought the urge to leap off Syvret's bed and get to his fighting position. But he didn't have a fighting position on this boat. His only duty was to keep out of the way. The same went for Cantor and Lucie.

Harry felt *Radegonde* surge away beneath him. God, but he was dying to know what was going on up there. He lay back on the narrow bunk and held his book over his face, trying not to think about anything. P.G. Wodehouse. He couldn't even concentrate on that.

There was a sharp rapping on the cabin wall. Harry reached over and switched back the curtain. A matelot was standing there.

'The Captain would like to see you on the bridge, Sir.'

Harry didn't need asking twice.

'Diesel thump,' said Syvret, his night glasses pressed to his face. 'Off the starboard bow. Big, but not that big. You can't hear it now with our diesels going.'

Harry, who'd been reading below, was totally blind. It would take a few minutes for anything approaching night vision to return, and Harry's night vision had never been good anyway. As he peered uselessly into the blackness, he was aware that Bassano was also on the bridge as well as four lookouts. All were scanning the darkness. It was very cold, and Harry was glad he'd stopped long enough on his headlong rush, to bundle himself into a duffel coat and mitts like everyone else.

There was a shout; a lookout pointed and orders flew about the bridge and were acknowledged. Harry didn't even try to follow, but he felt *Radegonde* slow, and saw a rating and one of the lookouts manhandle a small searchlight out of the conning tower hatch and on to a gimble on the bridge wing. A couple of big Hotchkiss machine guns with their gunners and ammunition then appeared, and suddenly the big conning tower was crowded.

Harry slipped to the back behind the periscope stands. If he leaned outboard, he could just make out the crew on the casing for'ard. The heavy fawn material of their duffels made everyone slightly easier to see. They were working at the 75mm gun, taking out the tompion, preparing it to fire. With her mine racks now empty, *Radegonde* was obviously preparing at last to indulge in the *vandalisme* Syvret had been so looking forward to.

This would be Harry's first proper action aboard *Radegonde*. He was curious rather than frightened. He had no idea where *Radegonde* was pointed, or of their target's course; and even though what night vision he had was returning, he could make out nothing in the immaculate, cloud-banked darkness. Not a star twinkled, and even the submarine's wake, as it swirled down its huge saddle tanks, could barely raise itself to iridescence. Muffled orders came from the bridge front, and suddenly there was a stab of light, and, caught in its cone, was the shape of a small, coastal trading steamer. Where Harry came from, they called them coasters.

Someone had spotted the ship's blank shadow, eyes sharp enough to train the searchlight directly on a target no more than a dark shape against a darker coastline. She was big, but not that big, just as Syvret had predicted, maybe 600 tons – 800 at the very most. She was not more than half a mile away. Down in the water, so heavy laden, her high fo'c'sle pointed diagonally towards *Radegonde*.

Well, well, well, Captain Syvret, didn't you handle that fine and dandy? said Harry to himself.

There was a bright flash at the corner of Harry's eye, and then in an instant . . .

BOOOM!

Radegonde's 75mm gun had been fired. Harry peered into the night, and there, a half-ship's length in front of the coaster, a plume of water punched up like an inverted golf tee. The coaster's bow wave immediately began to lose its white froth – she was most definitely slowing. The shot across her bows had done its job.

In the spectral glare of the searchlight, Harry could see an angular steel superstructure perched midships, with a flimsy wooden wheelhouse. Then, what appeared to be a huge figure emerged from it. The coaster's Skipper.

'Good evening, Captain!' It was Syvret bellowing in French through a speaking trumpet. 'The French Navy would like to pay you a visit, Captain!'

Silence. Then out of it, in heavily accented English, came a strident bellow from the figure, now leaning over the coaster's bridge wing.

'We do not understand you!'

Syvret's head turned inboard and began to scout among the heaps of duffel around him. 'Mr Gilmour!'

Harry stepped briskly to his side.

'Ah ha!' Syvret grinned over his muffler. 'Tell him in English who you are and who we are . . .'

'Me?' asked Harry, surprised. Syvret spoke the best English he'd ever heard from a foreigner.

'Yes, you,' said Syvret, irritation in his voice at being challenged on his own bridge. Then he grinned his dangerous grin. 'You English always sound more official. And if they don't like getting stopped, it'll be you English they'll blame. So go on, quick now.'

'Captain of foreign merchant ship!' called Harry through the trumpet. 'I am the Royal Navy Liaison Officer aboard this Free French submarine. Our Captain has instructed me to ask you to heave-to and receive a boarding party!'

———

Four of them sat round *Radegonde*'s wardroom table in red light, out of courtesy to the Norwegian Skipper and his Mate's night vision. Both Norwegians had very large tumblers of brandy in front of them. Also out of courtesy, so did Harry and Captain Syvret. The Norwegians gulped, however, while Harry and Syvret sipped.

The Norwegian coaster was called *Tryggve*, her Skipper had said, through a beard bigger than a bear's backside. They were en route from Trondheim to Oslo with general cargo – barrels of salt fish, hides and pelts, that sort of stuff. No war material or Jerry gear; and no Jerries on board either. Facts that had just been confirmed by Aldis lamp from *Radegonde*'s boarding party, who were still on board the *Tryggve*, and had just been whispered into Syvret's ear by Bassano, who had promptly slipped away again back to the bridge.

Syvret smiled. 'So, if I sink you, Captain, it will do nothing to blunt the Third Reich's war effort,' he said, in English, 'and leave a lot of Norwegians out of pocket, out of work, and out of pickled herring.'

The Norwegian Skipper grunted. His mate, a cadaverous, grey creature who sat hunched, with his head poking out of a black rollneck sweater and pea jacket, took another gulp of brandy.

'I won't sink you then, Captain,' said Syvret, 'if you promise not to tell anyone.'

There was a pause, as if both Norwegians were considering whether they were being made sport of, then . . . then it was like an electric charge had been passed through the two men. Their faces opened up; smiles, laughter, toasts, handshakes exchanged, and solemn promises made. When the rumpus died, Syvret, still smiling, gripping the Norwegian Skipper's fist in both of his hands, said, almost as an afterthought, 'There is however, one more thing you could do for me . . .'

Two nights later they were back. Not quite in the same spot, but two miles further up the coast, inshore, tucked into a shallow bay where the deep water let them hug the rocky outcrops and blend with their shadows; her diesels shut down, silent. It was pitch black and cloudless, with a brisk breeze from the south-east; it couldn't have been better. The sound of the expected freighter would be wafted up to them from miles away. And there she was, burbling under the sound of the wind.

Once every week, she ran up from the big German military depot at Stavanger, coast-hugging to all the main German garrisons with everything from mail to condoms; small arms ammunition, replacement socks, treats and essentials. A Norwegian ship, Norwegian-crewed, nearly 2,000 tons, but with at least half a dozen Jerries on her, and two 20mm gun mounts.

'And you can get a message to them?' Syvret had been keen to establish that fact with the two Norwegians from the coaster while he still had them in *Radegonde*'s wardroom. 'The crew? I wouldn't want to be going and blowing them up too, if I didn't have to.'

The Norwegian Skipper's beard had rippled with the emphasis of his reply. The Mate was nodding too, but his attention had been more on the little barrel of brandy Syvret had donated to their 'welfare fund' that his Skipper was clutching too precariously for his liking. Timings and signals were exchanged, and then the two Norwegian sailors had slipped back into *Radegonde*'s inflatable for the trip back to their ship.

And now here they were, waiting for their quarry; and here it was, to within half an hour of the Norwegian Skipper's prediction. That was Jerry for you: everything really did run on time.

It was to be another surface attack; a gun action, no torpedoes despite the depth of water being entirely suitable for a submerged attack, which would have been considerably less risky given that the target was apparently mounting a couple of 20mm canons. The guns weren't big, but they were quick-firing, and, well-handled, could easily put holes in *Radegonde*'s pressure hull. And holes in the pressure hull meant she would be unable to dive; and being unable to dive would mean her inevitable destruction.

Harry had learned his lesson about questioning the Frenchman's tactics and kept his mouth shut and his face blank. But Syvret already knew what he was thinking. Syvret knew everything.

'We in the French Navy will always try to avoid killing the sailors of our Allies if it can be helped,' Syvret observed to no one in particular, with Harry not two paces from him. He did not mention Mers el-Kebir. He didn't have to. Now that they had all gone over the details of his plan for the last time, Syvret stood on the bridge, his night glasses stuck to his face, staring into the darkness.

Orders were barked, preventing Harry from brooding upon the Captain's comment. *Radegonde*'s diesels grumbled to life and he felt the boat begin to move under him. Out there in the dark, someone had seen the shadow of the freighter pass their lair, and now they were creeping after it. Down on the casing, the gun crew had loaded the .75 and were waiting for the order. *Radegonde* gathered way, nosing out into the fairway between their bay and the islands. And as their nose swung past a stretch of open sea, Harry saw it: the ragged silhouette of a big ship against the lighter line of a faint horizon, and the vague hint of a phosphorescent propeller wake.

The minutes crept by. Harry moved back to his usual position by the stands, unsure why he'd been allowed on the bridge for the attack. Syvret was there, with two lookouts and two men to man the big Hotchkiss machine guns. Too many bodies to get down the hatch in the event of having to dive quickly, thought Harry.

They crossed the freighter's wake and were now to seaward of her. Then Syvret called the order, and Le Breuil with the gun crew echoed it.

There was a *BOOM!* from *Radegonde*'s .75. And another swiftly after, but no gouts of flame and light. *The projectiles are using flashless powder*, Harry thought. He leaned outboard to see the gun barrel, still at a very low angle, being reloaded, then traversing left, away from the shore and on to the silhouette of the freighter. As the questions formed in his head – *Where are the hits? The fall of shot?* – one, then two dazzling blooms of light appeared low over the far head of the bay, illuminating the rocky bluffs close below in a fierce sodium glow, and throwing into sharp, jagged silhouette the freighter close off their starboard bow. In the final frames before his night vision was obliterated, Harry was conscious of the rest of the bridge crew, heads down, shielding their eyes from the sudden chemical glare. *Radegonde* had fired two star shells on a low trajectory to fall fast and burn on the land; and draw every eye on the freighter to their light.

Harry, blinded by the flash, did not see what Syvret saw through his night glasses: the flurry of bodies dashing out of the freighter's bridge wing and down the companionways leading from the midships superstructure, and how they appeared to merge with another ragged charge of bodies coming up out of the ship, rabbling together on the well-deck where the cargo hatches were. Other figures remained on the bridge, different in what looked like big, light-coloured bustiers and coal-scuttle helmets – they were Jerries in life jackets; you couldn't hear them, but from their gestures, they were obviously yelling, and not happy. The same with the crew around a 20mm gun mount on the stern castle; leaning and peering, first towards the burning lights on shore and then for'ard at the riot on deck.

Harry heard Syvret give the order to open fire; no jargon was going to disguise that.

The starboard-mounted 13.2mm Hotchkiss opened up at a rate of 450 rounds per minute, every sixth round sent a red tracer into the freighter's flimsy wooden wheelhouse. Even Harry could see the red arcs reaching out across the water, and the wheelhouse splintering into satisfying shards that spun and tumbled and bounced off the funnel, ventilators and rails, before splashing into the water in little ploppy gouts all around a hull that was most definitely slowing down. What had once been the radio aerials came snaking down in coils, and then the flow of fire halted.

There was another *BOOM!*, and when Harry looked towards the freighter's stern, he was in time to see an explosion; not huge, but a nasty little splay of smoke skittering out, all red inside. The freighter's stern Samson post teetered, then toppled aft, dragging with it the derrick. They fell, straddling the aft 20mm gun mount, its crew, arms waving, trying to shield themselves, only to get tangled in falling rigging. They fumbled only for a few short seconds before the second round from the .75 exploded in the stern castle beneath them, and they and the gun went pirouetting most artistically up into the night and out over the side to vanish in a series of splashes.

Radegonde was turning so that she was now bow on to the freighter, at an almost perfect T to her, so that her port Hotchkiss mount could now bear. But before the gunner could open up, the freighter's fo'c'sle began to sparkle, and the air above *Radegonde's* bridge began to fill with sickening zipping sounds like tearing linen. A pause, then several things happened in very quick succession, so that it would be hard to line them up in order when all the din finally stopped.

The freighter's fo'c'sle began sparkling again and *Radegonde's* jumping wire, the one that ran from her bow to her periscope stands, parted; three jolts hit the conning tower beneath their feet, and in them were definitely two explosions; smoke began to curl up either side of Harry, and somewhere in all that pandemonium, the port side Hotchkiss opened up, sending its little red spits in a lazy arc to cause sparks to splatter all over the freighter's fo'c'sle where the Jerry 20mm had been.

'Anyone hurt?' yelled Syvret. The right number of 'OK's came back at him. And then there was silence. It lasted a few short moments, then from across the water came shouting and Harry looked up to see the Norwegian crew lining the freighter's for'ard well deck, waving and cheering furiously in the now stuttering reflections from the two star shells.

'Mr Gilmour!' shouted Syvret, leaning back to look for Harry. 'Time for you to do the talking again, Mr Gilmour!'

Harry, in his finest Royal Navy bellow, ordered the Norwegian crew off the freighter, pronto. He didn't ask if there were any Jerries left among them, and the crew didn't offer to enlighten him; nor did he congratulate them on following instructions and getting off the bridge and out of the engine room the minute the star shells went up. He didn't know who might be listening. Then *Radegonde* manoeuvred to lie off the freighter, and Le Breuil and his crew began firing high explosive shells from the .75 into her hull on the waterline, right where the engine room was.

Steam began jetting out of the top of the tall, natural draught funnel with a terrible screech, and as the big engine space filled up with water, the freighter began to list towards them, further, then further still, and then all in a rush she capsized and started going down by the stern until her bow was vertical in the air and she plunged from view in a welter of bubbles and oil and was gone. Beyond the frothing water, the freighter's whaler could just be seen, filled with men and towing a big carley raft with a dozen or so more perched on it, heading for the shore. Some of them could still be seen waving. Harry guessed they were all Norwegians. There would have been no German survivors, he was pretty certain of that.

Chapter Five

The topic for the following night's dinner discussion turned out to be communism, and how a communist state could possibly justify aligning itself with a fascist one. It was a very glum meal, even before the subject was lit upon, seeing that all that was on offer were cold sandwiches with sardines and singe – a highly dubious French version of tinned meat. Of the three 20mm cannon shells that had punctured *Radegonde*'s conning tower compartment, one had exited out the other side and the other two had exploded, wrecking the Captain's little attack periscope, the minelaying console and the bloody galley! The sacred domain of their saintly chef was now mangled metal! The Jerry bastards! The fact that the damage itself had very serious consequences for the boat's stability seemed to matter a lot less than the outrageous atrocity committed against their dining arrangements. Harry could have almost found it funny, if his life hadn't been at risk.

The only good news out of the action was that the conning tower lower lid had not been breached. However, a leaking conning tower . . . a conning tower full of water. You could forget your centre of balance or trying to maintain any kind of trim. If *Radegonde* dived, it would be like trying to balance your way across Niagara

Falls on a tightrope . . . while carrying a hod of bricks above your head . . . on the end of a long pole.

A team of what Harry would've called Stokers, armed with collision mats and wooden battens, went up into the conning tower as *Radegonde* sped away from the scene of the attack. The holes themselves had not been huge; no bigger than dinner service saucers. The mats had been used to mask the holes, and the battens to create a monkey puzzle frame, each hammered home against the other to hold the mats in place. Meanwhile, the Captain had ordered both diesel throttles opened wide and laid on a ninety-degree track from the coast to get as far away as possible before daybreak.

By the time the *Radegonde* did dive, the lower conning tower hatch had been sealed and high-pressure air fed in to help reduce the rate of the leaks; but leaks there were, so a jury pump had been rigged and kept running, and once dived they'd stayed shallow to keep the pressure off. They could hear the pump running as they sat round the wardroom table. And if they could hear it, so would Jerry if he turned up anywhere near them now.

'There are no communist states,' said Captain Syvret with all the authority that command could bestow upon him, as he nursed his glass of red wine.

His officers barked outrage. 'The Soviet Union is not a communist state?' said Le Breuil.

'No,' said Syvret. 'It is a country with a Communist Party in control, trying to create a communist state. They haven't achieved it yet. Don't take my word for it. Read the texts from their annual congresses. It's what all that Lenin "two steps forward, one step back" gibberish is all about. Although if you had been reading the later texts, you'd have realised Comrade Stalin has gone very quiet about "achieving communism" lately.'

'Is that how he manages to square his deal with the Nazis?' the so far silent Bassano asked. Bassano, the oldest of *Radegonde's* three watch-keeping officers; the taciturn, watchful Bassano from Marseille, who, Harry noticed, never quite seemed to get on with the other two. Bassano, of the dark complexion, slick-smooth, swept-back hair and the flat stare, who never rose to the odd sarcastic dig of the others, nor responded to any comradely gesture.

'Comrade Stalin doesn't square anything with anyone, my dear Bassano,' said Syvret after another sip of wine, 'because he's not a comrade. He is a Tsar . . . without a bloodline.'

'How can you talk like that about another communist?' asked Poulenc, the First Lieutenant.

It was not a question Harry would have expected from this very serious young man. Poulenc, with the looks of a *fin-de-siècle* poet and the manners of a diplomat, always spoke up for his opinions at these debates, but never to provoke. Precise, spare in his language, he pointedly never questioned his Captain, unlike others aboard. He stroked his moustache while he awaited a reply.

'Especially after you called your dog after him,' Harry heard himself butt in, immediately wondering whether he should have said anything at all. But everybody laughed, even Syvret. And Le Breuil said, 'Of course!' and they all laughed even more.

In the mirth Harry began to be aware he had just steered the talk away from some unseen precipice. Even the dog, who looked like he'd been following the debate, seemed to be smiling at him. Syvret ruffled his neck, saying, 'I call him Stalin to remind me.'

'Remind you of what?' asked Harry.

Syvret turned his smile on the dog. 'He is *very* clever. Just like Stalin. But he's still a dog.'

Chapter Six

It is a wet afternoon in early March, and once again Harry is standing on the pier at Gourock, watching the sheets of rain slant and dance across the spume-scuffed waters of the Tail o' the Bank in an endless procession of shades of grey. Unusually, the anchorage is almost devoid of shipping and the raft of escorts that are normally lashed together alongside at the far end of the pier are gone; they are at sea somewhere in the North Atlantic, some convoy's last bastion between a safe passage and the U-boats.

In peacetime Gourock Pier, served by the railway line direct from Glasgow, was a bustling port for all the steamer lines that plied their trade the length and breadth of the Firth of Clyde. In the summer it would be decked in bunting and packed with holidaymakers heading to the coast's resorts; now it's all just peeling paint and random mounds of essential freight under glistening tarpaulins, awaiting transport to all the little piers and jetties from Innellan to Troon and Rothesay; Ardrossan, Broddick and Campbeltown.

The gulls swoop and cry, the rain patters on his oilskin coat and the wind shakes the cast-iron lamp standards that mark where the sodden wooden planking of the pier meets the puddled flagstones of the covered railway platforms. Everything is wet and rimmed with gummy moss. Life in wartime, thinks Harry. Everything and everybody weighed under by the boredom of waiting for events to happen elsewhere; waiting for the day when normal life can go on.

Harry is heading home on leave, awaiting the little wheezing paddle steamer that is now approaching to carry him back across the firth to the small resort town of Dunoon, where his father is a teacher at the local grammar school, and his mother, a housewife.

Three weeks, he's been told; three weeks to patch the holes in *Radegonde*'s conning tower and re-reeve the jumping wire and do all the other myriad tasks to make the submarine operational for her next war patrol. Harry, as LO, has no role in this ritual. He might serve aboard *Radegonde*, but he is not ship's company. So he might as well be out of the way. The Captain (S) cut him a rail warrant and a leave pass and here he is. Off to be reunited with a mother who loves him; a pacifist father consumed with rage at his son's role in this war; and Janis, a girl he's known from school, who is beautiful, fashionable and completely cocooned in the security of her father's self-made wealth, and who says she is his girlfriend. And Shirley. The Honourable Shirley Lamont, a scruff with a mane of chestnut hair and a casual indifference to convention; wayward in a way only the aristocracy can carry off and who, according to her last letter, is now a volunteer ambulance driver in Glasgow, and so likely won't even be there. Harry doesn't know whether to be thankful for that, or sad. In fact, if he's honest with himself, Harry would rather be back aboard *Radegonde*.

Harry queued with the press of sailors filing up the gangway in rain-coats and dark blue caps with bands that read 'HM Submarines'; they were heading back to the submarine depot ship HMS *Forth*, Dunoon's new neighbour; anchored round the corner on the Holy

Loch, and home to the Third Submarine Flotilla, from where Harry had sailed on his last patrol as Fifth Officer aboard HMS *Trebuchet*. *The Bucket* to her crew, now familiar throughout the fleet because of what had happened up there off the Arctic coast of the Soviet Union; the neutral Soviet Union.

Harry was sitting out on the little paddler's deck on a carley raft that doubled as a seat, trying to work out in his head how long it had been since they had sailed into the Russian fjord and kicked over a hornet's nest, when suddenly he was right there again. It might have been broad daylight around him, but he was back in that Arctic night; right back there with it all happening, in full gory, noisy technicolour. A flashback; right down to the exploding depth charges, the *rabummm-babumm-bumms!* that had punched his diaphragm, and made his eyes lose focus and his eardrums sing and his gorge rise and jaw lock from fear. He doubled forward, his fists grabbing his knees, and his eyes scrunched shut. As he did so, he could even feel the paint flakes pitter on his neck just as they had in *The Bucket's* control room where he'd stood at his post, crammed together with Malcolm Carey, the Jimmy; Kit Grainger, the navigator; and the Skipper, Andy Trumble, always so cool, pulling his bottom lip, calmly pondering some imponderable as the world ripped apart around his ears. All of them so close, nose to ear with the ratings and Petty Officers, their backs to you, as they faced the trim board and the plane controls and the helm; sitting so you could rest your elbow on their heads and see the dandruff flakes and the roots of their hair; until the next concussion ripped and smoked the fetid air around you.

He forced himself to sit up, hands still on his knees, rigid, and stared hard at the mountains along Loch Long. He focused on their greens and purples, until his breathing started to calm again and he caught the sideways glance of a grizzled, three-badge Stoker; looking at him with an expression of complete understanding. They exchanged the briefest of smiles and Harry was OK again. He desperately wanted a cigarette, except even now he still hadn't got into the habit of buying them. The Stoker, a submariner by his cap band, stepped over.

'You needin' a smoke, Sir?'

'Yes. Yes, please,' said Harry, and the next thing he was breathing the acrid blast deep into his lungs.

'Rejoinin' yer boat, Sir?' The Stoker knew where he'd been, needless to say. He'd probably been there himself a few times.

'No. I'm heading home on leave. I actually live here.'

'Really? Nice, Sir. Very nice. What a lovely place to come home to, Sir.'

And then Harry was off the boat and in the back of a navy three-tonner taking the sailors to the crew tender pier at Sandbank. He was dropped off in Kirn, and then walked up the hill, through his front gate and up to his front door; a boy again, still thinking of his parents' house, their front door, as his own. Looking at it before he turned the handle, because the door was always open – people didn't lock their doors in mid-Argyll, there was never a need to. And there it was, another flashback, a little more benevolent this time, to the student he used to be when he would sit on the steamer, on the weekends he would return for his filial visits, and use the time to adjust his frame of mind from bohemian undergraduate to compliant only child.

Life at Glasgow University had seemed a world away from here back then. But, my God, what kind of world was he coming back from now? How did you adjust your frame of mind after that?

And how did you adjust your frame of mind to walking into the house you'd grown up in, to find your father, and mother, and the girl who said she was your girlfriend, all sitting round the kitchen table, frozen in a scene that should have been intimate, but one you knew immediately wasn't? He'd caught them talking, and it hadn't taken a genius to work out it had probably been him they'd been talking about. And that they hadn't been fondly reminiscing. But whatever questions he might have had were immediately lost in all the hugging from his mother, and from Gordon, the family Labrador, who kept jumping up to slobber on him. The hellos from his father and Janis were more subdued. Catching up, chucking Gordon under the chin and small talk took care of the rest of his arrival.

Later, when the rain had stopped, and patches of blue sky appeared, Janis and Harry sat out in the back garden. Harry had suggested a walk with Gordon, but Janis was in her heels, couldn't he even see that?

'Of course,' said Janis, 'that's the trouble with you. You're just so . . . completely . . . selfish.'

Of course. Where had Harry heard that before? Was he starting to get little Aspirant Faujanet's joke, at last? But he said nothing. Although Harry was still a young man, he had learned to understand when a woman doesn't want to listen.

'I wrote and wrote and wrote. Your mother wrote. No reply from you. Then you just . . . turn up . . . and expect to be waited on and fawned over. You think just because you put on a uniform and go swanning off in your little boat, you can forget to behave like a gentleman; you can forget about those who care about you. Self! Self! Self!'

She had him there. All those weeks in Raigmore Hospital, he never wrote. He couldn't. It wasn't that his wounds were so bad: a gashed forearm; puncture wounds in his back, none of them deep; a slash on his neck caused by glass from a depth-charge-shattered gauge. And then the blast damage from that 20mm cannon shell on the bridge of the Soviet tug – *your brain's been rattled around like a pea in a can,* the doctor had said. He'd laughed at that. So had Hank the Yank.

It was that he hadn't known what to write. His head had been full of the story he had just lived through. The story he'd been ordered on pain of Court Martial never to tell; an epic story of a secret German base in a neutral Soviet port; of a threat to Britain's convoy lifeline; and a foray into those neutral Soviet waters by two Royal Navy submarines, against the rules of war, to sink German ships and thwart a German plan; and of the aftermath, being hunted by German destroyers, the loss of one submarine and the all-but-wrecking of his own. He had no idea what had happened to *The Bucket* after they had limped back into a remote Shetland harbour, her crew to be lorried away and the entire, epic battle swept under a carpet because His Majesty's Government couldn't admit it had violated the Soviet Union's neutrality; and because the Soviet Union probably hadn't wanted them to anyway. Because the Soviet Union had violated its own claims to neutrality by offering base facilities to an enemy belligerent. Nothing in this war was straightforward.

Even when he'd got to Dundee, he still hadn't written. He'd tried to; had the pen in his hand.

'I was so worried I couldn't think of anything else,' Janis was saying, while he sat, wretched. 'Every . . . waking . . . hour. All I did was worry. That's why I'm here today. To tell your mother. To explain,' she continued. 'To tell her I just can't go on like this. I can't be treated like this. And then you turn up. Like nothing has happened. Well, I'm telling *you* now . . .'

There was a pause, and Harry looked up from his pose of bowed contrition. Janis was staring hard at him, as if daring him to . . . to what? He couldn't read it.

'I have found someone else,' she said, unblinking.

Aha! He thought. She was daring him to . . . beg? Plead?

'Edward has been comforting me.'

Who's Edward? he thought.

'He's a doctor.' She said it as if this explained things. 'I wish you well, Harris.'

Harris. His full name. She *was* being formal.

'But I don't want to see you anymore.'

Another pause. Harry bowed his head again.

'Aren't you going to say *anything?*'

'I can't think what to say, Janis.'

'Of course not. You're too busy thinking about yourself.'

And with that she was gone; a swish of nylon stocking as she uncrossed her impossible legs, and she was out of the garden chair. He wondered momentarily how she managed to get nylon stockings when rationing meant no other woman could. Her back disappeared around the corner of the house and she was heading for the gate. She hadn't gone via the kitchen, where his mother and father still sat, to say goodbye to them, the people who'd shared her terrible worry all those weeks, along with Edward; Dr Edward, rather, whoever he was.

The only sound now was of the three evacuee children who had come from Glasgow to live in his parents' house, away from the bombs: two little girls and a boy; poor, with a mother working in a munitions' factory, and a father in the Argyll and Sutherland Highlanders, dead in France Three children who Harry had forgotten about.

They were playing beyond the bushes at the bottom of the garden. He couldn't see them, but he could hear the shrieks of laughter and giggling, and the splashing coming from where the burn ran. What did he feel right now? Nothing. He felt nothing. So he went indoors again, to his mother's love and his father's anger.

That evening when his father had retired to his study, Harry steeled himself and went to see him. He'd wanted to, and he hadn't wanted to. The dread of again having to sit under the leaden burden of his father's disapproval vying with his need to try and reach out to the old man; to offer his father some solace for the hurt he seemed to bear.

He didn't knock when he went into the study; he was carrying two whisky and sodas, so he just butted the door open with his bum, put a tumbler down on the fireside table by his father's leather armchair, and sat down on the matching one opposite. The room was dark, lined floor-to-ceiling with bookshelves and never a painting. The only light was a standard lamp behind his father, spilling light over the paper he was reading. A huge Afghan carpet covered most of the polished marquetry flooring, and in the bay window was a huge desk, locked now, and sealed from the world. Only a large, framed portrait photograph of Harry's mother graced its top.

'I thought I'd come and talk to you,' said Harry.

His father, Duncan, gripped his paper more tightly by way of reply.

'You do want to talk to me, don't you?' Harry persisted.

'Depends what about,' said his father.

'How about how I am?' said Harry.

'How are you?' said his father, his voice as flat as if meeting a tedious acquaintance.

'Oh, you know. The usual. Committing atrocities. Carrying babies around on the end of my bayonet.'

'As long as you're enjoying yourself.'

To the uninvolved, this exchange might have sounded quite amusing; an ironic, sarcastic baiting between sparring partners, old in their drollery. But it wasn't. And even a sensitive witness could not begin to sense the fathomless hurt behind the words from both father and son. But Harry could. So he stopped.

'I know how you feel about the war, Father,' he said. 'But King Canute stood an odds-on better chance of stopping the tide than you do of ignoring this war, and what it is about. You're far too intelligent a man not to know what is at stake . . . this new dark age that threatens us . . .'

'*Threatens!*' bellowed his father. 'It's not threatening us! It's here already! We're in it, you stupid, self-deluding little lemming! *Nnngggrrrraagghhh!*' And in his impotent fury, the newspaper Harry's father had been scrunching in his fists fell from his hands, and he started thumping the big leather armrests of his chair, eyes squeezed tight as tight, like a child in full tantrum. And then, as shockingly as he had begun, he stopped. Harry sat frozen, appalled by this brief glimpse of the full embrace of his father's torment. His father looked very old right then, and was very quiet. Then, as if after an age, he began to speak very softly.

'You cannot imagine the joy and love in which you were conceived,' he said, not looking at his son, but at something very far away. 'Or the joy and love you brought with you when you entered the world. Yes, you are right. I am an intelligent man. Which is why I have never deluded myself that such feelings have been mine alone to experience.'

Harry's father had stopped speaking, but his words still seemed to hang in the room. Then he looked up, straight into Harry's face, his eyes so deep and hard Harry couldn't read them.

'And then I look at you,' he said finally. 'In your uniform. The fruit of my loins. And I think of every other father who has had a son. And of every other father whose sons you have taken from them.'

And then, at length, he looked away again; but he wasn't finished. 'And for what? Some historical imperative. They come and go, believe me. So do not presume to tell me I do not understand what is at stake in this war.'

The two men sat in silence, until eventually Harry's father bent to try and rebuild his newspaper from its crumpled sheets. 'Shouldn't you be getting back to the killing?' he said, shaking out the centre section.

Harry left the room and sought refuge in the mayhem in the kitchen. Young Arthur Clunie, the lad from down the road who sailed with the Port Line, was recently back, and Arthur's mother had brought round some sugar from the cache he'd smuggled ashore in his dunnage, so Harry's mother and the evacuee children were making scones. Harry joined in, and the shrieks and laughter and the mess helped him bury what he'd just been through. Gordon looked on from his basket in the corner, his baleful eyes surveying this gross disruption to his peace.

Chapter Seven

Harry was looking down from *Radegonde*'s bridge at Leading Signalman Lucie – who was lolling in a wheelbarrow, while Leading Telegraphist Cantor pushed him along the Dundee quayside – wondering why he'd been so eager to get back aboard. A telegram boy had delivered the news to the Gilmour household. Harry was to report to HMS *Ambrose* within three days. Harry knew what it meant: *Radegonde* was about to sail on her next war patrol. He could have squeezed another forty-eight hours out of his pass, but he left immediately. Couldn't get away fast enough, after what had happened. Not between him and Janis; he couldn't have cared less about her. No, after what had happened between him and Shirley.

And now he was back, watching as a drunk and incapable Lucie returned from leave, with barely fifteen minutes to cast off. He had made it only because young Cantor had known where to find him, lying passed out as usual.

Watching Cantor, Harry couldn't help but feel the young man appeared rather adept at recovering his older shipmate, and that this was a familiar routine; for the *Radegondes* too.

The inevitable gaggle of Brass that always gathered to wish the flotilla's submarines bon voyage were there right now, at the forward gangplank, in last-minute conflab with Captain Syvret. Only a crane and a tarpaulin-covered heap of stuff on the quay shielded them from the terrible truth – that Leading Signalman Lucie had still not managed to rejoin. His superiors would have taken a dim view if they'd noticed. From where he was perched, Harry could see there were a couple of *Radegondes* on the casing aft and another gangplank; the final act in this farce was about to unfold – the getting of Lucie up the gangplank and down the aft hatch without the Brass seeing.

Harry couldn't stand to watch any longer, so he looked away across the Tay, where the sinking sun was throwing Fife into shadow and dappling the waters. In another mood he would have found all this as hilarious as the two French matelots back there. But he wasn't feeling very funny these days.

Later, with Bassano, the navigator, upstairs on watch, Harry sat down with Captain Syvret and all the other officers for the first meal of the patrol. Stalin was elsewhere. Harry had learned from their first patrol that Stalin had the run of the boat and was courted with what amounted to competition by all the other messes on board, from the Petty Officers' to the seamen's. The chef had prepared a huge turbot with pommes frites and some kind of pudding that involved lots of tinned peaches, meringue and cream. The vin rouge was flowing, and tonight's debate was about artists who had remained behind in France to live under the Germans. It hadn't taken long for the word 'collaborator' to arise, and the argument to become heated; and the greater the heat, the faster they talked, and the less Harry could follow.

Some actress called Arletty, and Maurice Chevalier, appeared to be coming in for some stick. Then Picasso was mentioned by Captain Syvret to a clamour of outrage from Faujanet and Le Breuil. But Poulenc interrupted with a lot of 'Non, non, nons!' The lugubrious Poulenc had a touch of the aristo about him, and managed to stay as close to manicured as Harry had ever witnessed aboard a submarine. Harry had never seen Poulenc without his navy cap – a cap that seemed impervious to all oil drips and grease smears, the hair that peeked beneath it cut so close as to appear no more than a dark five o'clock shadow. Poulenc's French, Harry could follow.

'I heard from Carlton Gardens, a story about M'sieur Picasso I think you should hear too, before you start hanging him in his absence,' said Poulenc. Carlton Gardens was de Gaulle's headquarters in London, home to all Free French forces.

'M'sieur Picasso apparently does not hide from the Boche. He flaunts himself. And they hate it because they know they cannot touch him unless he does something obviously anti-Boche. He is too famous to just randomly disappear. But they search his places. All the time. Looking for an excuse. I was told during a recent search some senior SS officer uncovered a print of *Guernica* in Picasso's studio. He asked, "Did you do this?" and Picasso replied, "No, you did."' Poulenc let his eyes pass round the table.

Guernica, Picasso's painting marking the first terror bombing of the Basque town of that name by Luftwaffe pilots and planes flying for Franco during the Spanish Civil War. Harry knew all about that. The entire civilised world knew about that.

'Picasso stays in Paris not to collaborate, I would suggest, but to remind the Germans that the world is watching what they do,' Poulenc added. Everybody shut up. A first for *Radegonde's* wardroom, thought Harry.

But before Le Breuil could whip off the wardroom table top and get at the gramophone, Harry decided he had something to say. That last subject for discussion had been controversial, so maybe he could try out his controversial topic too. Harry had been rehearsing the something he wanted to say over the past few weeks. It was a matter that had been on his mind since he had joined *Radegonde* and he hadn't been able to stop nagging at it. He'd always told himself he was going to have to pick his moment, but what with everything else that had happened, now he couldn't wait.

So much for his moment.

'Never mind about what Picasso or Arletty did. What about the Royal Navy?' he asked, assertively loud, speaking French; always French around the wardroom table.

Everybody affected to look puzzled, but Harry knew they weren't.

'Mers el-Kebir,' he said, so as to leave no one in any doubt. Nobody looked pleased that he'd raised the subject.

'What about it?' said Captain Syvret.

'The Royal Navy sank—' but Harry did not get to finish.

'We all know what happened.' Syvret's interruption was just sharp enough to brook no argument.

Third July, 1940, Mers el-Kebir, the French naval base near the Algerian port of Oran. There had been four French battleships, a seaplane tender and a flotilla of destroyers in port. The British feared they would be surrendered to the Germans under the armistice that Vichy France had signed with Hitler two weeks before. The French Navy had said no to the Germans. But neither would they surrender the warships to the British.

The British, not trusting this new, pro-German government to resist German pressure forever, had then issued an ultimatum: join us and fight on against the German invader or face destruction. The French ignored it. The result: a Royal Navy squadron had bombarded Mers el-Kebir, sinking one battleship and damaging two others as well as four of the five destroyers. Almost 1,300 French sailors had died. The British Admiral in charge had objected strenuously to his orders and had only opened fire under a direct command to do so from the new Prime Minister, Mr Churchill. In the aftermath of this action, word got round about what the Admiral thought about the whole sorry story. He said he felt 'ashamed'. And that pretty well summed up the feeling throughout the Royal Navy.

At the same time, other French ships in British ports had been boarded by Royal Navy crews; in Alexandria, and Portsmouth and Plymouth too. Several sailors had died, on both sides. That was why, serving aboard *Radegonde*, Harry had decided he had to know what the French Navy felt about it. Same old Harry; on his first posting, in the wardroom of that ancient, bloody battleship HMS *Redoubtable*, the Harry who wouldn't sit and take all the bull and ragging; and on his first submarine, *Pelorus*, the Harry who wouldn't collude with her drunken Skipper to help him cover up her needless loss. Harry; he just couldn't let it lie.

'How do you feel about it? About what happened?' he persisted.

All the officers, even Poulenc, looked at Syvret, who blew out his cheeks.

'Feel? Feel?' said Syvret, sounding almost tired. 'Are you being serious? Don't answer that. You'll probably say something unforgiveable.'

There was a long pause, and the thump of *Radegonde's* diesels – a sound you got so used to, you normally didn't notice – was loud now in the wardroom. From where Harry sat, he caught a glimpse of the chef's face poking round the bulkhead door, curious at the lack of noise from the officers, before he thought better of it and withdrew.

'How do you see this conversation ending, M'sieur Harry?' resumed Syvret. But his question was rhetorical. 'You say you're sorry, and we say we forgive you?'

There was another pause as if Syvret was gathering his thoughts.

'My parents have a town house in Lyon,' he continued. 'I grew up there. A German is in it now.'

And yet another pause.

'Poulenc,' he added, nodding at him. 'There is a German sitting in Poulenc's house in Chartres.' Then Syvret pointed at the other two officers. 'And a German in his house, and his house. And the crew, in their houses and on their streets.' And one pause more, and then a grin. 'I don't know about Bassano's house; I don't know if any German is brave enough.'

There was a laugh at that, a laugh that Syvret's changed expression quieted.

'We're fighting the Germans,' he said. 'You're fighting the Germans. And we'll both do what we have to do to win. We understand that. But what do we feel? That's none of your business.'

Chapter Eight

Harry was lying on Captain Syvret's bunk, in his tiny cabin, out of the way while *Radegonde* began her first lay. Three days had passed since the conversation in the wardroom. For Captain Syvret and his officers it had been as if nothing had happened. They carried on as normal; a different debate every night over the evening meal. Only Faujanet or Le Breuil paid any kind of attention to Harry, religiously intoning their 'of courses' every time Harry spoke, followed by the usual adolescent giggles, and always an indulgent smirk from Syvret. No one mentioned Mers el-Kébir, and, indeed, Harry got the impression that Bassano didn't even know any such conversation had taken place; that no one had bothered to tell him.

The rest of the time Harry had sat with Lucie or Cantor – watch on, watch off – on the surface through the night up in the conning tower by their radio set, as they monitored the radio frequencies; or when *Radegonde* was submerged, down in the wardroom decoding their trawl of signals. Sometimes, like now, he hid in Captain Syvret's cabin, when Syvret was on the bridge or in the control room.

At last, after a tortuous approach, dodging some overly zealous Jerry anti-submarine activity, *Radegonde* was off Stavanger, in the process of laying her minefield. Harry could hear the mines go; the reverberating trundle and then the short *ting!* as each dropped off the end of the rack and fell to the sea bed.

But he wasn't really paying attention. Harry, with nothing to do, was back in a minefield of his own.

Harry is walking up the Camel's Hump behind his parents' house – the little hill you got to by cutting through Dunloskin Farm – his wellington boots well-caked in the yard's mud; a bright, hazy day, with high cloud, and cold. He's in civvies, in his duffel coat, with a herringbone cap pulled down to his ears so you can't see his face as he trudges, dull of step, on up the hillside parallel to the tree line, a man with a burden he does not want.

You don't want to look inside Harry's head right now. It's not a place to be. No one's a hero all the time. Out there, there are plenty of people who've had harder wars than him, but Harry's not telling himself that right now. It's not just the depth charging he's endured aboard the old *Bucket*, or the fight in that Russian fjord, or the whole injustice of the Royal Navy and all its bull and nonsense, and the ship's company it scattered and buried on a dozen other boats just to hide what they'd done, when they should've all been made heroes; the *Buckets* – his ship's company – who he should be with now. And it's not the friends he's lost or the wounds he's suffered. Or his father sitting behind his paper, and Harry's realisation after his conversation with him that night in the study that it's not anger the old man feels for him, but despair and fear. Despair that *his* son is fighting in a war. And fear as to what might happen to him. His pacifist dad: huge, utterly remote, viciously intelligent, cold to everyone but his mother, and dispensing the judgements of Jove to everyone else.

His father; what is he to do about his father?

It isn't as if his father never fought in a war. He had; the last world war, and even won a medal. So he knows why he is afraid for his son, and why he despairs. But Harry knows nothing about what happened to his father on the Western Front, and no one, not even his mother, will tell him. She is still trying to be serene in the middle of this rift that has opened up in her family.

So there he is, our Harry, full of resentment for the people he should be turning to for succour.

It's not even the fact that the first submarine he had served aboard, HMS *Pelorus*, had been sunk with him still trapped inside, or that it had been mere happenstance that he had survived while so many of her crew had not.

No, it's not just one thing for Harry. He's twenty years old and it's all of them. The whole bloody war, and everyone in it.

And when he gets to the summit of the Camel's Hump with all this churning within him, and he looks out over the firth, the town, the ships, the whole seething little diorama; the whole, pointless, stupid, mad, inconsequential, irrelevant . . . that's when he sinks to his knees, rolls over, clutching himself and begins to sob; deep, wracking, wallowing, unfettered sobs. Like a thwarted child.

He's still doing it when Shirley Lamont comes up the hill behind him, and sees.

⌣

There is an enormous *clang!* and he's back aboard *Radegonde*, off Norway. Then the sound of grinding metal; he can feel it through the hull. It goes on too long before it stops. Harry is lying in Syvret's cabin, no longer on that little hill above his home, and he is wondering what the hell has just happened.

71

He sits up, but knows better than to go crashing into the control room when the crew will likely have more pressing things to do than to give a running commentary to a useless bystander. He can hear the shouting already. The *Radegondes*, he has learned, are an efficient crew, but they aren't half bloody noisy. Running feet go to and fro in the passageway. Then Cantor sticks his head into the cabin.

'Something's gone wrong with the lay, Sir!'

Harry gestures him into the tiny cabin. There's barely enough room for them to sit side by side on the bunk.

'I admire your confidence in me, Cantor,' says Harry, with his lopsided smile, 'but I'm not sure there's anything I can do about it.'

'I think there might be, Sir.'

The cabin curtain is unceremoniously whisked back a second time by a matelot in his bobble cap and striped vest – a uniform that is still too comically inappropriate for Harry to take seriously, despite the time he has spent aboard *Radegonde*. He smirks. But the rating isn't smirking. Captain Syvret wants him immediately.

'It's the minelaying mechanism, Sir,' says Cantor as Harry rises to follow. 'The instruction manual is in English.'

Harry hadn't far to go to meet Captain Syvret. The matelot had told him to wait at the wardroom table, which was just the other side of the passageway. The senior Petty Officer in charge of *Radegonde*'s engines came hurrying from aft; and Syvret and Le Breuil appeared, running from the other direction, clutching a large binder, paper and pencils. They slipped into the banquette either side of Harry and Syvret slapped the binder on the table. All three of them looked grim.

'A mine has come off the track,' said Le Breuil, all suggestion of his usual frivolity gone. Speaking in French slowly, to make sure Harry understands. 'That's what I think, but we can't know until we surface. Whatever has happened, it has jammed the mechanism and there are eight mines backed up—'

Le Breuil had more to say, but Syvret interrupted, his voice flat and scrupulously polite: 'It is your shit British mechanism. And your shit British mines. That you British insisted fitting to a French boat and then giving the French crew a shit set of drawings and your even shittier book of how it works – all in inconvenient English!'

After a pause, Le Breuil continued, 'And all the measurements, tensions, everything; they're all in imperial and not metric. We're not sure how we're going to be able to deal with this without your help.'

'I'm not an engineer,' said Harry.

'That's all right. Beyfus here is,' said Syvret nodding to the rather bovine, lumpen-looking Petty Officer, who was wearing greasy dark blue overalls, and had more grey hair sprouting over his collar than was on his head. Beyfus smiled obediently. 'He is not, however, a linguist.'

Syvret spread a set of drawings that showed a plan view of *Radegonde's* hull, with the two mine racks running down either side. Below it was a side view that gave more detail of the mechanism. Beyfus pointed with a dirty-nailed finger at what looked like some extended loop system that connected to a large, toothed gear wheel.

'It's a basic rack-and-pinion system,' he said in heavily accented French that Harry struggled to follow even though the middle-aged engineer was going slow. A rack and pinion system. That meant nothing to Harry. His heart sank. He looked round the grim faces that were looking back at him, swallowed, pulled over the binder and opened it. The language was in English all right, but it was densely technical.

'Isn't there some manoeuvre you could do to shake it loose?' Harry said brightly.

Syvret, sitting next to Harry, crooked his neck round to appraise him, then, sitting back, in rapid French that Harry didn't quite catch, he dismissed Beyfus. Le Breuil rose from the table too, but continued to hover while Syvret gave him instructions; it sounded like a course change; then in a loud voice he called for two coffees, before turning back to Harry.

'Harry,' he said, very calm now and speaking to him in English. 'Let me explain.'

Much of the initial stuff Syvret told Harry was about the boat and how it worked; most of it Harry had already learned from de Maligou, the boat's sea-weathered Maître principal, on his initial tour. But what followed made Harry's stomach sink even further. *Radegonde's* mine racks held a total of thirty-two contact mines and were open to the sea, so that the racks that held them did not form any part of the boat's buoyancy. There was one inspection panel on each side that you could enter, at the forward end of each rack, and holes at the aft end where the mines dropped out. Those were the only ways into the racks.

The mines they were carrying this time were standard British Mark XVs, each almost three and half feet in diameter, with eleven contact triggers on their casing – 'horns', Syvret called them – and 320 pounds of explosives in their guts. The mines sat on boxes holding a coiled tether; when the box hit the sea bed, the clips holding the mine released and the mine floated up on the tether to wait, unseen, at a set depth beneath the surface for some unsuspecting ship to come along, hit one of the horns and set the whole bloody thing off.

The only good news was that the mines didn't go live until the clips were released; and even when they were live it took a very hefty impact from a lot of tons of moving steel to fire the horn triggers. Because nobody wanted odd bits of flotsam, or a curious seal, setting off the damn things. This much Harry knew.

'So, we are going to have to surface and take a look at what is jamming it,' Syvret continued, sipping his coffee. He grimaced, and looked over to Harry's cup, which was still half full.

'If M'sieur Le Breuil is correct,' he added, leaning back to the little cupboard where he kept the wardroom brandy, 'and it is a derailed mine, then someone from the engineers is going to have to go in there and fix it . . .'

'Beyfus?' Harry interrupted. 'Your engineer chap?'

'Too fat,' said Syvret, topping up Harry's coffee with a shot of brandy, then his own. 'He couldn't squeeze in.'

Syvret raised his glass, 'Salud!' and he drank. Harry followed his lead and returned Syvret's lopsided grin with one of his own.

'It'll have to be one of the lads. That's where you come in,' Syvret continued. 'You are going to have to explain to whoever's going, how to do it. What nuts to loosen on the rack and what end of the pinion to hit with a hammer. So you better get reading. Oh, and the weather upstairs is even shittier than your minelaying mechanisms. I'll let you know when we get into the lee of something and can start work.'

And with that, Syvret patted Harry once on the shoulder and was gone, back to the control room. Harry pulled the binder towards him, opened it again, and with the plans by his side, began to read.

Meanwhile . . . Syvret nosed *Radegonde* inshore. The weather was indeed shitty. The back end of a spring gale, with driving rain and a chopped and confused sea running from the south-west. Even at this time of the year, dawn was starting to break early at this latitude, so it would soon be light. Not the best of times for a submarine to surface in enemy waters.

As far as Harry could see, the system worked on a toothed chain – the rack – which was set into and looped along the deck of the mine chamber, for'ard to aft. Resting vertically on each rack were the boxes holding the mines. The boxes ran on rails either side of the rack, and were clipped on to the rack's teeth by A-rings, which to Harry's eyes, were just bigger versions of the little chrome thingies that held the bath pug to the overflow.

The mechanism was driven by two big cog wheels – the pinions – one for each rack, and each was driven by a pair of actuators that could draw power from either the batteries or the diesels. When you turned it on, the pinions' teeth locked with the rack's teeth, and what followed was the elegance of simplicity; round went the pinion and around went the rack, pulling the mines to the hole at the end; and when the rack turned under, the mines fell off. Bob's your uncle.

That was how the mechanism worked. How you fixed a jam – fixed it without wrecking the mechanism – was another matter. There was the step-by-step procedure for disengaging the pinion; there were the pressure points in the system where leverage could be applied to loosen the rack, unseat it and remove blockages, then shift it back; procedures you had to follow so as not to break links, or damage teeth, or reseat the mechanism out of alignment. Harry was an intelligent lad and with a lot of sweat generated on his brow, jabbing his finger between the text and plans to keep his place, and careful, lip-moving concentration, he could visualise what might have to be done. But to explain it in French, to a loose-limbed grease monkey whose education had probably never extended beyond three years of secondary schooling – schooling that had probably only been completed months previously rather than years – that's when Harry knew how this had to play out.

Apparently there was one other task expected of Harry before the unjamming of the minelaying mechanism could begin. He learned of this when Syvret summoned him aft to the crew mess. Harry stepped through the watertight door, clutching his set of plans – it would have been a waste of time bringing the binder for what he was intending – and was confronted by a tall, pasty-faced and pimply youth, with a matted mop of curly hair and a vacant expression that Harry took to be fear.

The boy was encased from neck – and wrists – to ankles, in a black rubber suit, sealed at the extremities, and with splatters of chalk dust round the holes. When he moved, puffs of the stuff would appear where it wasn't quite snug. Beyfus, de Maligou and several matelots in foul-weather gear were crammed into the compartment too. So was Captain Syvret, and he was holding out a Davis Escape Set. Harry stared at it.

'Nobody knows how this . . . thing . . . works,' said Syvret, loosely dangling the set. 'You need to show him.'

Harry looked blankly at him, then he noticed that above the rubber-clad youth was the aft escape hatch. He stopped breathing. A wave of old fear washed over him, until he noticed how the boat was rolling, and realised they must already be on the surface. He started breathing again.

'The mine chamber will be as good as flooded,' added Syvret. 'He'll need this if he's going to work in there.'

The Davis Escape Set was a Royal Navy device for assisting submariners to escape from sunken submarines. It consisted of a rubber bag with a rubber corrugated tube sticking out of it and an oxygen bottle fitted to its bottom. Inside was a canister of CO_2-absorbing chemicals. You breathed in and out through the tube. The chemicals scrubbed what you breathed out, so you could breathe it in again without dying of CO_2 poisoning. The oxygen was there to fill the bag as a life jacket, if you needed it, or to give you something extra to breathe if what was going in and out of your lungs wasn't quite doing the trick.

Harry had encountered the damned things twice in his career. Once, in the training tank at Fort Blockhouse, when he thought he was going to drown; and a second time, off the Firth of Forth, getting out of his first submarine, its bows in the sea bed in 150 feet of water and a bloody great hole in her.

The Davis Escape Set Syvret was holding out to him was the first one he'd seen aboard *Radegonde*. It didn't take long to work out why. *Radegonde* had been equipped with this piece of kit, but because it was British they'd never worked out how to use it. Just like the bloody minelaying mechanism. None of that mattered now.

'He's not going,' said Harry, nodding at the boy.

Syvret held back the set. 'What do you mean?'

'I'll go,' said Harry.

From the look on Syvret's face, Harry knew he didn't have to spell out the logic of his decision. But Syvret had to make at least a show of having to be convinced.

'What if you make a mess of it? You are, after all, at your own admission, not an engineer,' said Syvret. 'How do I explain to your Lordships of the Admiralty that I have lost one of their Liaison Officers?'

'There's over 300 pounds of explosives in every one of these bloody mines,' said Harry. 'If I mess up, the only person you'll be explaining anything to will be St Peter.'

Everybody laughed. Even Harry.

Syvret gestured to de Maligou. 'Get the boy out of the suit.' Then to Harry, 'A moment with me, please M'sieur Harry.' And they squeezed back through the watertight door into the motor room.

'When we load for operations, they load the mines first,' explained Syvret, with his hand on Harry's shoulder, 'while the mine chamber deck is still above the water. Then they load everything else: fuel, food, torpedoes, my brandy, the vin rouge, the crew; and pretty soon the chamber is under the water. I explain this to you, just so you know we're not doing this on purpose, making you have to splash about in very cold sea.'

'Thank you, Sir,' said Harry formally, but with his lopsided grin. Syvret decided the grin didn't actually make him want to kill

Harry as he'd feared. In fact, he quite liked it. Royal Navy sangfroid. Why not? They had to be good at something, these damned rosbifs.

'Just one other thing,' Syvret said, no longer sharing the grin. 'About only having to explain to St Peter . . . that's not strictly accurate. If, when you're in the chamber, and Jerry shows up . . . I'm going to have to dive the boat and get out of here.'

Syvret didn't have to explain any further.

'I know, Sir,' said Harry. He hadn't. Hadn't even thought of it. But he knew what it meant. Still, Royal Navy sangfroid dictated 'I know' was the right thing to say.

'Well, let's get you kitted up,' said Syvret, this time in English, out of politeness. 'Do you like our frogman suit, by the way? It's Italian Navy; made by Pirelli, the tyre people, apparently. De Maligou purloined it back in 1939. We use it for harbour work; the boy goes down and checks all the valves and vents, untangles Stalin's lead from the props, that sort of thing . . . What? You look surprised?'

'Stalin has a lead?' Harry said, drily, and Syvret laughed and slapped him again on the shoulder, which Harry found bloody irritating.

Chapter Nine

Harry cannot remember ever being so cold. They gave him beer before he went into the water. He had frowned at that. 'Piss in the suit,' de Maligou had explained. Harry had looked revolted; de Maligou had raised his eyebrows, and said again, 'Piss in the suit.'

Harry had resolved it would never happen. After hitting the water, his resolve had lasted less than ten seconds.

And now here he is. Suited up, the Davis Set looped round his neck, nose clips and goggles fitted, the bone of his skull creaking with the cold, and his extremities burning painfully with each slap and dip into the water.

He creeps along, clinging to the submerged section of *Radegonde*'s casing and lowers himself down into the mine chamber's launch chute. The chute itself is underwater and follows the line of the casing as it tapers towards the stern in a lip; if you look for'ard, it disappears into an elliptical void, chopped off at the top and bottom, and the hole angled back. Just inside it he can see a mine sitting, black and menacing, on its rack. Each time his hands and feet make contact with the slick steel it feels like blows on wounds already numbed by shock. The weather is indeed grim. A group of swaddled crew are on the casing to supervise Harry's efforts; they are hunched against it. Among them are de Maligou, Beyfus and Le Breuil. Syvret is on the bridge, and below, Poulenc stands over the hydrophone operator, listening for Jerries.

To port is an islet, about 150 metres off; all grey rock and shiny green moss. An endless roil of pearl-grey cloud hangs low over everything There should be no aircraft up in weather like this to spot them from the air.

———

Boat and land are rimed with skeins of moisture, and it drizzles, like it's been drizzling since the beginning of the earth and will do so until its end. But if Harry is looking at the view, he's not aware of it. He's only aware of the cold, and a sea that is all confused chop, splashing his face repeatedly as he clambers into the hole. They'd tried the for'ard chamber inspection hatch, but a collective sticking of heads into that hole had concluded the errant mine, if that was indeed the problem, was not at that end of the rack. So it is up to Harry to go in the arse end, and sort it out from there.

Getting into the suit had been an epic task in itself, involving an incredible amount of chalk dust to force his limbs into the obscenely clingy, cold rubber. Despite the sealed neck and cuffs, the suit is far from watertight, but after the beer passing through him, and the initial amount of water seeping in, what is there has started to warm up courtesy of his body heat. But the cold is still making him slow and clumsy.

Attached to lanyards, Harry has a torch; a prise bar, an adjustable spanner and a hammer; the lanyards run from a belt on his waist to a webbing bag slung diagonally over his left shoulder. Toes, numbly clinging now to the tumblehome of the rack, only his head is still above water, the Davis mouthpiece gripped in his teeth as much to control his chattering; his goggles endlessly being splashed and slapped by seawater, he shines the torch into the chamber; and there they are. The mines: big black dinosaur eggs, bristling with spikes, receding into the dark. He feels himself rocking slightly to the roll of the boat. Harry tries at first to clamber over the top of the mines – anything to be free, even for moments, from the deep chill grip of the sea – but the clearance between the mines and their horn triggers, and the chamber head, is too narrow. He must go down, where the depth of the mine boxes will give him all the room he will need. The water closes over his head, and the cold is like a pressure, crushing his skull until his jaws feel locked.

He pulls himself through a green gloom that ripples in torch-light; hauling himself along by the mine boxes on the outboard side of the rack. The boxes themselves, so close, yet they seem to loom. And he keeps banging himself against steel – his knees, elbows, even his head – but the blows have lost any sharpness in the cold. He is counting the mines as he passes them, as they curve over his head; no horn triggers on the bottom to snag on his Christmas tree of kit; a silent thank you. He is aware of the coils of line peeking from the mine boxes, and the boxes, like vegetable crates with little engraved Bakelite plates on them – 'Hoist Here', 'Release Clip I.P.' – and although he is counting, the cold makes him forget.

He has no idea how many he has passed when there, in the torch beam, lies the derailed mine. Oh God. What a bloody mess. At least the mine lies on this side of the rack. He mouths another silent thank you. He will not have to go back down and up the other side to wrestle it back on to the rails. He must stop and look. What has happened? But his brain feels like congealing tar, and he is having trouble turning what he sees into thought. It's the cold; he knows that. But it isn't helping. Con-cen-trate!

The picture is slow in coming, but he sees eventually; it is the mine in front of the derailed one that is jammed. The one behind has hit it, and been itself hit from behind, causing its inboard wheel to jump out of the rail, distorting the A-ring pulling it, which in turn has toppled the mine box off the rails completely, jamming the mine by one of its horn triggers against one of the mine chamber's ribs. The trigger, Harry sees, with a dull, throat-tightening fear, is bent; and with every roll of the boat, the mines behind are giving it another push.

He manhandles himself back down the chamber, shining the torch around the mine in front, looking for the cause. He finds it. Its A-ring, which attaches the mine box to the rack and looks for all the world like a percussionist's triangle, except made of High Tensile steel, has failed. He can't see why, but it has. It is now just a twisted steel bar, peeled off its mine box, almost straightened, free of the rack's teeth, but now jammed tight into one of the rack's links, bringing the whole bloody mechanism to an abrupt halt.

Harry looks closer, the bar has been bent by the pressure of the link's spindle and it's well and truly in there; there's going to be no pulling it out, and with it stuck, nothing's going to be moving anywhere. There is the sound of metal scraping together very close as the boat rolls again; it is the derailed mine's horn trigger, being ground against the rib.

Oh god, oh god, oh god. I can't do this, he thinks. He is too cold to scream it. Maybe the mine will just go off, and the cold will stop and all this will be over. He doesn't know what makes him go on. Brain first; work it out. To free the twisted A-ring you need to uncouple the link. The drawings; think. The links are not riveted are they? If they are . . . Don't think about that. Think about . . . yes, it is a bolt and nut . . . and the nut is on this side of the rack! Yes! That's why you decided to come up this side. Remember. It wasn't random. The adjustable spanner. Yes, yes, yes. Just undo the nut and prise out the bolt. Yes.

He fumbles for the spanner, forcing his numbing fingers to be steady. He finds it, and its lanyard is fouled by the prise bar's lanyard.

He has to stop and untangle them. Take your time. He stretches out on the chamber's deck and peers in to where the twisted A-ring is sticking out, bent from the rack. He leans in with the spanner. There is no space between the rack and the bottom of the mine box to attach it to the nut and get any leverage on it. He wants to smash and smash and smash the spanner against the twisted A-ring. But he doesn't. He pulls back.

The prise bar. If he levers this side of the mine box off its rail, he can create more space. The cold has leached every ounce of strength out of his arms. He tries to raise the box. Pressing down with arms that have no power, and pushing up with a shoulder he can't feel any more, the box comes up a fraction. But how does he keep it here? The box drops.

The hammer! He fumbles the hammer out of the webbing bag, and undoes its lanyard. If he loses it now into the rack's sump . . . but he doesn't think about that. He levers the box up, and with his foot pushes the hammer under one of the box's wheels. It doesn't work. The box comes down and the hammer skitters from under it. He just manages to trap it with his foot. He is getting very, very cold now. Sleepy cold. Think. The hammer. The rail. He tries fitting the hammer's head into the rail and when he does, he immediately wants to kiss whoever designed it. The hammer's head fits, almost neatly, into the groove. He pushes it in, leaving the handle sticking out at an angle, close to the mine box's wheel, and using strength he doesn't have, raises the box again . . . higher . . . a bit more . . . higher. And with his foot, he pushes the hammer upright and under where the box's axle should be . . . and lowers, slow, gently, feeling the hammer taking the weight, but still going slow, slow, until the fucking, bastarding . . . BOX! . . . is resting on the hammer. He feels for the spanner again, and stretches out again, and leans in under the box, groping for the link nut.

tcom

Harry will never really remember everything he did in the mine chamber on that morning in early April 1941 somewhere off Stavanger. How he got the nut off, eventually, using the prise bar at some point to lever the spanner; or how he managed to catch the nut when it twirled free, before it vanished into the rack's sump; or how he remembered to get the bar out, and not leave it lying there to jam up the rack later. It would all forever be a blank. So would how he'd managed to realign the bolt into the link holes and rescrew the nut so the rack would work again.

All the heart-stopping, slow-motion fumbles, working between the shadows and the sickly light cast by the torch, all diffused by the dark water. There were dim memories of heaving the second mine back on to the rack, but nothing about how he'd prised its A-ring apart to get it out of the way, or how he had the presence of mind not to leave the ring behind, but to jam it with the other one in his belt; or how he'd levered and pushed the mines apart to create enough space to get the derailed one back in line.

When he came out of the hole at the end of the chamber, several hands grabbed him and pulled him from the water, out on to the casing and into the freezing air. He couldn't talk; could only, with great effort, unclench his jaw to let the Davis Set's mouthpiece fall free. He couldn't even make a proper thumbs-up gesture, but the deck crew were all still grinning. All that shivering and wheezing for breath; at least he was alive.

The sequence of events that happened next, however, those would stay etched in his mind forever. The noise first, and the scattering of figures, but mostly that single, vivid snap; that face, so clear and sharp that he knew he would recognise it out of a street full of people were he ever to see it again; and of course the sure and certain knowledge that he never would. Ever. Because the face he had looked at was about to become the face of a dead man.

He was in a crush of matelots, all bundled up in their pea jackets, mufflers and bobble caps on tight. They had gathered round Harry where he lay on the wooden deck slats and torn off all the equipment he had slung around him: the Davis Set, webbing bag and tools, the lengths of bent steel and the torch. Harry was gazing, dazed, at the sea and at the electric green of the islet through the drizzle, as if he never believed he'd see such a sight again; looking up and observing how the cloud base had lifted a bit too . . . an aircraft appeared out of the dense white fluff. Right there, before his eyes. One minute cloud; the next, an Arado 196 floatplane.

It was just off the end of the islet and so low, too. The sound of its engine was barely audible above the noise of *Radegonde's* own diesels, charging batteries. Needless to say even a barely conscious Harry recognised the aircraft immediately: its big, round, radial engine cowling; the dull green paint and the big black crosses on its side and wings; and the cockpit perched above those wings, long, like some extended garden greenhouse. In the back, a gunner, looking the other way; but in front, the pilot, his canopy pulled back, looking right down at Harry; right into his face. It was the Jerry's astonished expression – the immaculate incredulity – that Harry would always remember. He had no time to register aggression or fear; and he was young, a boy just like him. Frozen, then gone in a blur of wing as the aircraft went over *Radegonde's* periscope stands with no more than thirty feet between her and the Arado's two huge floats, suspended on their cat's cradle of struts. Harry thought the eggshell blue of its underside looked almost fairgroundy.

Out of the corner of his eye he could see the port side Hotchkiss gunner wrestle with his gun. But the Arado had appeared too close for him to get in a shot. The starboard gunner, meanwhile, who'd been facing the wrong way, looking aft, had dragged his gun all the way around, and as he swung it, there was the distinctive Hotchkiss rattle. Harry watched as the Jerry powered away over *Radegonde's* starboard bow; transfixed, as its trajectory converged with a running red stitch of tracer rounds rising from *Radegonde's* conning tower, from the starboard Hotchkiss.

A section of its cowling exploded away; an inspection panel; lumps of wing root and skin, and a gout of black smoke, immediately snatched by slipstream. And then the Arado's nose shot up, almost vertical, and it was as if the whole aircraft had been suddenly snatched away by some giant, unseen puppeteer from above; disappearing up into the cloud, as if the entire piece of theatre had never happened at all.

Captain Syvret was at the aft end of the conning tower, gesticulating, ordering everyone below. Harry, half carried, half shoved, was being dangled over the aft hatch, when he looked up again. Way away, off the starboard bow, the Arado suddenly reappeared out of the cloud base, but like some entirely different aircraft, trailing smoke and diving vertically, straight into the sea in a gout of white water. Harry was down the hatch and *Radegonde* was already diving before the last of the water finally subsided.

When Harry woke up he was lying flat on a pile of thin mattresses dragged from matelots' bunks and piled on the deckplates. He could see he was in the engine room, between *Radegonde's* two silent diesels. The silence meant they were submerged, and running on electric motors.

Harry felt his head being raised, and one of the many matelots kneeling around him pulled a thick, knitted woollen hat over his ears. A commotion developed at his feet. When he focused, he saw de Maligou, still in his pea jacket, attacking the seals of the frogman suit with a bolt cutter. Behind him was another matelot with a huge knife, slicing the suit open as if he were flensing him. And suddenly Harry was naked, being dabbed with towels. He wanted to shout:

Your good Italian frogman's suit! But his jaws were going like a pneumatic drill. He couldn't speak. And then there was the pain; he felt as if his whole body were on fire.

The next thing, the matelots' many hands were pulling a sleeping bag round him, and Faujanet's face was leaning over his. Faujanet, naked apart from his skivvies, crouching down and grinning sheepishly.

'We all love you, Harry. I love you, Harry,' he was saying, then suddenly frowning, as he seemed to be about to try and get in the sleeping bag with him. 'But like a brother. OK? No kissing, Harry. No kissing and I promise never to say "of course" again.'

Harry's eyes went wide with alarm; but he couldn't talk to tell Faujanet about the pain in every limb and extremity, and how he couldn't bear to have the Frenchman kick and elbow his way into the sleeping bag beside him. But Faujanet didn't see; he was too busy planting a big kiss on him, landing somewhere between his eye and the bridge of his nose.

Harry wanted to shout *Stop!* but couldn't. Somebody else did, however. Captain Syvret had stepped into the engine room through the bulkhead door behind Harry's head. Harry eyes rolled with relief.

'What are you doing, Faujanet?'

'I'm getting in to keep him warm,' Faujanet replied, huffy that his sacrifice wasn't being appreciated.

'He won't thank you for it, Philippe,' said Syvret. 'He'll be hurting, and it won't do any good right now.' Then, to the others, 'Blankets. Get lots of blankets round him.'

Syvret knelt down, brandishing a flask. 'Hot chocolate. You can have some as soon as you are able to tell me you can swallow it without choking.'

He ran his eyes over Harry's shuddering, slimy white body as the sailors mummified him in coarse wool. 'You look like something from a St Malo fishmonger's slab,' he said. 'Well, almost.'

Harry, his eyes starting to roll again, looked up at Syvret. 'A-a-alm-m-ost?'

Syvret blew out his cheeks in his usual, reassuring fashion and smiled. 'You're not dead,' he said. 'Thankfully.'

Chapter Ten

'Somebody should write to the Luftwaffe warning them about you,' said Captain Syvret. 'Every time you see one of them, someone shoots them down.'

He and Harry were in the wardroom, the little glass light fitting on the deckhead above casting a dim, cosy light over them. Both men were hunched over mugs of something steaming, leaning on the table. Harry was bulked up in several sweaters and had a blanket round his shoulders. He still looked slimy white, but was at last beginning to believe he might one day feel warm again. He forced a mirthless smile.

Syvret was talking about the Junkers 88 over Dundee, and now the Arado. But Harry wasn't in a reminiscing mood. He was thinking about other things. What he'd done and why he'd done it. It wasn't as if he'd had to do it. It wasn't as if he was one of them, a *Radegonde*, ship's company and all that. No, he was a supernumerary. It wasn't his navy, he told himself, and it hadn't been his job. He'd nearly died; which seemed to be a pretty good reason for asking himself: *What in God's name were you thinking, Harry?* Did he really have the right to be so careless of his life now, just because he was no longer saving it for Shirley Lamont? Was that what all this was about? Trying to get himself killed just because he was ashamed of how he'd treated a stupid girl. Except she wasn't stupid; he was . . .

And that was what was going around and around in his head, like a scratch on a record.

The boat was quiet. Three days had passed since Harry had freed the mine. Not that Harry could have told you; most of that time he had spent in a kind of pain-addled, semi delirium. Nor did he have much memory of his actual deeds down in the mine chamber. But he must have done something right. Because when he'd finished, all the mines had been back on the rack and the mechanism was working again. And now they were motoring away from a successful night-time surface minelay on their alternate target. All the mines had been deployed and were out there now, bobbing about, ready to blow the arse out of any unsuspecting passing Jerry.

The Captain was happy; even the crew seemed happy. No one had actually said thank you, but there had been all those toothless grins when the *Radegondes* had popped in to see him in ones and twos as he lay mummified in blankets on the Captain's bunk, his arms so bundled up he was unable to fight them off when they insisted on ruffling his hair.

He was aware of the Captain considering him. He took another warming gulp from his mug; coffee and brandy. He felt it warm its way into his belly.

'Everybody is still going to hate you . . . of course,' said the Captain, that last bit with a wry smile. 'Nothing will change that. It's nothing personal. You're English. Everybody hates you.'

Harry made no comment. Actually, he found the idea of being hated, even if it was for the wrong reason, quite comforting.

'You hate me?' he asked.

'Of course!' said Syvret. When he realised what he had said, he heaved with suppressed laughter for a moment. 'Oh, dear, I'm becoming tedious.'

'Certainly not,' Harry said drily, 'you're very amusing.'

Syvret considered him for a moment, then said with that glint in his eye, 'I hate you, because you're English; because your climate is insipid, your food inedible, your manners ludicrous', like he was ticking off a shopping list of ingredients for a nice dinner, 'and your women are icicles. Because of your wretched class system, and your affected superiority. Because you do not know how to enjoy pleasure; you're not allowed to dip your toast in your coffee, or in your boiled eggs – you deny yourself! Eating chicken legs or lamb chops with your fingers – you deny yourself! You do not know how to make coffee. Instead, you make sludge. That is all I've ever tasted in England. And what do you drink instead? Tea.' He paused to smile at Harry; his warm, twinkly, devilment smile. 'And don't even mention your women's fashions. I cannot look at their hats and still believe in civilisation.'

Harry, too, was smiling now. 'Is there anything you do like?'

'I like some of your traditions; like the way, down through history, you name your warships for the attributes of your women . . . *Illustrious . . . Formidable . . . Indefatigable . . .*'

'You know I'm not actually English,' said Harry.

'Yes. And that's another thing I hate. I constantly insult you, and you don't even have the common courtesy to be annoyed.' He paused again, musing. '*Implacable . . . Colossus . . . Thunderer!*'

'Aspirant Faujanet said everybody loves me now,' said Harry.

'He was humouring you.' He emptied another slug of brandy into Harry's mug. 'You know, Harry, now that you are a *Radegonde*, you're going to have to learn how to take a joke.'

Radegonde lingered on the Norwegian coast for a few more days for the sake of some *vandalisme*, but no suitable target for their torpedoes presented itself. Harry was sitting with Lucie at the radio inside the conning tower. Both Lucie and Cantor had barely been able to contain their pride in Harry after his deed of epic derring-do. 'Saved the boat, you did, Sir,' Lucie had confided in him at one point, his chest puffed out like a mating pigeon. And later, when Harry had caught the two of them giggling like girls together, and asked rather coolly what was so funny, Cantor had leaned in to tell him. 'The boys up in the for'ard mess, Sir. They're trying to get one of the Torpedomen to fix you up with his sister, Sir.'

Harry managed to look both scandalised and intrigued.

'She's a dancer in that Folly Berger, Sir. They've got a pin-up of her on the bulkhead. She's really nice,' grinned Cantor. 'They really like you, Sir.'

Harry had decided to be haughty. 'The Folies Bergère is in Paris, Cantor, and the last time I looked it was full of Jerries.' But all he was thinking was how he might plausibly get a glimpse of this pin-up.

'For after the war, like, Sir,' said Lucie. 'Not right now.'

But Harry was thinking right now would be better.

When their recall came over he ripped off the full message from Lucie's signal pad and went down to the wardroom to decode it. Captain Syvret was at the wardroom table when Harry slid in.

'Our recall, Sir,' he said, ferreting about for the secret books in the cubby he used for his feet when sleeping. Syvret had a chart on the table and was drinking coffee and eating toast while he peered at it. He looked up, then stuck his head into the passageway and called the steward for coffee and biscuits for Harry.

Harry finished the decoding and pushed the message over to Syvret. While Syvret read, Harry sat back to dip a digestive biscuit in his coffee. He ate it, then slurped some coffee to wash it down. That was when Stalin padded up, skipped on to the banquette beside Harry, and began a conversation.

'*Grrnngungnnm,*' said Stalin, reflectively, while looking from Harry to the plate of digestives.

The intimate little tableau struck a thoroughly contented Harry as the epitome of domestic bliss. To complete it, Harry lifted one of the biscuits and offered it to the dog. Stalin peered closer, then recoiled.

'*Rrrrnngrumnngr,*' it said.

Harry offered again, and Stalin looked positively accusatory.

'I've just offered Stalin a biscuit, Sir, and he's refusing it,' a stunned Harry said to Syvret.

Without looking up, Syvret asked, 'Did you put any butter on it?'

'No.'

Syvret sighed, rolled his eyes, then went back to reading the signal. Curious now, Harry, biscuit still in hand, slipped out of the banquette, took two steps down to a little second galley, then brought the biscuit back, buttered. He sat down again, his every movement being followed by Stalin. He offered the biscuit again and without a moment's hesitation Stalin took it and in two chomps and a lick of his lips it was gone.

'Well, bugger me,' said Harry.

Syvret was still reading the signal, not even looking his way.

'There is no law,' he said, distractedly, 'that says communists can't be sybarites too, you know.'

Stalin meanwhile had nuzzled up against Harry, his eyes devouring him adoringly. And right there and then, Harry had one of those epiphany moments where the possibility of an entirely different world, of another life, suddenly becomes plausible. Looking down at that bloody dog, he had never felt so distant from the Royal Navy; so far away from all the discipline and the duty, and the expectations and traditions of his service. From the war, even. Instead, he found himself in the company of madmen. And he quite liked it.

In fact, for the first time in a long time Harry felt . . . happy. He chucked Stalin under his chops, and Stalin nuzzled him back.

'You haven't seen a little girl wandering around here?' he asked the dog in English. 'Answers to the name of Alice?'

Syvret squinted up from his chart, gave Harry a sideways look, shook his head despairingly, and went back to work.

According to the signal decoded by Harry, they were to rendez-vous with a Royal Navy armed trawler just after dawn, outside the coastal minefield protecting the Firth of Tay. The exact position was pricked on the chart, and over the ensuing hours, while Bassano navigated them to X-marks-the-spot, Captain Syvret composed his patrol report. It was a more time-consuming task for him than for a Royal Navy Skipper, as he had to compose two – one for the FOS and another for Carlton Gardens – and they were not always exactly the same report. All Harry had to do was decide what he was going to do with his leave. In the previous world, there would have been no debate. In this one, the thought of going home held no charms for him at all.

Radegonde, like all submarines coming in off patrol, was abuzz. Her crew went about their duties with a certain briskness. Nothing was too much trouble, smiles were everywhere you looked and bonhomie and good will were all-pervasive. Stuff to go ashore was trussed up and made ready; inventories were completed; anything was attended to that might impede their dash down the gangway once they were alongside.

As always, Harry kept out of the way when *Radegonde* was performing critical evolutions, such as diving, or surfacing, but once the boat was up, diesels engaged and her course shaped for Dundee, Captain Syvret invited him on to the bridge. And there was the trawler, off the starboard bow, ready to escort them, not because of any threat from the Germans but – as Harry knew all too well – because of the threat from the RAF. There had been many a Jack who had come to grief because he believed pilots could tell one submarine from another. This was not so. As far as the Brylcreem boys were concerned, all submarines were U-boats. This was a truth every submariner had to learn.

It was a bland, grey day, with high white cloud and a stiff breeze buffeting in from the north-east. *Radegonde* and her escort cork-screwed in rhythmic echelon across a long, rolling swell. Harry scrunched himself down into his duffel coat, behind his muffler and waved gratefully to his protectors; members of the trawler's aft gun crew, lounging round their 20mm Bofors mount, goofing at *Radegonde*, returned the wave. The Angus coast was still just a smudge. Harry had plenty of time to decide what he would do when they docked.

The Honourable Shirley Lamont, youngest daughter of the late Viscount Cowal and the eccentric – or demented, depending on your point of view – Lady Cowal. Shirley, sister to Hamish, the new Lord, and Cameron, the younger son; her brothers Hammy and Cammy, whom Harry had known vaguely since childhood. The local, impoverished aristocrats. Both the sons were cavalry officers now, in the same regiment the family had bred officers for since the days of the Covenanters. Maybe that said all there was to say about them.

It didn't begin to cover Shirley. The girl with the pre-Raphaelite explosion of chestnut hair; the girl whose face he couldn't get out of his head – the face that had been with him when the German depth charges were raining down and he thought he was going to die. Knew he was going to die.

Harry leans over the bridge rail and stares into the water, seeing himself on top of the Camel's Hump that day, blubbering; and then seeing Shirley suddenly appear.

In his mind, he hovers over the scene; he doesn't want to get too close, to hear the words again. He couldn't bear that; hearing his words again. He has enough trouble continuing to look, knowing what he is about to see. The Harry on high contents himself with just looking down on the Harry below. He watches as he stifles his own sobs; pulls himself together; watches Shirley as she steps forward to comfort him; watches as they sit and he begins to talk. He knows he is talking about himself, about his war, while she says nothing about hers. And he watches while she throws her arms around him, not saying a word, and clings to him like she's saving him from drowning. Except, standing where he is now, knowing what he knows now, he's not sure whether maybe she was trying to save herself.

They seem to remain like that for an age, before she starts to fumble with his coat, and then his trousers; and then her own layers of clothes. And Harry, watching from above, starts to feel sick all over again; sick and excited.

Harry, poor Harry; he isn't a completely inexperienced young man. He has been with women before; but here we have no Nijinsky of coitus, or a Donne in the art of seduction. Because this is back then, in a time before sex; where nice girls didn't, and what a boy could get, he had to cajole and negotiate for, hard. And even then, where was there to do it?

Not that any of that matters, because this is not Harry's show. Yes, he has always wanted Shirley; ached for her sometimes, but not like this. Romantic Harry has had his own imaginings as to how it should be, one day.

But this is Shirley's show. And she's taking what she needs because it is the only life-affirming thing she can think of after what she has seen; after what she has lived through on the bomb-shattered, burnt-out streets of Clydebank. This poor, shattered young woman needs her life reaffirming, right now; here, with her Harry. The only boy she's ever trusted. She doesn't know how to ask for it; who would? How would you ask? What words would you use? How can she ask him to prove to her that her body is still whole, and that life still courses within it, unlike almost every other body she's seen in the town she's just come from?

Like any smash and grab, it's messy and over quickly; and no one knows quite what to say afterwards. All Harry guiltily notices is that from the little splatters on his shirt tails, he is her first.

Harry, still replaying it all in his mind, follows as they both eventually descend from the Hump. He sees Shirley walk to her bicycle and cycle away. He knows there are tears in her eyes, but he dare not go so close as to see them again. It is not easy to relive the scene, even when all he has to do this time is watch it, from afar.

He knows what has happened; and he doesn't know. Which is why he runs. When he'd got back to Dundee, all the letters that had been chasing him around the Royal Navy postal system had finally caught up with him.

From the pouty, stylish, Gorgeous-with-a-capital-G Janis, who said she had 'written and written and written', there had only been one letter. He didn't read it, just dropped it in a wastepaper basket, unopened. But from Shirley; there was a parcel of them.

He started with the oldest one. In it she had at last turned eighteen and she was joining up, like she'd said she would, to be a volunteer ambulance driver in Glasgow. It is the thread that runs through all of her letters. A thread that starts with the excitement of it all, bubbling up through the other news and chat about politics, music, the war, books, them; and then the other news becomes less, and pretty soon it is all thread. Her war, under the bombs. Picking up what's left.

The letters end with a deceptively short little note, written a few days before Harry had returned on his first leave after joining *Radegonde*. The letter set out everything she wanted to say about two nights she had spent in Clydebank, and their aftermath. She didn't write much. The letter wasn't graphic; there was no self-pity; she's not that kind of girl.

March 13 and 14; the Clydebank Blitz. Two nights of sustained Jerry attack. It was all over the newspapers while Harry was at sea. Everybody knew the papers didn't tell everything; everybody knew it had been bad. And everybody probably knew Shirley had been there. But nobody had told Harry.

In a previous Gilmour household, before the world went mad, the talk would have been of little else. But in this world, the Gilmour household is no longer a place where people talk in the same old-fashioned way. His father sits behind his newspaper; he cannot talk to Harry, he is defiant and impotent against a world at war. His mother, the talker and the peacemaker, cannot talk because the house is full of other people's children; in the daytime, loud and excited and full of fun in a new world away from the bombs; but at night, sleepless, tearful, frightened, they are the orphans of a father dead at St Valery and a mother still in the city doing war work.

And into it all had walked Harry, home from the sea, too busy thinking about his war to listen to stories about anyone else's; giving nobody a chance to tell him anything. Selfish.

Gazing blankly into the foaming white of *Radegonde*'s wake, Harry sees it clearly now, all right. Everybody is in this war, not just him. But he hadn't seen it when Shirley had needed someone to talk to, more than talk to; all Harry had done was talk about himself. Who was the arse who said it is always better to face up to things as they really are? A mere few hours ago, Harry had felt happy. Now he's faced up to things, all he feels is shame.

He had been staring so intently into the water, he hadn't noticed Bassano leaning companionably on the rail beside him. By the look on the Frenchman's face Harry could tell he knew Harry had been brooding.

'So, what're you going to do on your first night ashore, Harry?' said Bassano, looking towards what was firming up to be Carnoustie Bay.

'I thought I was going out to get blind drunk with you, Henri,' said Harry, turning to look at him.

Bassano pursed his lips and rocked his head from side to side in that reflective way only a Frenchman can.

'*D'accord*,' he replied.

Chapter Eleven

Harry was on *Radegonde*'s bridge – not on watch, but adding his own set of binoculars to the constant scanning of the horizon – when the radio traffic started up. It was a beautiful spring day, with only a few scattered, high cirrus clouds against a vivid blue sky and a steady south-westerly breeze scudding the tops off the long rolling swell.

Radegonde was at forty-five degrees forty-nine minutes north, forty-four degrees thirty-eight minutes west, deep into the mid-Atlantic, cruising at a steady twelve knots, with just over 600 miles to run to Halifax, Nova Scotia, where she was scheduled to refuel before heading south for Martinique. Leading Telegraphist Cantor was on radio watch down in the conning tower's radio kiosk when the first signals started to come in. Leading Signalman Lucie was off watch, but was up there with him with nothing better to do than sit about reflecting on the excesses of their last leave. Cantor got him to go and call up through the conning tower hatch for Harry.

Harry, meanwhile, in between scanning the horizon, had been reflecting on his own excesses of the last leave. Exact convoy routings weren't broadcast for obvious reasons, so seeing as *Radegonde* was in the middle of convoy waters it was a good idea to keep an eye out. Being run down by a phalanx of up to a 100-odd merchant ships could, as the Yanks would say, ruin your whole day. Yes, visibility right now might be gin-clear, but the sooner you spotted a convoy, the more time you had to get out of its way. You might be on their side, but you were still a submarine, and having to engage in long explanations with a jittery escort was a problem you could do without. Especially on such a nice day.

So in between horizon-scanning, snapshots from his run ashore played out in Harry's head: out on the town in Dundee, arms linked, stepping out like Tiller Girls down the High Street with two other Free French officers from the other French sub in the flotilla, *Minerve*, belting out 'The Marseillaise' with a lung-bursting gusto; being thrown out of the dance at the North British Hotel for starting an impromptu conga line; then navigating deftly away, untouched, from the fight that had erupted in their wake on Castle Street between a bunch of Royal Navy lads and some Brylcreem boys coming it all superior. And then the waxing philosophical bits too, when it was just Harry and Bassano, just as the evening was getting going, before they'd topped off their alcohol tanks; leaning against the bar in Mennie's up on Perth Road, Bassano saying, 'So who was the woman you were thinking about? Or is it women?' And Harry, smiling to himself, replying, 'Isn't one enough?' and suddenly feeling all grown up, just like Humphrey Bogart.

'So what was the problem, Harry?'

'Beyond fixing, Henri,' Harry had replied. Definitely like Bogart, especially when he then got to say, 'And you? A woman?' And Bassano had nodded, in that way that only Frenchmen can. And that was when Bassano went all lyrical, in a way Harry had never dreamed him capable, easing open a door to a cultured and educated Bassano that Harry doubted any of the *Radegondes* ever imagined existed.

'Are you a reader, Harry?' he'd asked.

'Yes.'

'Ford Madox Ford. One of yours. Do you ever read him? *Parade's End*?'

'Yes.'

'In *Parade's End* there's a description of the hero's wife . . . "the more she has made an occupation out of torturing him, the less right she thinks she has to lose him . . . she will tear the house down and the world will echo with her wrongs . . ." That was mine. What do you do about that?'

'Drink heavily.'

'D'accord.'

It hadn't been the only philosophical excursion that leave. Unable to even think about going home, he had decided to take up an invitation extended months ago to go and see Sir Alexander Scrimgeour at his club in Edinburgh. Old Lexie, financier through the week, yacht-master at the weekend; owner of that magnificent twelve-metre sailing greyhound *Tangle*, and indulgent mentor to a young Harry for whom no task had been too menial to bag a berth aboard her as crew.

Lexie was a member of the Aristotelian, of course he was! That discreet bastion of intellect, philosophy, money and claret-swilling that had sprung up on the corner of Hanover Street and Queen Street in the aftermath of Great Britain's great defining victory in the Seven Years' War to provide a retreat for men the likes of old Lexie, where leisure could be taken after the exertions of building an Empire. Past alumni included David Hume, Adam Smith, Walter Scott and Alexander Fleming.

It had been a weekday when Harry had caught an early train from Dundee and rattled across the Forth Bridge to Waverley, to present himself in front of the Aristotelian's deliberately innocuous front door. Inside had been infinitely more grand. How very Edinburgh, Harry had thought: all genteel modesty on the outside. He was led through a high-ceilinged portico whose paintings he didn't have time to study, to a Chesterfield-populated library, book-lined floor to ceiling with one wall segmented by long deep windows, each pane starred with strips of masking tape against bomb-blast. Old Lexie was standing with a group of men of similar age, all in morning suits, cradling whisky snifters and toasting their backsides before a huge fireplace. The wall mirror above it was angled just right to reflect the varied array of balding pates below.

Harry was presented with his own snifter and then gently quizzed on the progress of the war, which he found amusing, seeing as every one of these men of business probably had a much better idea of how Britain was faring than he had. Then Lexie and Harry peeled off to dine alone.

Sir Alexander Scrimgeour was a man who looked taller than he really was; not because of any erect bearing, but his slight stoop. He was a spare man, more skin than flesh these days, flappy more than jowly; a face made up of sheets of legal parchment, and a strong chin that jutted out as if stretching to touch the plunging tip of his magnificently hooked nose. His neck dived into his starched collar without touching the sides. Not the best canvas to write his character on, but his smile, when it broke, which was often, worked wonders, aided and abetted by the devilment in his twinkly eyes. You knew right away then, this was a man who loved life and certainly knew how to make the most of it.

The old fart nodded his appreciation when Harry thanked him again for the sextant he'd presented him with when he'd signed up for the RNVR, but it was the French he really wanted to hear about.

'It's verr-y important work you are about, laddie,' he said. 'Keeping them in the war. They're a great, great nation who've gone a wee bit astray these days. Not to mention the sore strait they've plunged us gentleman into. To have our access to claret so suddenly denied. I'll tell you, this war better be over before the club's cellar gets any emptier.'

Harry assured him, if the *Radegondes* were anything to go by, they wanted to fight.

'Aye, aye. All well and good,' said Lexie. 'And long may it continue.'

Then he paused, ruminating, before starting up again. 'They might have prevailed in the last war,' he said, carefully bisecting his rabbit, 'but it cost them dear. Cost both of us dear. And we've both lived in dread of another, which is why we were so unprepared for this one. But such a magnificent country; a place of culture and prosperity and peace. Not all that unlike us in these islands. The only thing about the French, though, is they are prone to two very different types of violent disaster.'

'What would those be?' asked Harry, wondering whether the old man was beginning to ramble. He should've known better.

'Avalanches in the Haute-Savoie,' said Lexie, 'and their national politics.' And he washed a forkful of rabbit down with a glass of the aforementioned claret. Harry followed him. The braised rabbit really was rather good – and so was the claret.

'They do like to get into their respective trenches, when it comes to their politics,' said Lexie. 'And, of course, communism was a big threat to them, especially after the crash. I can't remember how many governments they had before war broke out. And, of course, all the time their Right was listening to Mr Hitler and only hearing what he was going to do to the communists. And there's still too many Frenchmen think he's a good thing. Even now.

'Marshal Pétain and his Vichy cronies believe they're still dealing with the Germany of 1871. They think once the Hun's beaten us, they're only going to hang around in France long enough to impose some punishing but bearable treaty, exact reparations and then bugger off. As they did back then. They don't realise who this man Hitler is. That this is a different war, and they're in Hitler's empire now. That's why it is so important that we back this bumptious big scrapper de Gaulle; and so should the French people.'

Tangle had been towed up the River Leven, and hauled ashore for the duration, Harry then learned. Sir Alexander hadn't even bothered to check whether there were new regulations regarding pleasure boats, he was damned if he was going to risk his precious lady among all that naval traffic, or venture out anywhere on waters choked with assembling convoys. The conversation drifted on until it was almost five, and Harry had to think about getting a train back to Dundee.

'One more wee balloon of this most elegant Armagnac,' he had said, and who was Harry to argue? He had just spent one of the most agreeable lunchtimes of his life. And not really because of the setting he'd been treated to, or the matters he had discussed with the man, although his view on how matters stood politically with the French had been interesting; it was because of the way he had talked to Harry. Like a grown up. Harry had stopped being the boy who 'did' aboard this man's yacht. Harry, in his uniform of a Sub-Lieutenant, RNVR, had been addressed as just that. And more; there had been an undisguised pride in Sir Alexander when presenting his protégé – his dashing, young submarine officer protégé – to his cronies. Harry had liked that. So much so that he'd stopped thinking of him as old Lexie, and started thinking of him as Sir Alexander instead. He chose not to think about how he had left matters with his father.

Harry, back on *Radegonde*'s bridge, rolling on the Atlantic swell, was still smiling at the memory when Lucie's shouting interrupted his reverie and he had to trot to the conning tower hatch.

'What?' he said, irritated, glowering down to where Lucie stood at the bottom of the ladder peering up.

'Scuse me, Sir. But there's a lot of stuff goin' back an' forth on the radio, Sir. We think you should take a listen to.'

'If it isn't Glenn Miller playing "Tuxedo Junction", I'll be extremely upset,' said Harry, backing to clamber down the ladder. The rest of the bridge team, from the Captain to the lowly lookouts, cast little smirks at each other on seeing Harry annoyed.

Cantor was perched at the radio set, earphones scrunched on his head, scribbling furiously as more Morse code was coming in. Harry pulled up one of the little wooden stools. On the table in front of Cantor was a growing pile of torn-off signals from his pad, all awaiting identification and decoding.

'A lot of this stuff is Jerry,' said Lucie, tapping the pile.

Harry frowned at him; what was he supposed to do with piles of Jerry signals? Better minds than his were off somewhere, buried in deep bunkers and even deeper secrecy, trying to break those Jerry codes, and if they were struggling, what did bloody Lucie and Cantor think he was going to do with them?

But Lucie was old in the ways of the navy, and well used to bloody officers jumping to wrong conclusions.

'Sir, when I say lots of Jerry stuff, I mean *lots*. And Lionel here thinks the sending stations are close, and more than one fist, Sir. And there's stuff from Western Approaches. And from Kernevel too, by the bearing and signal strength.'

'Fist' was a wireless operator's signature; the distinct beat in the way he tapped out his signals. Unique to every operator, if you had the experience and the ear to hear it. And Lucie was saying Cantor did.

Also, at the mention of Kernevel, Lucie now had Harry's full attention.

'I've jotted down the exact times and bearings to the Jerry stuff, Sir,' said Cantor, taking a break from scribbling his Morse, and pushing a pile of signal slips to Harry, 'for you to compare with our position. The stuff from Western Approaches is there.' He prodded the pile of signals Lucie had his hand on. 'And the Jerry

stuff from France, from Kernevel. But there's more than one station transmitting the Jerry stuff out here,' he added, nodding in the
general direction of north. 'Four, I reckon, Sir. At least. And these,'
he added, spreading several slips from the rest, 'these are from the
same station.'

'You're certain?' said Harry.

'You can bank on it, Sir,' interrupted Lucie, with what sounded
like paternal pride. 'He's good with his fists, Sir, is young Lionel.'

So, considered Harry, we have traffic from Western Approaches
Command, the new joint Royal Navy, RAF Coastal Command HQ
set up back in February in Liverpool to run all the convoys to and
from home waters. And from Kernevel – how did the likes of Lucie
and Cantor ever hear of Kernevel? How does anyone ever hear anything in wartime?

Kernevel was the French villa in Lorient from which Karl
Donitz, the German Admiral in command of the Kriegsmarine's
U-boat arm, ran his show. Funny how word gets out, thought
Harry, as he scooped up all the slips, turning his mind now to the
four other possible transmitting stations, out here somewhere, in
mid-Atlantic.

'I'm going below,' he said, slipping out of the conning tower
and down into the control room. 'Keep listening in, Cantor . . . and
good work.'

When Harry got to the wardroom, that bloody French Marines
officer – or le Fusiliers Marins, as they would have it – Enseigne
de Vaisseau Thierry was sitting there, hogging the banquette and
sharpening a bayonet. What an arse, thought Harry, who did he
think he was going to be stabbing any time in the near future?
Harry, on the bridge in the sunshine, had forgotten all about him
and his platoon. In fact, since the day they'd stepped on board back
in Plymouth, he had tried to forget about them as often as he could.
He especially wanted to forget about them right now as he wanted

to get at his code books and work out what was in the signals from Western Approaches. He'd had an idea, but the books were in the little cubby behind the banquette, and Thierry was in the way.

The French youth looked up at him. He could only have been about Harry's age. His hair was buzz-cut to a dark shadow, and his chin was another that had yet to feel the need of a razor, but it was the rest of his face that was truly arresting; not for any particularly distinguishing feature, but for its blandness. It was flat, character-less and if you stared long enough, chillingly lacking any human quality you might appeal to. He was certainly a bumptious little bastard, full of outrage at le Boche, and all who were collaborating with them. And no one was permitted to have more contempt for the Vichy government than he. The self-righteousness would gush forth as if you'd turned on a tap. If there was any fighting to be done against Jerry and his lackeys, Thierry was first in the queue to do it, and everybody had better understand that, especially any jumped-up, stuffed-shirt, little English shopkeeper. Which was why Harry had cottoned-on early to the fact that Thierry didn't like him.

Harry asked to be allowed in to get at the cubby. Thierry the-atrically continued to sharpen the bayonet for a few more strokes, then wordlessly moved aside, just enough for Harry to retrieve the code books, and no more. It would have been handy for Harry to spread his stuff over the wardroom table and get to work, but he didn't have the energy or the time to get into one of these little gavottes Thierry seemed to revel in, over who had the biggest dick. So Harry went into Captain Syvret's cabin – something he was allowed to do, and Thierry wasn't, which, needless to say, infuriated Thierry even more.

Enseigne Thierry and his platoon were *Radegonde*'s cargo, and her reason for heading to Martinique; they were on their way to enforce the writ of the new Free French government on France's Caribbean colonies.

It had all started with the black Humber staff car waiting for Captain Syvret when they'd come alongside after their last patrol. Nobody aboard had thought much about it at the time. If anything they probably assumed someone in the flotilla offices had had a sudden attack of concern for Captain Syvret's wellbeing and had sent a car for him so as he could make his patrol report and get off on leave faster. Then Captain Syvret had turned up again days later, looking very grim, and all leave was cancelled, the crew recalled, and they headed off, amid great secrecy, for a destination unknown.

Three days later, the secret destination had turned out to be Devonport Dockyard in Plymouth, where *Radegonde* was taken in hand, and fitted with four welded watertight tubes designed to fit in her mine chambers. The tubes were capable of carrying all the kit and weaponry required for the landing of a Fusiliers Marins platoon, fully equipped and ready to carry out operations on a foreign shore.

Then Thierry and his platoon had come aboard, its twenty men instantly transforming what Harry had felt had been quite a roomy boat into an ocean-going Black Hole of Calcutta; and equally speedily managing to annoy and then render downright hostile the entire crew.

Captain Syvret had been absent for most of that interlude, along with the First Lieutenant, Poulenc; both of them closeted in a secret conclave ashore with senior Free French officers and men in dark suits and homburg hats. It was rumoured even de Gaulle had attended some of their meetings.

By the time Captain Syvret and Poulenc returned, the discipline aboard had deteriorated to the point where confrontations between the crew and their guests were regular, and on two occasions they had already come to blows. Throughout all this Harry, Cantor and Lucie, with no responsibilities aboard, had hidden in a dockyard hut. Afterwards, Harry had heard that Thierry had buttonholed Captain Syvret the minute he had stepped off the ladder into his own control room, to inform him that while he, Thierry, was aboard, he alone was in charge of his Fusiliers Marins, and that it was Captain Syvret's job to get his unruly crew back in line and get Thierry and his detachment to their objective without any further ado.

Captain Syvret had politely invited the Enseigne into his cabin and pulled the curtain. Nobody had actually heard what was said, but when Thierry had emerged, his bland face was ashen, and all discipline was quickly restored. Then they had put to sea, and on the second day out Captain Syvret had briefed everyone on their mission. They were going to spend the summer in the Caribbean. Harry thought that should have made *Radegonde* a happy boat, but resentments between the crew and the Fusiliers had continued to simmer.

But Harry didn't have time to brood on any of that. He went straight to the signals from Western Approaches and opened his code books. There were four messages. The first was addressed to a convoy escort Commander, copy to convoy Commodore, for a convoy designated SC, indicating it was an east-bound slow convoy, originating in Sydney, Cape Breton, on Nova Scotia. It also gave its number. *'Be aware: 3, repeat 3 U-boats, now believed operating in your area.'* That was message one. Message two was a weather report which indicated the weather in this area would continue fine for the next twenty-four hours. Message three raised the number of U-boats to five, and message four, to six. Harry looked at the timings: ten hours since the first U-boat warning.

There was nothing from the convoy, but then there wouldn't be – it would be observing strict radio silence. No point in helping Jerry to find you.

Then he looked at the Jerry traffic. Each signal was made up of random blocks of four letters each; Cantor had marked the bearing of each one. The ones that came from points to the north of

Radegonde's course, Cantor had designated targets 1, 2, 3 and 4. Target 2 had transmitted more than once. Then there was the other set of signals; their bearing was constant and from the east, and Cantor had pencilled a 'K' on them. For Kernevel, presumably. Harry scooped the signals up and headed for the control room and its chart table.

Bassano had been marking their course. He was leaning against the table, sipping from a mug of coffee.

'Been chatting to Joan of Arc's love child, have we?' he said, grinning. 'Is he enjoying his cruise?'

'Help me with this,' said Harry as he slapped down the signals. Bassano glanced down at the paper slips and saw the bearings, and his expression changed. Down went the cup, and out came the parallel rulers, dividers and a pencil. He began tracing back *Radegonde's* course, and from the slips he marked the timings of the Jerry transmissions, then from each transmission time, he drew a line in pencil from *Radegonde's* progress out along the bearing, and way off up the chart. Somewhere along that line there had been Jerries doing the transmitting. Exactly how far along the lines however, they would not be able to tell without a cross bearing, unless . . .

'These slips marked Target 2, we know they were sent from the same station?' said Bassano, holding several of Cantor's annotated intercepts.

'Cantor says he's confident they came from the same fist,' said Harry. Bassano nodded intently. He started scribbling Cantor's target IDs on the pencil lines, then looked at the chart again.

'He's transmitting here,' said Bassano, stabbing at the chart with his pencil, 'and then here, and here. He's moving. East.' Bassano then began adjusting his dividers. 'If our heading is westerly . . . at twelve knots . . .' Bassano took up a slide rule and started to work it, then readjusted the dividers and drew them down between two of the pencilled lines until the tings spanned the gap. 'Target 2 is less than thirty miles nor'-nor'-west of us, and doing . . . eight knots.'

Bassano looked up at Harry's sharp intake of breath.

'Eight knots,' said Harry. 'The speed of a slow convoy. That's a wolf pack assembling.'

'What?' said Bassano, studying the chart more closely.

'Target 2 is a U-boat that has spotted one of our convoys and is trailing it,' said Harry, excited now. 'Instead of attacking right away, he's held off and started yelling. Those other transmissions are other U-boats telling him and Kernevel, they're coming to the party. My God! And Western Approaches knows. They must be doing D/F on them . . . direction finding . . . they've got stations that can triangulate the signals . . . and they're flashing warnings . . . there are U-boats in your area. It's a wolf pack all right. I knew it. I've got to tell the Captain.'

Less than a minute later, Harry and Captain Syvret were leaning over the chart table.

'Surely the escort will double back and engage them,' said Syvret, pushing his cap back and squinting at the starburst of bearings pencilled on his good chart.

'They can't leave the convoy,' replied Harry, staring at Syvret intently. 'Standing orders. They don't know how many U-boats might be out there, so they have to stick close to the merchant ships.'

'So?' said Syvret, turning now to stare back.

'Jerry doesn't know we're here,' said Harry, staring back too.

'And long may that continue,' said Syvret. '*Radegonde* has her own mission.' He paused, before adding, 'I do hope you're not suggesting we add our voice to the warnings and radio the convoy there are Jerries sneaking up behind them.'

'No,' said Harry. 'Then Jerry would know we were here.'

'Oh God!' said Syvret, his face doing his hangdog expression. 'You are going to suggest that we engage these U-boats, aren't you?

Like we're the US Cavalry, and I'm John Wayne.' Syvret stopped in mid-flow the minute he'd said that, and smiled a little as if he were considering the point; then he went grim again. 'Look at you. There's practically bloodlust in your eyes. Down, Fido!'

Harry didn't say anything.

'And now you're going to tell me about the lives that'll be lost if we don't,' Syvret added. 'And ships that can be saved, and that this is a once-in-a-lifetime chance to get back at the Boche. Orders, Sub-Lieutenant Gilmour. Don't you understand orders? I have my orders.'

Bassano, who was leaning back against the table watching the two of them, shrugged, and then said, 'If you did go after them, Sir, you'd be delaying little Miss Thierry back there from getting to grips with all those accursed Vichy collaborators sitting about on Martinique, oblivious to his immanent descent, and you know how much that'll piss him off.'

Without taking his eyes off Harry, Syvret sighed and said, 'I know.' Then, after the silence that followed, he said over his shoulder in a formal voice, 'Helm. Starboard twenty. Make your course three four zero, full ahead together. Pass the word for the Torpedo officer. I want to see him in the control room, now.'

It was still daylight by the time *Radegonde* had worked her way up behind where they had now estimated the wolf pack was gathering. They were still running on the surface, and were roughly west-north-west of the target area, their main periscope extended to its maximum elevation, with Bassano keeping a permanent watch between ninety and 150 degrees. It was a tactic that Syvret hoped would allow *Radegonde* to remain hidden under the U-boats' horizon, but allow *Radegonde*, with her periscope extended above that horizon, to see them. Also, Syvret was hoping that since the U-boats were concentrating on the convoy, their lookouts may not be paying as much attention as they should be to what might be approaching from astern.

Faujanet, on the bridge, called down that he could see a smoke smudge just topping the horizon on 135 degrees. Some dirty smoke-stack undoing all the secrecy. It must be the convoy. Advancing at this speed, it would be a slow one. Probably with the designation SC. Harry had no idea how many merchant ships it would number – three dozen at least, likely many more – all laden with vital war supplies. A slow convoy also meant they would probably be older ships; rust buckets many of them, with clanking, reciprocating engines, some maybe even coal-fired. Crewed by ordinary blokes, civilians, just doing it for a living, except the war meant they no longer had the option to chuck it in and look for work ashore. Their country needed them now, whether they liked it or not. The ships would be marshalled in rows, in a big oblong box, moving broadside on. If it were thirty-six ships, there would be nine ships abreast, four deep. The shape was easier for the convoy's Commodore to control with his signal flags and Aldis lamps; more ships could see him when it came to wheel and manoeuvre. And the escorts; half a dozen if they were lucky. Flower Class corvettes, smaller than half the steamers that plied the Clyde in peacetime. A few dozen depth charges a piece, and a pop gun on the fo'c'sle. And maybe one V&W Class destroyer; a relic of the last lot, for the escort Commander.

And somewhere between it and *Radegonde* there were likely six or more enemy submarines, following on the surface, waiting for night, when their low, black silhouettes would help them sneak inside the escort screen, into the big oblong box, where they could begin their work, sinking ships.

And right now, all that stood between them and their prey was *Radegonde*; not the best type of warship for the job at hand.

For *Radegonde* was first and foremost a minelayer. The mine was her principal weapon. Yes, she had torpedo tubes, six in fact, but hunting down her enemies and sinking them with torpedoes was not what she was designed for. Her torpedo tube layout told you that if nothing else did. Four 550mm tubes faced forward, two either side of her centre line, with each tube holding one torpedo, plus one reload stowed in the forward mess deck, which doubled as the main torpedo room, and which some of the crew slept in. Then over the stern, there was the most bizarre weapon he'd ever seen on a submarine: two 400mm torpedo tubes mounted on an external swivel device that sat above and abaft the two minelaying chutes. Those could be trained astern through 180 degrees, but there were no reloads for them. The first time Harry had set eyes on it, he began trying to imagine how you'd manage to accurately aim the damn things. He was still none the wiser.

The 550mm torpedoes were of 1920s design and carried a 300kg warhead; they were alcohol-powered and had a range of 3,000 metres at forty-five knots. The 400mm torpedoes were slightly less impressive, dating from the same vintage, with a 140kg warhead and a range of just 2,000 metres at just thirty-five knots. Harry had first been introduced to *Radegonde*'s fire power by de Maligou way back when he first joined her. After *Pelorus* and *Trebuchet*, Harry hadn't been much impressed. He certainly never imagined he would be going head-to-head with a clutch of German boats, armed with such puny weaponry.

U-boats were proper hunting submarines, and their crews were almost certainly far more experienced in submarine warfare than the *Radegondes*. It would be fantasy to hope they could sink all the U-boats now ranged against that hapless convoy. For a start, they couldn't be sure how many they might be up against. But it was certainly possible that *Radegonde* could disrupt their attack, spread confusion and maybe let the convoy break contact with the U-boats and get away. That was doable. And, anyway, regardless of whatever was going to happen, there was always the damage they could wreak to look forward to.

One's dander, said a grinning Harry to himself, *is definitely up!*

And even as this thought formed, Harry brought himself up short; wondering to himself who it was doing all this talking inside his head. It didn't sound like the chap in the tweed jacket and varsity scarf, who quite enjoyed spending hours in the library; whose idea of a wild time was having a sixth pint on a Friday night; and who liked looking at girls' legs when they showed in a twirl at the Saturday dance. He had quite liked him. Now, apparently, he was being replaced by another Harry, who was looking forward to killing other people; with bloodlust in his eyes. He refused to think about what he'd done to Shirley; blanked her, utterly. But he couldn't stop himself from thinking that this Harry didn't seem very likable at all.

Chapter Twelve

'If they're grouped tight together, Sir, it could be a pretty brisk action and the fruit machine really could help,' Harry said, his hand patting the top of a box of dials and knobs.

Syvret was leaning back against the chart table, and regarding Harry like he was some kind of tempting demon. 'Its range read-outs are imperial, not metric,' said Syvret.

But Harry was a man on a mission. 'I'll worry about speeds and ranges. What you need to know is when to fire, and for that, all you need is the right periscope angle. The fruit machine will give you a firing solution faster than working it out on a slide rule, especially if you're moving from one target to another quickly. I know how to work this thing. Let me help.'

The fruit machine was a basic electro-mechanical angle solver and it had been fitted to *Radegonde* just as Harry had joined her. The Boffin Box, they called it; the latest addition of many items of Royal Navy kit, all of it now cordially loathed by her crew. None of it was up to Marine Nationale standard, they said, so how could they be expected to know how to use it. And they were buggered if they were going to learn. You'd have thought it had been foisted on them, but nothing could be further from the truth. The stuff had been fitted because the French Navy's entire inventory of spares was now held by the Germans.

Harry pointed at the smaller dial on the device, with its little icon of *Radegonde*'s hull etched on it in Bakelite. 'This is us. There's a feed from the log plugged into the back giving our speed, and another from the gyro giving our heading. This other one is the target. You're on the periscope. You call out to me the bearing to the target, drop your stadimeter on the target and call out the range – I can do a good metres to yards in my head – and then you use your trained nautical eye to estimate its speed, and call that. I then crank all that into the machine here and out comes the periscope angle. Once you've got that, you turn your periscope to that angle and just wait until Jerry putters across the little black line, then you shout, fire one!'

Syvret scratched his head, and looked to Le Breuil and Bassano, then back to Harry. 'OK,' he conceded. Then added, 'If the U-boats are tight together. But if we come on them spread out over an area of sea we do it the old-fashioned way.'

To the west it was already night when *Radegonde* sighted her first U-boat. Syvret had hoped to get north of where he thought they'd be so he wouldn't be silhouetted against a setting sun, but Jerry had thought of that too and, not wanting to be caught likewise by the convoy, was running at speed, nor'-nor'-east of *Radegonde*'s track. Two more U-boats quickly slid up the horizon beyond the first target.

'Down periscope. Start a plot, M'sieur Bassano,' said Syvret, and he called out the enemy's heading. 'They are working their way around to the head of the convoy. I mean to put us between them and it, and be waiting as they angle in to attack.' He looked at his watch. 'We'll go to Action Stations in half an hour. M'sieur Faujanet, inform Thierry that I have ordered that he and his men are to move to the aft mess and remain there until I order otherwise.

119

And take Maître principal de Maligou with you. Tell him he is to growl a lot.'

There was a ripple of heads and shoulders around the control room, as officers and men suppressed their laughter. *Oh, Captain Syvret,* thought Harry, *you know how to lead men into battle.*

Radegonde remained on the surface, running flat out. Syvret was on the bridge with four lookouts instead of the usual two – one set, eyes peeled for Jerry coming from port, and the other for steering clear of the convoy, particularly its escorts, to starboard. In the control room, Poulenc was on the trim board, Bassano the plot and Le Breuil in the forward torpedo room. Faujanet was with the gun crew, under the forward hatch, waiting. Syvret didn't want them up yet; he wanted to see how the fight was going to pan out, and didn't want any more bodies up top than necessary in case he had to dive in a hurry. Harry sat at his fruit machine. Its log feed showed *Radegonde's* speed as seventeen knots, and the gyro showed their heading at 100 degrees.

With their high superstructures and tall masts, the convoy would've been in sight from the bridges of the gathering wolf pack, even as darkness fell. And the wolf pack's low silhouettes made them invisible to the convoy. *Radegonde* might be running closer to the U-boats, but she was a submarine too, and equally low in the water. Syvret was banking on the curve of the earth to keep her below the German night glasses now scanning the horizon; banking on how easy it is for a lookout to miss something he does not expect to see. And Jerry was not expecting to see *Radegonde.*

Now, with the night closed in, the only difference between the dark sky and darker ocean was in the subtlety of shading. Syvret and his lookouts had to strain to pick out even darker smudges against their backdrop. In the control room, and forward, beneath the gun hatch trunking, they were all bathed in red light, to preserve their night vision. No one spoke, in case they might miss the call of 'enemy in sight' because they were chatting. The only noise now was the thundering of the diesels. Harry felt the atmosphere in the control room: it was like being a raw recruit in the middle of a cavalry squadron at full charge, intoxicated by all the mad, blind, bursting confidence and *elan*. So overweening it kicked aside a doubt that had been nagging at him.

'Control room!' Syvret called down through the bridge mic. 'How far have we run on this course?'

Bassano, without having to check his watch or chronometer on the chart table, called out the distance and time.

'Reduce speed to 200 rpm. Come to zero-six-five,' came Syvret's curt, staticky command. Harry remembered thinking, *What's wrong? Three U-boats are out there. You saw them. Aren't they where they're supposed to be anymore?*

The questions clamoured in his head as Harry felt the hull lean as the boat curved to port, and the noise of the diesels again became the only sound.

Then, suddenly, a shout. But it was not the shout the boat had been straining for; more like an intrusion from a parallel universe. Syvret's voice was barking from out of the squawk box positioned over the chart table. And, so far, the Captain's French was not so fast or jargon-filled that Harry couldn't follow.

'Surface contact on three-five-zero! She's coming on fast', and he paused. *Must be using the stadimeter*, thought Harry. And indeed then came another call, 'Range 3,500 metres . . . It's a U-boat!'

As good as 4,000 yards, decided Harry, and cranked it in.

'From his bow wave, estimate speed at twelve knots plus.'

And Harry cranked that in too, thinking, *You need to take your foot off the accelerator now, Skipper, you don't want us crossing in front of him, instead of him crossing in front of us.*

And, as if he'd been listening to Harry's thoughts, Syvret called, 'Five knots!' And Harry physically felt *Radegonde* drag in the water.

Then Syvret called down another range. The U-boat was closing fast. Out of the corner of his eye, Harry caught Bassano working his slide rule, then Syvret called again, 'Estimate target's course is one five five', and Bassano nodded to himself, and began plotting its course. 'No, zigzag,' added Syvret with Harry thinking, *Why would Jerry zigzag; he is closing on his target; he doesn't know we're here, he thinks he's the hunter not the prey.* 'It's going to be a track angle of one-zero-two degrees,' added Syvret, with a degree of glee. A perfect set up. If all held good, *Radegonde* would be sitting at right angles to Jerry's advancing course.

All that was needed now was for Harry to crank out a good periscope angle on his fruit machine; the firing solution. It was all about angles and speeds: the U-boat, and *Radegonde* closing it from starboard; the invisible line reaching out from the U-boat, down which it would travel, charging out of the night; the course *Radegonde's* torpedo would take to cut that line; and the point on the U-boat's progress where Syvret had to shout fire, so that the torpedo and the U-boat would arrive at the same place at the same time.

So far, Harry's command of French had allowed him to follow the barked commands. So far, so good, but he started to feel a certain anxiety; events were moving, and the tactical picture changing, but as yet, not too fast. Nor had the navy jargon yet become too technical; nor too *French* navy. So far.

Then Syvret made another range call in metres. Harry translated it as 1,800 yards, and cranked it in. Enemy course still steady on one five five. And then another call, he translated that one as 1,200 yards. But that was too soon. The U-boat couldn't have travelled 600 yards in that time. What was Syvret calling? Bassano, working over the chart, paused and ordered speed increased to eight knots. Was the 1,200 call the range Syvret wanted to fire at? Harry was losing the tactical picture, getting confused. He was also aware of Poulenc on the trim board, suddenly unusually active.

'Periscope angle!' It was an order from Syvret, not a question.

That was for Harry; but he was caught unawares, watching Poulenc and wondering what his last inputs were. Realising he didn't have the time, he calculated from the inputs he had. This was not the moment to start interrogating the Captain about updates. 'Periscope angle is red one six.'

Bassano repeated Harry's call over his mic, but before he'd finished the call the air was rent by the diving klaxon – two guttural bellows, and the lookouts were tumbling down into the control room, and Syvret's voice could be heard, not through the squawk box, but from the conning tower kiosk immediately above; loud staccato orders in French that Harry could *not* follow. He caught Syvret yelling, 'One hundred metres!' and assumed that was where they were heading down to. And from the decibels, he assumed the Captain meant fast. Very fast. Harry felt *Radegonde*'s hull begin to fall away. But only begin. She was definitely going down, but there was no angle developing on her. It was all far too sedate. He should have been hanging on to something by now.

The nagging doubt came back.

He couldn't help it now, wondering if the *Radegondes* had ever done this before. A torpedo attack for real. Especially a surface torpedo attack. She was a minelaying boat, and for all the time he'd been aboard her, it had never entered his head to be so rude as to enquire whether they'd ever sunk anything with her torpedoes. But even if they hadn't, surely they knew how to get their boat down in a hurry?

Syvret was yelling again, and Poulenc on the trim board was yelling back. Something about how he couldn't get her bows down, how she was insisting on going down on an even keel, and no amount of increased revs and down angle on the planes was driving her off it. And that was when Harry realised what was wrong, and so did Syvret and Bassano: Thierry and his platoon jammed into the aft crew mess. *Radegonde* was stern heavy and wasn't going to be rushed.

Harry was out of his seat and sprinting aft, swinging through the bulkhead doors like a macaque. He was already heading through the motor room, when his and the Electrical Petty Officer's eyes met in understanding; the Petty Officer on the sound-powered telephone from the control room was being ordered to get *everybody* for'ard, now! Harry shot past him, as he started yelling at the motor room crew.

Harry, as he undogged the bulkhead door leading to the aft crew mess, could hear the pounding of feet, and feel them through the deckplates, as *Radegonde*'s crew charged off towards the bows. He pushed the door open, hitting an outraged Thierry a glancing blow. The Fusiliers Marins had been sulky when originally ordered aft into this confined space that smelled of matelots' socks and other things; had been angry when they heard the bulkhead door's dogs being secured on them and realised they were being locked in. And they had become increasingly alarmed as they first felt the boat slew, then slow, and then they had heard a klaxon blare for no apparent reason. Now they were being screamed at in bad French by that arrogant rosbif. It was all too much. French Fusiliers Marins would not be ordered about on a French boat by some jumped-up foreigner. Thierry drew himself up to argue.

Harry did not have time for this. *Radegonde* needed everybody in the bows, right now. She needed her nose down, and to be powering deep if she was going to get out of the road of whatever harm was undoubtedly coming her way. He needed to get Thierry's attention, right now, and motivate him and his men to follow him forward. Right now! So he punched Thierry right on the end of his nose, turned and ran. Completely outraged now, the Fusiliers Marins pursued him without requiring any further persuasion.

Their weight made all the difference. *Radegonde* started going down. Fast.

Her bows, now too heavy to control, meant she was heading all the way down into the abyssal depths of the mid-Atlantic, driven onwards by her twin electric motors going flat out. Syvret ordered full astern, together; but to no avail.

It was the ever-poised and unflappable Poulenc on the trim board who saved them; who kept his head, and in a series of precise orders, none of which Harry understood, had blown the forward ballast tanks and the bow and aft planes to maximum rise; he'd ordered the crew – including the incensed Fusiliers Marins – aft again, at the run.

And at last *Radegonde*'s bows had come up and the boat was brought back into trim at a hull-creaking 212 metres. The sudden halt in their dive allowed Harry time to divert his thoughts away from blind fear, to trying to work out in his head the tactical picture; to try to understand exactly what had just happened. Then the sickening *ricka-chicky-ricka-chicky!* of high-speed screws above them began echoing through the boat. It was a U-boat, going flat out. At some point during Syvret's attack, Jerry had turned towards them. The U-boat went over the top, and then there was a roar as the U-boat too, began diving.

Minutes later, after all the chaos had subsided, back in the control room . . . 'Some damn, carrot-topped, carrot-chomping, bat-faced, box-swede, master-race, with his fucking hat on backwards must have seen us!' ranted Syvret, to no one in particular, in his designed-to-be-irritating, matter-of-fact voice.

'He means a U-boat lookout,' Bassano helpfully translated sotto voce for Harry.

Everyone was still bathed in red, and the shadows cast by Syvret's frown made him look demonic, while every other face looked condemned. One last look around and Syvret clambered back up into the conning tower kiosk, getting ready to put the periscope up again. 'The U-boat turned towards us,' they heard him continue. 'Directly towards us. But look on the bright side. If we had fired our torpedoes, he would have combed them.'

Radegonde was on her way back up after three minutes of what seemed to Harry total confusion.

A constant call and counter call was now playing out between Syvret and the matelot on *Radegonde's* hydrophones which allowed Harry to work out that *Radegonde* wasn't running; she was still in the fight. There were obviously other propeller sounds out there in the water, and it looked like Syvret was deciding which one to go after. He would have a choice too; this close to their target the U-boat Skippers wouldn't be chatting to each other, alerting each other. An eagle-eyed escort might notice a blinking Aldis lamp, but using their radio transmitters this close would deafen any radio operator listening out in the convoy.

But Harry was no longer trying to follow the action.

Silly Billy Harry, he told himself in a quiet fury. *Trying to work that fruit machine had been a bad idea . . . submarine warfare moves too fast for you to stop and do translations in your head, and then start fingering your way through your jargon crib to make sure you've understood the last order but three . . . you should've tried ordering a nice cup of coffee while you were at it.*

Harry, when he'd untangled himself from where he'd been clinging on to stop himself from ending in a heap on the forward bulkhead, did not return to sit at his fruit machine. He went and squeezed himself between the aft control room bulkhead and the chart table; out of the way, with Bassano between him and any Fusilier Marins not yet completely terrified by what was happening around them, and still out for retribution for that punch. From where he was, if he looked up, he could see Syvret at the small attack periscope in the kiosk through the hatch above.

There was a lot of noise in the control room now: people shouting out the revs on the motors; the charge left on the battery; the angles of the diving planes; the boat's heading; the bubble on the trim, to the point Harry couldn't work out how Syvret could think, let alone tune out all the din that wasn't relevant, but he seemed to be managing. The main conversation was still the one between Syvret and the hydrophone man about HE effects to port. Harry glanced at Bassano's plot. *Radegonde* was at periscope depth twelve metres, on 100 degrees when Syvret called out for *Radegonde*'s speed. 'Three knots,' came the reply from the matelot on the engine room telegraph. There was more shouting: the hydrophone man called out, and then Bassano amended the plot. From what Harry could see and translate, it appeared they were on a converging course with another target advancing on 135 degrees. He didn't catch the range, but the enemy was apparently doing twelve knots and Bassano was hurriedly working his slide rule. 'Nine red!' he called. *Was that a periscope angle?*

There were more yells between Syvret and a Petty Officer down here in the control room, then the Petty Officer repeated them down the sound-powered telephone. More shouting; Syvret looked up from the 'scope, his eyes hard. The PO on the phone was wild-eyed. Then nothing. Nothing was happening, no one was shouting. And the impasse went on and on and on; Harry's mind racing ahead; thinking, *what the hell is happening?*

A voice, like a distant crackling of brown paper could be heard from the headphones; the PO shouted something Harry didn't understand and Syvret had his eyes back on the 'scope again. Harry thought, *I know it's dark, but you've had that periscope up a helluva long time!*

Syvret's head came back from the periscope, and Harry could see him, half face down, mouth the word '*merde!*' He hit the periscope handles and ordered it down, calling out once again; not angles or depths this time, but something . . . aft, it sounded like. Something else had gone wrong.

God, but it was infuriating not being able to follow the action. The PO appeared to be ringing another number on the phone, and Syvret called out again. It was a course change. Starboard four-zero, and he was calling for more revs; a lot more. Harry watched Syvret look at his watch, then look down directly at him, and, dearie me, was there no end to this Frenchman's bravado, he smiled a smile, as if to say: are we having fun yet?

The PO on the sound-powered phone began speaking into the mouthpiece. Syvret checked his watch again, studying it this time. And the control room, unnervingly, was allowing him silence in which to do it.

'Up periscope!' said Syvret. He stepped forward to grab the handles, then swivelling it to port, scanning briefly, he settled on a bearing and called, 'Check!'

De Maligou's frame appeared in the hatch behind the Captain; he had been following him around, leaning over him, hands on his shoulders, squinting at the angles marked on the periscope's bezel. He called, 'One-two-zero, red!' And the shouting started up again.

Harry looked from one face to another, trying to work out what was happening. He could see from Bassano's plot, *Radegonde* and the U-boat were diverging. Another shout, and Bassano was over the plot, changing their heading to a wider angle, and marking their speed beside it. They were doing nine knots now and the amps must be draining out their batteries like water out of a tap. And then Syvret shouted, 'Fire!'

Fire, what? thought Harry, until he felt *Radegonde*'s back end judder, like a nightclub dancer's shimmy, and then it repeated itself. That's when he knew, when it dawned on him: that infernal contraption on the casing aft of the minelaying chutes – the two swivel-mounted torpedo tubes. Which was why Bassano had his stopwatch out now; they had just fired the two aft tubes, and he was timing them to target. Syvret still stood glued to the periscope, his head fixed on the bearing. *Bad tactics*, thought Harry, *to have that 'scope still up, even at night.*

'First one, missed,' said Bassano, taking his finger off the watch, Harry thinking, *Christ that must have been close*, and then after two beats, Bassano just managed to say, 'Second one . . .' before he was interrupted by Syvret shouting, 'AHA!' And then just a half beat later, *BUUD-DUUUDDUUMMM!* It came reverberating through the hull, shortly followed by a surging, swishing sound of water as the shock waves shuddered through the sea and rocked them gently on their beam ends.

They'd got a U-boat.

But Syvret wasn't cheering. 'Bring us back to one-zero-four, revolutions for three knots, down periscope. Hydrophones, let me know who else is in the water with us when that din finishes.'

It was a teeth-grating din of tearing metal, when it got started; its sound coming through the hull, as if some giant was in a tantrum with his toys. It was a sound Harry had heard before, but not this close up. It made him shudder, and from the looks on the control room crew's faces it was having a similar effect on them. No rejoicing over their victory here while they listened to their enemy die. And it seemed to take forever for the tangling, twisting wreckage of the U-boat to sink beyond their hearing.

'Propeller sounds, bearing one-five-zero,' the hydrophone man said at last.

'Far away,' he continued. 'Twelve thousand metres, maybe thirteen thousand, I think.'

That's well over thirteen thousand yards, Harry calculated; too far for a shot.

'New target is on a similar heading . . . no, wait,' said the hydrophone man. 'Slightly divergent. Angle is widening, but not much.'

Bassano had already started a plot. Syvret leaned over to peer down the hatch and Bassano slid the chart so he could see. Harry took a peek too. What they saw was a pencil line marking *Radegonde*'s course at 140 degrees, and behind her, to port, her target. Bassano marked the target's general course with the edge of his parallel rulers.

'Definitely diverging now,' called the hydrophone man. 'I estimate it between one-two-five and one-three-zero. Speed . . . twelve knots.'

'Bring us on to zero-four-zero,' said Syvret. 'Let's aim for a track angle of ninety degrees. If we're going to go after him, we might as well do it with a touch of finesse. Once on track, give me turns for nine knots.'

Harry felt *Radegonde* go into her turn, while Syvret, standing back from the periscope, began a harangue with Le Breuil in the forward torpedo room – relayed through the PO on the sound-powered phone – none of which Harry could follow. Then it appeared to be the hydrophone man who was being berated, and Harry couldn't quite follow that either, except it seemed to be about whether there were any other targets lurking out there.

Bassano had pencilled in *Radegonde*'s sweeping turn to port, marking her progress against his watch, and pricking off her position relative to the approaching U-boat.

'Up periscope!' ordered Syvret. 'Bearing?' he cried, and de Maligou, still shadowing him round the 'scope, called it. Bassano measured and marked the chart. 'Down periscope,' said Syvret.

'It will have to be a long shot, Sir,' said Bassano, after busying himself on the slide rule.

'Five thousand?' asked Syvret.

'More like six, six and a half,' Bassano replied.

They were talking about range. In thousands of metres. Jesus, but that was long.

Syvret fired another bark at the hydrophone man. Harry didn't catch the exact words, but it was obvious it was a question, and equally obvious the answer was a negative. Syvret let his irritation show in his next bark at the PO on the phone. Something about the torpedoes. All four. They were going to fire all four. And depth settings? Yes, Syvret was giving out depth settings; and gyro angles too?

Harry, brows knitted, trying hard to work out what was being said; the torpedoes were going out fast, their spread to be dictated by the adjustments Le Breuil was to make to their internal gyro compasses. Bassano was talking now. Syvret leaned into the chart table; Bassano had scribbled timings and angles on the two converging pencil lines. 'Track angle zero-nine-two,' was all Harry could follow.

Both Syvret and Bassano consulted their watches. Syvret ordered, 'Up periscope!'

'Red one-six,' called Bassano, and both Syvret and de Maligou called it back. *That must be the periscope angle*, thought Harry, as Bassano called, 'Your range on firing will be 6,400 metres.'

Christ, thought Harry, *almost four miles! That must be close to the torpedo's maximum range. Too far! Far too far!*

Radegonde's bows were pointing almost at right angles to the U-boat's projected course. Travelling at forty-five knots, it would take her torpedoes less than two and a half minutes to be where the U-boat would be. It was plenty of time for the U-boat's lookouts to spot the tracks; time and distance for tiny miscalculations to become huge. De Maligou, still standing behind his Captain, had his hands over the periscope's handles too, as he kept his eyes on the bezel that indicated the target's bearing; he was holding a stooped Syvret, whose eyes were glued to the periscope eyepiece on red-one-six, his shoulders showing how he held the 'scope slightly to his left, waiting for the U-boat.

Seconds passed, then, as it entered the cross hairs on the periscope viewfinder, Syvret called, 'Fire one!' A moment later, a little bump in the water, indicating the torpedo had gone out, and then a call came from the hydrophone man that Harry didn't understand, something about the torpedo running smooth and accurate, probably, because no sooner had he called it than Syvret ordered, 'Fire two!' And then with each launch, a bump, and out of the corner of his eye, Harry could see Poulenc deftly touching the trim board, compensating for the 1,400kg-worth of torpedo that had just left its tube. One, two, three, like clockwork. Harry felt a mounting elation as the torpedoes went on their way.

Syvret had barely managed to finish calling, 'Fire four!' when there was a huge *BUUD-DUUUDDUUMMM!* and *Radegonde* lurched as if she had been punched on the nose; a teeth-rattling judder ran through the fabric of the boat, smashing lights and gauge dials and knocking hats from sailors' heads. Then there was a distant follow-on of smashing crockery from the galley in the conning tower kiosk, and then from the second galley down the passageway; and a hiss of high-pressure air from ruptured pipes.

For a fleeting moment, there was complete darkness, as all the red bulbs shattered; then the insipid yellow of the emergency lighting suffused the control room, and Harry felt *Radegonde*'s bows rising, and rising even more. There was a cloudiness in the air, as if the air itself had been shaken, or was it his eyes had been knocked out of focus?

Then the shouting started all over again!

The loudest shout came from Syvret, 'Get her bows down Poulenc, before we broach!'

'I'm flooding everything for'ard!' he yelled back.

But Syvret wasn't listening to explanations or excuses, he was yelling at Bassano, while other people shouted damage reports at him. The bows began to go down again and the PO on the sound-powered phone relayed calls from compartments throughout the boat. Syvret was half way down the kiosk ladder, half in the control room, gripping Bassano by the shoulder, bending to yell in his ear; then he pushed him on his way, and, without thinking, Harry went to follow him. Syvret caught his eye, then nodded his approval as he shouted at the PO, 'For'ard torpedo room! Put through the for'ard torpedo room to me up here!'

By the time Harry caught up with Bassano at the torpedo room bulkhead door, acrid smoke was billowing out of it, and so were crewmen, all of them choking and coughing. No one could hear anything except for a high-pitched mechanical screaming coming from one of the torpedo tubes – the tube with the smoke billowing from around the top of its seal with a thin fan of water jetting out round the rest of it. And then the smoke suddenly stopped, and the jet of water formed a perfect bloom around the entire circumference of the tube's inner door, like a blanched daffodil in the poor wash of the emergency lighting. One of the senior rates, a Maître, was bent over Bassano, yelling in his ear.

Harry didn't need telling what had gone wrong; whatever had exploded had jammed a torpedo, half in, half out of its tube, with its engine running, and its arming prop running too, no doubt, powered by water that *Radegonde* was accelerating into, to get more flow over her diving planes and drive her bows down to a decent depth. The explosion had also sprung the torpedo tube's rear door.

'Everybody out, Maître,' said Bassano, 'except the three of us. Dog the aft watertight door shut behind them, M'sieur Gilmour. Maître, bleed some high pressure air into the compartment, let's see if we can discourage that water.'

The water stopped to a dribble, but the pressure made Harry's eyes and ears hurt, and the screaming of the hot-running engine made it difficult to think. The Maître was at the torpedo tube's drain valve, but Bassano waved him away. He couldn't shout above the screaming of the engine, but the Maître understood. Of course he did; no need to check the tube, it was obviously flooded, otherwise where had all the water come from? All three of them paused to get their breath in the smoke, and to try and think against the din.

And then suddenly it stopped. The engine must have run out of fuel, or, more likely, the motor burned out. Then, in the immediate silence, there were two distant explosions, bare seconds apart. Harry and Bassano looked at each other, but it wasn't until Bassano smiled that it dawned on Harry what they were.

'Torpedoes one and two,' Harry said, stating the obvious.

'Bravo, torpedoes one and two,' said the torpedo room Maître. 'Not so bravo for torpedoes three and four . . . three must have prematurely detonated seconds after she left the tube. Blew four back into the boat, and all of us on our arses.'

Now that he had the time to notice, Harry could see blood matted in the Maître's blue overalls under his collar, and a huge welt on his left forearm. The initial blast must have thrown him around the compartment. Bassano gestured Harry to a first-aid box on the bulkhead, while he lifted the sound-powered phone receiver and called the control room. Bassano made his report to Syvret, as Harry sat the Maître down, pulled away his overalls and began swabbing blood away from a gash at the top of his left shoulder blade. Now that they had all found something to do, it gave them time to contemplate the fact that none of them had the slightest idea how to deal with the live torpedo jammed in the number four tube. At that moment none of them could have cared less that *Radegonde* had just sunk a second U-boat.

'We'll blow it out,' said the Maître. 'We'll get the First Lieutenant to bleed a huge charge of high pressure air into the tube's launch bottles, and we'll blow the damn thing right out the tube. Let it sink.'

Harry was applying a dressing to the Maître's wound, but because it was deep in blood-matted hair on his back, nothing was going to stick, so he was unwinding a bandage that would have to go under his armpit and over to attach it. Harry studied the man who was looking at him now from a face the consistency of sawed wood through eyes that could not disguise his displeasure.

The Maître was a middle-aged man, not fat, but with a middle-aged paunch, accentuated by his blue-and-white-striped vest. His tattooed arms, that were their own testament to his years in the Marine Nationale, rested on big thighs. Put a beret on him, thought Harry, and he would have looked like he was taking a rest after a hard day selling onions. Harry gave the bandage a last pull to get some pressure on the dressing, and pinned it.

'Thank you, Sir,' said the Maître through his now-clamped jaws, although his grimace conveyed something far from gratitude.

Bassano was still holding the phone. 'That would get it out all right,' he said, 'but we wouldn't live to congratulate you on your brilliant idea, Maître.'

'The fucking thing'll be live,' said the Maître, finishing Bassano's argument.

'Why is that bad?' asked Harry.

'The charge of high pressure air hitting it will probably be enough to set off its impact fuse,' explained Bassano. 'And if it doesn't, and the thing sinks, the pressure will. So if the blast from the damn thing going off doesn't get us right on the nose, it'll get us under the chin. Christ, even if we try going half ahead, it will probably trigger it.'

The crackle of a voice came from the phone. Bassano listened, then explained their predicament. Then they waited in the sickly, artificial light of the debris-strewn compartment, with Harry half thinking the unthinkable thought – *could it all really end here, like this, with all of them waiting on the inanimate whim of a bent torpedo, deciding whether or not it wanted to go off?*

The phone crackled again, Bassano put it back to his ear, and then he smiled.

'What?' said Harry. What could be funny about this?

'We're going to use high pressure air to push it out after all,' said Bassano. 'But when we do, we'll already be going the other way.'

The Maître grinned, as much as he could with the pain still sawing at his shoulder.

'What?' repeated Harry, irritated that he could be treated so cavalierly on the edge of his own oblivion.

'The Captain is going to ring up full astern, and when we're doing it, he'll tell us to blow the torpedo out the door,' explained Bassano. 'So that if or when it does go off, we'll already be moving away from it. Far enough away, hopefully. That's why he's the Captain. He can think of things that should've been obvious to the rest of us, but for some reason wasn't. What a clever fellow. How long do you think it would have taken us to work that one out, Maître?'

'Oh, I don't think you should be so hard on us, M'sieur Bassano,' the Maître replied. 'We'd have worked it out, by the second bottle at least.'

Harry stood beside the Maître at the firing lever for the number four tube. Below it was the tube's bow door activator switch. When the torpedo went out, the Maître was going to hit it, hoping the actuator that powered it was still working, and that the bow door would shut, holding the sea at bay and allowing the tube to drain. If the actuator wasn't working, in the middle of the compartment, between the two sets of tubes, were a set of heads that you fitted an operating handle to so you could hand-crank the tubes shut; a task equal to Hercules, but only if he'd been in training, the Maître assured Harry.

They felt the vibration through the boat as *Radegonde* went to full astern. Bassano, phone to his ear, cord fully stretched, had wedged himself on the deck, against the starboard torpedo storage rack. Harry had the operating lever free, just in case, and crouched between the tubes. The Maître had one hand on the firing lever, while he held on with the other. The vibration subsided, as the boat settled on her speed astern. The phone crackled with the Captain's voice.

'OK Maître, give it its blast,' said Bassano, and they all braced. The Maître hit the lever and there was a tremendous *whuuump!* of air that they all felt in their guts, rather than heard; the boat jumped, and there was a grinding of metal. The Maître hit the outer tube door activator. He waited to hear the sound of its motor running, and see the little hand on the indicator move. Nothing. He hit it again. Still nothing.

Harry, meanwhile, was counting in his head and was about to mouth, 'A thousand and six', when the air in the compartment was rent. None of them actually heard the explosion; it was too close for sound. It hit them. Everything physical moved briefly out of its space and for an instant all things were no longer where they should have been. Harry could see, in an eerie kind of gelatinous motion, the torpedo tube door lift entirely out of its seal, and long, rippling fingers of fire extend and grope into the compartment, then he and the Maître were in a bundle, collided in the middle of the torpedo room floor. Bassano was wrapped bodily round the storage rack, obviously, and seriously, winded. The bows of the boat kept rocking, but the fire, if there ever had been fire, and not some trick of concussion, had gone. There was a fan of water from around the torpedo tube door, and a jet of it, like a steel blade extending from a tiny fissure in its rim, and the water was generating a tremendous noise.

Harry and the Maître groped themselves to their feet and lurched to the tubes. Harry was still clutching the operating handle. It took both of them in their shaky state to fit it to the correct head; then together they began to turn. The Maître had been right about it needing Hercules. We're at periscope depth, thought Harry – thirty-five feet; one atmosphere – the sea was coming in at just under thirty pounds per square inch instead of the normal fourteen. Not too bad. Just keep leaning on it. Every turn of the threading is another fraction shut; every grunt, the closer we are to home. And then Harry felt the bump as they came up against the backstop, and both he and the Maître collapsed, leaning on each other. As they lay, draped over the handle, the jet of water started to die, and the solid fan collapsed to a sluice and then a dribble, as the torpedo tube drained itself of seawater.

Bassano was on his feet, but still bent double.

'You two can stop cuddling each other,' he rasped. 'The door's shut now.'

'I love it when the Captain has these bright ideas,' said Harry, creaking his body upright. 'They're always such fun.'

Chapter Thirteen

Harry was in his favourite spot at the back of the conning tower, behind the periscope, sunning himself and sharing a smoke with Thierry. They weren't exactly friends, not after the punch on the nose incident, but profuse apologies and the intervention of the Captain had brought about a truce. That, and the impression Harry had made on the young firebrand Frenchman with his efforts in the forward torpedo room, wrestling a hot-running, 1,400kg, live torpedo, and helping to get it out of the boat before it exploded and blew them all to kingdom come. Thierry had also rather admired Harry's self-deprecation when the Captain had complimented him on always seeming to be on hand when it came to saving the boat from being blown up.

Harry had blushed, thanked the Captain, and hurriedly denied any heroic intent behind his actions.

'It's down to being a Liaison Officer. It's not a proper job,' Harry had explained to the wardroom. 'Which has its advantages. Don't get me wrong, Sir. I'm not complaining. You do get a lot of time to lie about, picking your nose and scratching yourself. On the other hand, when emergencies crop up, as they do from time to time, well, everybody else, having proper jobs to do, tends to be very busy; so there's only you left to do the stepping in. Can be a bit of a bugger, really, but it's the price one has to pay for all that picking and scratching, I suppose.'

Thierry could still see Harry, as he sat there, plonked on a stool in the passageway, with only a corner of the wardroom table to call his own, and that stupid grin he had, spread all over his face, as he self-deprecated away, furiously. It was the way these rosbifs didn't seem to mind people laughing at them; he'd never understand such lack of pride. God only knew how they were going to win the war.

Thierry took another drag on the Lucky Strike Harry had proffered him from his duty free stash. The morning sun was warm on their backs as they leaned on the rail and looked towards the distant, sandy smudge that was the Delaware coast, and discussed all the ways they had hated cold, drab, joyless Halifax, Nova Scotia – and that was just the women.

They were back at sea with all the drudge and entanglements of the shore left behind, and a clean run south under clear June skies, with the air warm and the soporific lullaby of the long, placid oceanic swell beneath their keel. A steady twelve knots on the surface, with the eastern seaboard of a still-at-peace United States never more than fifteen miles on their starboard beam, and a huge Tricolour streaming from the top of their aft periscope stand to a cleat at the very back of the conning tower rail; just in case any nosy US Navy warship patrolling on the fringes of international waters was in any doubt as to who they were dealing with.

A three-watch bill, meals at sensible hours throughout the day, and Harry's evenings taken up rehearsing the *Radegondes* for their very first sods opera, scheduled for the forward torpedo room on Thursday night after the last dog watch. It was enough to have made everyone on board quite philosophical now about the sheer cross-grained, bloody-mindedness of their reception in Halifax, Nova Scotia. Fresh from having just sunk two U-boats and thwarting a wolf pack attack, thus allowing a fully laden eastbound convoy to escape scot-free, they had expected something a little more benign.

The port authorities had begun the farce by attempting to confine the entire crew to the boat for the duration of her stay; a nasty, vicious thing to do to any crew arriving damaged after an action at sea, but downright bloody impossible for a submarine, where there is nowhere to put the crew if you intend to repair the boat.

Admittedly, the armed motor yacht that met them coming in – commandeered off some millionaire and painted grey – had been very welcoming, with lots of cheers and whoops from its ageing Royal Canadian Navy crew as they escorted *Radegonde* into the narrow neck of Halifax harbour. But there the pleasantries ended. They had been perfunctorily bossed about via a speaking trumpet from a disreputable Harbour Master's launch, finishing up at a berth almost too tight for *Radegonde* at some general cargo quay; hemmed in by a pair of Lakers. Then some vast, black, American sedan, carrying an impatient Royal Navy Lieutenant had come to whisk Captain Syvret away – the RN bod didn't even shake Syvret's hand as he bundled him into the back.

No one else came to greet them until eventually a young, fat Canadian customs officer waddled up the gangway, an attaché case stuffed with forms clutched over his wobbly belly, followed by two hayseeds in ill-fitting uniforms, looking like they'd just fallen off the back of a combine harvester. Tubby from customs had then peremptorily enthroned himself in the wardroom, and produced the first of his lists. If it hadn't been for his uniform, which bulged and creased over a truly considerable surface area, he could have been some cherub, adumbrating divine compliance in an Italian Renaissance fresco.

All the officers and senior rates had been ordered into his presence and then, in a grating nasal twang, he informed them the two hicks were there to search the boat once the paperwork was completed. He then began interrogating the crew as to whether *Radegonde* was carrying any of the following contraband; the list was as long as it was comic, but every box was going to be ticked, or he would see to it they would die while he was trying. By the time he got to '. . . are you carrying any pornography . . .' Le Breuil was so bored by it all, he gave way to flippancy. 'We don't even have a pornograph,' was all he'd said. But it had been enough. Flippancy had been the only excuse Tubby'd needed for the arbitrary exercise of his petty powers; a bullied boy at last conferred with a licence to bully others.

He had calmly folded the contraband form with an exquisite daintiness, and filed it back in the attaché case; then, with a smirk, he'd opened a cardboard-bound docket book, filled in a docket, tore it off with a flourish and handed it to Harry as, he sneeringly observed, the 'only English speaker here'. Then summoning all the dignity his bloated figure could command, he'd bestowed a final thin simper of satisfaction on them, and waddled to the conning tower ladder. A matelot had to apply direct assistance to his backside to get him up out of the boat.

Harry had read the docket: No crew or supernumerary would be allowed ashore for the duration of *Radegonde*'s stay in port, nor any stores, equipment or personal luggage to be unloaded. An armed civilian policeman would be posted at the gangway to ensure compliance.

Harry had shown Captain Syvret the docket on his return, expecting an explosion of outrage. But it had obviously been just one more bit of bad news in a day full of bad news for Captain Syvret. He hadn't even the energy to appear surprised.

'Brandy,' was all he said to Harry across the wardroom table. Then, when he had half emptied his drink, he had started to talk.

'I've met Canadians for the first time. A lot of Canadians. Bad. Then I got to meet one of your fellows. In fact, your Royal

Navy Grand Sublime Poo-bah for the port. Good. A very charming and remarkably forthcoming fellow.' At that he had paused and
wrinkled his brow before continuing, 'You Royal Navy fellows are
all ... very ... charming and remarkably forthcoming. And straightforward, yes, that's the word', and he nodded and smiled at Harry as
if conceding a significant point. 'And today that was a blessing. The
Canadians don't like us. Which I had already gathered. They don't
want us here. We complicate things somehow. Schedules. Dockyard
space. Being French. Apparently *Durandal* has been in before us.'

'*Durandal?*' asked Harry. 'Your big-gunned, submarine battlecruiser, and not the sword of Roland, I take it?'

Syvret gave Harry an irritated look, then went on as before: 'No
French Poo-bahs here in Halifax though. They're having to train
one in specially from Ottawa. Just for me. To discuss matters. So
your Poo-bah tells me. Tricky, that one. Politics meets propaganda
apparently. No good is ever going to come out of that.'

'Your government; they're not happy?' asked Harry.

Syvret laughed a sardonic laugh. 'Depends who you talk to,
according to your fellow. The diplomatic types want me guillotined
for not single-mindedly pursuing my mission. On the other hand,
the uniforms like the idea of two U-boats sunk. They like it a lot,
apparently. Who knows, we could be talking about them having
me replace Thierry as Joan of Arc's love child. Not bad for a first
attempt, eh?'

And that was how Harry had found out he'd been right to wonder whether *Radegonde*'s attack on the U-boat wolf pack had been
the first time she had fired her torpedoes in anger. It had.

He thought back on the shambles of that night; the utter, falling-
over-your-own-feet chaos of the attacks, and he still laughed at it.
It might have been Fred Karno's Army in the control room, and
Abbott and Costello in the torpedo room, but not only had they
sunk two U-boats, they had disrupted the attack entirely; had

allowed the convoy to veer away so that the U-boats had lost contact completely. *And you can't argue with success, Harry,* he thought.

'It's not funny,' Harry had said, laughing. 'You damn well bloody might have killed me.'

'Well, it was your idea we attacked in the first place. And we didn't kill you,' said Syvret, sighing. 'So what are you worried about. Have another brandy. There. That'll make everything better. *N'est-ce pas?*'

'My idea? You said you wanted to do it to irritate Thierry,' said Harry, adding, as an afterthought, 'Sir.'

Captain Syvret looked huffy. 'I lied.'

Harry laughed again, although he wasn't sure he should have. 'You lied, Sir?' He kept having to remember to say 'sir', because Syvret was the most un-sir CO he'd ever served under, and Harry was becoming concerned how easily he seemed to be slipping into insubordination. Also, there were times when Harry wasn't quite sure whether he was having a serious conversation with his Captain, or not.

'You know that repeating everything I say back to me as a question is very irritating, you horrid little rosbif Sub-Lieutenant?' Syvret had then said, in a very flat voice.

Harry, shocked by himself, and immediately contrite, had drawn himself up, coming to attention in his seat, not knowing whether to apologise, or keep his mouth shut. Syvret had offered no clue, glaring at him through gimlet eyes. Then he'd said, 'I did it because, from the look of the bloodlust in your eyes, you might have attacked me instead if I'd said no', and then he'd waited, with his eyebrows arched, as if daring Harry to ask another question.

Syvret himself had then broken the tension, laughing; he had thrown himself back on the banquette, all the gloom he'd come aboard with gone. Leaving Harry to reflect that they did things differently in the Marine Nationale; and he had still to work out where the boundaries were.

'You want to see the look in your eyes now, Harry!' he'd roared, and then added through his mirth, 'I like having you as my friend, *mon brave!*' Then he'd paused, gestured for more brandy, and said, 'That look you had, Harry. You remember. That look you have when you want their blood. You reminded me what we're all supposed to be doing here. Sinking Germans.'

Those words again. It had lodged in Harry's head, what Syvret had seen in him. So much so that he was thinking of them again now, as he leaned on *Radegonde's* rail, sharing a smoke with Thierry, this French marine he'd once punched, for God's sake! Thinking about something else when he should have been luxuriating in the simple joy of seeing the United States of America for the first time; being amazed, even, that he, young Harry from Dunoon Grammar School, was actually seeing the actual United States; the first of his class to do so.

Instead, here he was on the bridge, his thoughts taken up by the total shambles of this patrol, or mission, or whatever it was being called now by the people who had dispatched them.

First, they'd been ordered to make the transatlantic voyage as part of a convoy; in company with other ships so that an eye could be kept on her. The Admiralty hadn't been keen apparently, on Free French ships wandering all over the ocean like they owned it. But no, her errant Captain, and an ever-contrary Free French naval staff, had insisted on an independent passage.

Second, she was only supposed to refuel in Halifax. She wasn't there to take up busy dockyard space, or for her crew to go sight-seeing. And what had happened? She had sailed in with serious damage to her forward casing and one of her torpedo tubes; with cracked battery cells, ruptured high-pressure air lines and internal piping, smashed fittings and the 101 other tedious little breakages resultant from a damn good shaking.

And third, nobody from whore to port Admiral wanted to welcome another free-roving mob of Free French sailors after *Durandal's* stay. They hadn't liked having *Durandal* in Halifax. The officers being just as bad as the matelots. If indeed Free French they were. For, in between their brawling and refusal to pay for anything, from a nice time to bunker fuel, they all had a lot to say about Churchill, de Gaulle and the war in general; all of it linking both men, and events, to unnatural acts involving farmyard animals. As far as *Durandal* was concerned, Halifax hadn't seen a more ill-natured, tight and quarrelsome crew in a long time. They were even worse than Americans.

But whether the Canadians had wanted *Radegonde* or not, her crew had had to be put ashore, while the *Radegonde* herself went into dry dock, throwing schedules and maintenance plans out of the window. Harry had not had much to do with the boat after that. Most of the crew went into barracks and the rest, and her officers, spent most of their time on board, making sure the dockyard Johnnies did as little damage to her as could be helped. He'd later heard that the survival of the vin rouge tank and its plumbing had been a particularly hard-fought battle.

Harry, meanwhile, spent most of his time around the Royal Navy's wardroom ashore. In the weeks *Radegonde* spent in Halifax he was only once invited to dine at *HMCS Stadacona*, the Royal Canadian Navy's shore establishment; this was a better record of hospitality than offered by the Royal Navy's Third Battle Squadron, then in town for the purposes of escorting convoys. It was an oversight for which Harry was eternally grateful. For you can imagine his surprise when on entering Halifax Harbour, he'd first clapped eyes on the squadron's clutch of R-Class battleships anchored out in the Bedford Basin; and discovered that among them was his first posting, HMS *Redoubtable*.

He'd stared at her a long time, remembering how life had been, and might have been yet. She, and the other ships of the squadron, *Revenge* and *Ramillies,* had certainly looked impressive, there in the Basin. But Harry remembered what his friend Peter Dumaresq had called them: targets. As they sailed in, an astonished Harry had stared at the battleships' towering, imposing presence from *Radegonde*'s bridge, with the little Harbour Master's launch below, nipping and harrying them to a berth. And he remembered back to when his judgement had been far harsher.

His life aboard *Redoubtable* as a junior RNVR Sub-Lieutenant had been nothing less than preposterous; one endless round of futile ritual to sustain a weapon so blunt and unwieldy and slow as to be useless in modern warfare. Now, after that close encounter out in the Atlantic with the wolf pack, target was the word that again sprang to his mind; how could anyone imagine such a ship protecting a convoy from U-boats?

So Harry had steered clear of the Third Battle Squadron sailors; after all, they lived in a different Navy from him now. But that sight of the big ships had spurred something in him, a germ of an idea; a lesson he had learned, that needed to be considered and communicated. He'd had to commandeer the wardroom portable typewriter to type out his patrol report for the Admiralty, so once he'd finished it and before he sent it to the transatlantic teleprinter, he sat down to compose his thoughts.

Even in the dead, flat, effacing language of such official naval documents, Harry's patrol report was a veritable roller coaster; but what he was proposing to append under 'observations' was far more presumptuous. He hadn't even been sure whether he should mark it to be forwarded on, or even to whom; he, a mere hostilities-only RNVR Sub, the lowest marine life form, barely a step above the bacterial. But with nothing else to do except hide from the wardrooms of three capital ships, and only a small town in which to do it, he went ahead anyway. He'd read enough Admiralty bumf to know that 'drab it down' had to be the order of the day, and so the title he finally lit upon had been, *Proposals for the establishment of operational hunting/support groups along the north Atlantic convoy lanes and Western Approaches.*

There, he'd thought, enough to stun a mullet. But after witnessing *Radegonde's* reckless rampage through that assembling wolf pack, the idea had seemed to Harry to be so bleedin' obvious – so elegant and so simple. There had been no tactical forethought, they hadn't had a clue what they were about, but one rogue submarine among Jerry had wreaked havoc: sunk two U-boats and allowed a convoy to escape uninjured. Imagine what could have been achieved if they'd weighed in mob-handed?

Not submarines though, he'd decided, but surface warships. Something fast and with more endurance – sloops, say, or those old V&W class destroyers. Four of them, six even. The escorts could never leave a convoy to go off prowling for U-boats, but an independent hunting group could. Ranging ahead or astern of the bunched-up merchant ships, waiting for Jerry to pop up, then fixing their positions with D/F – their radio direction finder; getting in among them while they ganged-up to attack and were too busy drooling over the nice big fat convoy.

And so off it had gone with his patrol report. Harry had always found it odd that he'd been expected to write a patrol report at all. But for some reason, as the BNLO – British Naval Liaison Officer – aboard this particular Allied vessel, he was apparently expected to deliver his account to the Admiralty of what the aforementioned boat had been getting up to in the Allied cause.

Nor was Harry sure whether the Captain of his aforementioned Allied vessel was supposed to know that his BNLO was writing a report card on him, which was why Harry had decided to show his patrol report to Captain Syvret before he sent it. He'd finally tracked down *Radegonde*'s Captain to a dockside shed where he'd been sitting in oversized, greasy overalls, with a set of inventories before him and a flask on his desk that should've held coffee but held red wine instead. Syvret had looked mildly surprised, but he did not comment on the fact that Harry had been asked to report on him. He merely sat down to read it.

'What do you think, Sir?' Harry had asked.

'If they hadn't asked you, I'd've been surprised,' said Syvret. 'They'll want to know what we've got up to on our nice day away.'

'What about my observations, Sir. Should I send them?'

Syvret had looked him up and down. 'Well if you have to send them, you'll be doing the right thing sending them as a separate report. You don't want to confuse the poor operations people with matters of strategy.' Then he composed his face to look more serious. 'As for the observations contained therein, what can I say? For a start, they are an accurate and concise tactical appreciation of our action. They also offer well-argued and eminently sensible suggestions based on our tactical experience for future anti-submarine operations; and they are written by you. Well, it's not that it's you personally, but by the likes of you. As for whether you should send it – I wouldn't like to comment, except to say, good luck.'

'That bad, eh, Sir?'

'Oh no! It's not bad. It's very good. That's its trouble. Wine?'

So Harry sent his comments off with his patrol report. After that, glum, with nothing else to do, but thinking, *well at least I've tried*, Harry addressed himself to drinking in the town's hotels where the other RNVR officers off the corvettes and destroyers drank; and where the respectable but bored ladies of Nova Scotia would sometimes gather too.

In his life ashore, nothing happened for a while; then several things happened at once.

A pile of mail from home caught up with him, at the same time as, on the other side of the Atlantic, *Bismarck* came out, and then a week later got sunk, and here in Halifax, Harry received a summons to go to the office of the Royal Navy's Liaison Officer to the Royal Canadian Navy.

The Royal Canadian Navy's headquarters was in the town's Admiralty House. *My God! But that was quick*, he'd remembered thinking, assuming it was in response to his observations. However, it was only after he had arrived at Admiralty House that he discovered the summons had nothing to do with a junior officer's musings on the future conduct of the Battle of the Atlantic.

There were three men waiting for him; one in uniform and two in civvies.

The building itself was a Georgian pile overlooking the harbour, and he walked there on a beautiful, crisp spring morning along Barrington Street behind the dockyard, then up a little lane. There was a Royal Marine at the door, who inspected his little cardboard identity card with great care, sniffily regarded his single wavy braid ring and then stood aside to admit him, all without saying a word. He was eventually shown to an anteroom of considerable opulence, corniced with high ceilings, and garlanded with paintings, none of which looked a day younger than eighteenth century.

When a nondescript Wren, rendered into greater invisibility by her ill-fitting uniform, finally appeared to show him into his audience, none of the three men inside rose to greet him. They sat in the middle of a chamber of even more imposing gravity, behind a desk large enough to make each of them appear grand in his own right. There was an elderly Captain, bareheaded, so Harry was prompt in removing his cap to avoid any confusion over saluting; a fusty looking civilian, more vintage than veteran, in a morning coat, a pinned dark-blue spotted tie and turned down cellulose collar; and another civilian, of an altogether more dapper cut, age indeterminate, class, definite.

'Sit down, Mr Gilmour,' said the Captain in a commanding voice, toned down for indoors. 'I am Captain Embury, LO to the RCN, and the RN PNO Halifax. Thank you for coming.' This latter was said more by way of, let's get this over with and not waste any more of my time.

Harry said, 'Sir', and sat, knees together, cap in lap, like an errant public schoolboy in the headmaster's study, as he knew was expected of him. He was, alas, still expecting this meeting to be about something entirely different.

The Captain was tanned, with a full head of neatly trimmed, grey hair and an immaculately cut uniform with two neat little rows of medal ribbons recording what must have been a distinguished First World War career. In short, he was proper, up-and-down, squared-away Royal Navy, all the way through. So much so, just seeing him sitting there was like returning to the known world for Harry, after all those weeks aboard with the foreigners.

'What an exciting time you've been having aboard your tempo-rary berth, Mr Gilmour,' Captain Embury said with a thin smile. 'While I'm sure our esteemed French allies are to be congratulated on their sinkings, you have no idea of the problems they have caused the Canadians by their resulting demands on the dockyard facilities.' There was a sigh and a shuffle of the papers before him, as if to say, now to the business at hand.

'*Radegonde*, once her repairs have been effected, will pass out of operational control of Flag Officer, Submarines and will come under the direction of the Free French naval staff in London. That handover notwithstanding, you are to remain as BNLO aboard *Radegonde* until further notice. While FOS will have no fur-ther interest in *Radegonde*'s operations, apparently there will be a continuing diplomatic interest on the part of His Majesty's government; one which you will be required to serve. These gentlemen', and he gestured with a nod and a smile to the civilians, 'are here to acquaint you with your duties in that respect. Do you understand, Mr Gilmour?'

Harry did all in his power, first, to prevent his jaw dropping, and second, to stop himself asking all sorts of damn fool questions about what was happening to his ideas on future anti-submarine tactics. But he had been in a blue suit long enough to know when to keep his trap shut unless it was to say, 'Aye aye, Sir', which he duly did.

The old civvy peered at Harry over a pair of tiny, metal-rimmed glasses. 'Mr Dilnot. Foreign Office,' he said. 'Pleased, I'm sure', and then he went into some dirge about Anglo-French relations, the future of France's far-flung colonies and the potential of Vichy to muddy waters, before assuring Harry that the complexities therein were none of his concern. His mission was not to ask questions of the French, or to seek clarifications, or offer interpretations. He merely had to report. What was said and what was done; and by whom to whom, and when. All delivered in a voice that sounded like the pages of an ancient Greek Grammar being riffled. The exact mechanics of how all this was to be achieved would be explained by Mr Fleming, and Mr Dilnot nodded to the Savile Row suit with the carnation in his buttonhole, who'd been doing nothing but appraising Harry over steepled fingers since he'd sat down. What age was this one? Mid- to late-thirties? Older, God forbid? Harry always found it hard to guess the age of older men.

As soon as Mr Dilnot had finished, Mr Fleming shot out of his seat and came round the desk, his hand extended. Harry stood ready to put out his hand, but Fleming grabbed him by the elbow. 'It's all kilocycles and code books, so no need to detain these gentlemen any longer,' he said in a voice that managed to be quite steely, yet plummy at the same time. Harry disengaged by stepping back and putting his cap under his arm, he came to attention in front of Captain Embury.

'You are dismissed, Mr Gilmour,' said the Captain, looking somewhat balefully between him and Fleming.

'Sir. Mr Dilnot,' said Harry to the two seated men, before Fleming had him again and was leading him to the door. That was when Harry noticed Fleming was carrying a plain Admiralty canvas folder bulging with paperwork.

'Had to drag myself all the way up from our embassy in Washington DC just to see you, y'know,' Fleming was saying, like they'd been up at Oxford together. 'Hope you're suitably impressed,' he said as he ushered him across the anteroom, down the stairs and out of the door. 'Let's get a bloody drink', and he didn't stop talking all the way up on to Gottingen Street, where they found a colonial-looking hotel and made straight for the bar.

'Came up by train,' Fleming was saying. 'Actually bloody comfortable. Wouldn't know there was a war on. There isn't of course! Not here! Ha ha! Big, roomy buggers, their railway carriages – railroad cars, they call them – same gauge though. Same feet and inches between the rails, but they overhang by miles. That's why all their platforms are about three inches off the deck instead of the bloody great precipices we have. Gives them all the room they need. Wide as your Auntie Beattie's bum. Damn cunning, the Yanks, when it comes to accommodating big bums. Although a bugger getting on and off if you've got housemaid's knee, eh! Gin, I think. Two, with angostura bitters. We'll push the boat out. Got nothing else to do today.'

And he slapped down the canvas bag and flung himself in a big floral easy chair like he owned the lounge. Harry lowered himself into a similar chair opposite and sank back into its grip.

'It's all in there,' said Fleming, pointing to the canvas folder. 'You only need to transmit if there's something to say. You seem like a smart young chap, I'm sure you'll know. Send it via Halifax, 4,900 kilocycles, the usual Admiralty wavelength. Get your sparkies to tack it on to the end of the routine stuff. Wouldn't want to arouse suspicion. But make sure you mark our traffic for the attention of the call sign in the book. The book's got our own little code too, for you to dress our traffic up in. Piece of cake really. Now this Skipper of yours, Syvret, what's he like?'

The gins arrived. Fleming took a belt of his with deliberate relish. Harry didn't want to be so rude as to look at his watch but it couldn't be much after twelve thirty. Oh, well, when in Rome . . .

'Like, Sir?' he said, observing the niceties. 'I'm not sure I understand.'

'Like. You know; his politics . . . is he light on his feet . . . would you invite him to your club? That sort of thing,' said Fleming, still the affable chap, despite the more specific change in their conversation.

Am I being asked to spy here? thought Harry.

'Hard to say really, Sir,' said Harry. 'We don't really do much chit-chat. It's all very professional.'

He was buggered if he was going to blab about the wild blasphemies and treason talked at *Radegonde*'s wardroom table, if for no other reason than he somehow sensed he wasn't among friends.

'They like you apparently.'

'Sorry, Sir?'

'Mr Dilnot was all for swapping you for some other Johnnie who'd know his way around this sort of nonsense better than you. French would have none of it. Any idea what it was you said that's so endeared you to them?'

Harry didn't reply and Fleming, sitting cross-legged, didn't seem to be interested in any answer. He brushed the razor crease of his trousers absently. 'Know much about our Captain's background? You swap any fireside anecdotes? What life was like chez Syvret?'

'Life on board an operational boat doesn't leave you much time for that sort of thing, Sir,' Harry lied blithely.

'A good family, the Syvrets. Very society in Lyons,' said Fleming, toying with his gin. 'Commercial interests . . . pater big in local politics . . . mater, quite the salon führer. And our friend . . . an only child . . . and a very bright child to boot. Betcha didn't know that then?'

'No, Sir.'

'Won a place at the *École polytechnique*,' said Fleming, fixing his eyes on Harry, looking for a reaction. 'That's the shop where they cultivate their high flyers, the Frenchies. Strictly exam passes only. It's all very *égalité* over there. Just being the fruit of le loins of the Comte de Bon Bloodline won't cut it. Not like us with our old school ties. You have to be a proper clever-clogs to get in. Cut throat competition too, I believe. Very short on the *fraternité* in that department. He never tell you anything about that?'

'No, Sir,' said Harry, thinking, how does he know all that? And, if he knows that about Captain Syvret, what does he know about me?

'Hmm. So I suppose he didn't tell you why he never took up the place,' said Fleming, eyes now fixed on Harry. 'Ran away to sea. A woman. And not just any. The wife of one of their big politicos. Caught with *le pantalons* down. Had to give it the old body swerve pronto; if you get my meaning.'

And then Fleming seemed to lose interest in all talk about Syvret. Harry, later, would guess the open incredulity on his face that must have greeted all those revelations had convinced Fleming that Harry really did know very little about Captain Syvret.

But it was what Fleming wanted to talk about next that really took Harry aback.

'I also wanted to get a proper look at you, Harry,' said Fleming, with an extra spurt of oiliness. 'Especially as you haven't come with exactly glowing references.'

155

Harry felt his throat tighten.

'The Skipper of your first boat didn't think much of you.'

The Bonny Boy, thought Harry, and again saw that gargoyle figure, still half drunk, the pipe-cleaner legs sticking out of his shirt tails, pointing an accusing finger at *Pelorus*'s downright bloody marvellous Jimmy, Lieutenant Sandeman. Charlie the Bonny Boy Bonalleck, *Pelorus*'s Skipper, blaming Sandeman for pressing home an attack Bonalleck should have been in the control room to launch himself, instead of lying drunk. And it all happened on Harry's first submarine, on Harry's first war patrol. That had been one to remember.

The Bonny Boy, who later, in a royal strop against his crew, had allowed his boat to be rammed and sunk by a friendly merchantman on a pitch black night, blundering into a convoy lane where he should never have been.

But Fleming hadn't finished. 'Your boat was lost, and the only reason you survived was you deserted your post,' he added.

Fleming let that hang between them, until he was forced to say, 'Do shut your mouth, Harry. People will stare.'

Harry did as he was told. He couldn't think straight; how could Bonalleck have come up with such a lie? He wanted to blurt out his denial, but caution prevented him from saying anything. He should have been off watch when *Pelorus* had been rammed – in his bunk and not at any damn, bloody 'post'! And anyway, the word was 'station' in the Royal Navy, not 'post'. This ass didn't know everything. But he was right about one thing; indeed he hadn't been at his Diving Station. He'd been in the engine room spaces, conducting a spares' inventory with two of the boat's senior rates; on the Bonny-bloody-Boy Bonalleck's orders! Because *Pelorus* hadn't been at Diving Stations.

Fleming watched Harry chew his rage, then added blandly, 'Runs in the family, too, I discovered, when I was giving your record the once over . . . being not quite the proper chap.'

Still, Harry remained silent, taking some comfort from the little tell-tale twitches of irritation that he was detecting round the edges of Fleming's determinedly indifferent expression.

'Your father being a bit of a conshie . . . in the last lot . . . a blemish on any family's good name, I'd have thought,' added Fleming, delivering what he'd expected would be his coup de grâce when it came to putting this young pup in his place; showing him who was boss, and intimidating him into the necessary subservience for the job he wanted him to do. But the little shit had just smirked at him. He'd had to bestir himself on more than one occasion in the archives looking for some lever to use on this otherwise irrelevant little squirt, and he was smirking at him. Fleming wasn't happy.

Harry, on the other hand, had been . . . well, if not exactly happy, then relieved. Duncan Gilmour, head of languages at Dunoon Grammar School, and father to Harris John Gilmour, far from being a conscientious objector in 'the last lot', had won a Military Medal. Harry had even held it in his clammy six-year-old hands, having discovered it while rummaging, as children do, in the back of his father's wardrobe. Duncan Gilmour did not talk about his medal; was in fact very circumspect about his role in the Great War, to an inordinate degree; as was everyone around him. Nonetheless, and Harry hadn't needed anyone to explain it to him, the British Army didn't hand out Military Medals to conshies. Ergo, Mr smarty-pants here hadn't known everything about him after all.

Fleming had moved on swiftly, not wishing to dally over his miscalculation, whatever it had been.

'Your last Skipper seemed quite impressed, however,' he said, with an insouciant smile. 'And the French like you . . . Anyway, we can't have any surprises on this one, so we had to rake over the coals just to be on the safe side.'

Fleming, having regained his poise, continued: 'Now, regarding this mission your boat is on. We're picking up lots of flutters from behind the curtains. Apparently the French are very sensitive about it. Can't spell it all out to you, of course. All very hush-hush. Suffice to say the chaps at Carlton Gardens are all in a flap about ensuring it succeeds. They're very concerned your Skipper is going to behave himself . . . and do what he's told. And since even *Mon Général* de Gaulle seems to be flapping, we thought we'd better keep a weather eye out too. Just to be on hand . . . lest our esteemed allies should need us to step in.

'Also, something else to be aware of when you phone home . . . to keep an eye out for . . . You chaps might not be alone when you get down there to Martinique. The French have another submarine lurking about over on this side of the pond. *Durandal*. A bloody ridiculous great tub it is; with lots of big guns sticking out of it and an aircraft hangar strapped to its back. It's in the Brooklyn Navy Yard right now; the Yanks having kindly agreed to buff it up and make it fit for active service; with us having to pay for it, need-less to say, up front in hard-earned US dollars. Now I haven't a clue what it's intending to do or who is intending to do it, once it's back at sea . . . but it has come to our attention that the crew might have some ideas of their own.

'When it was in here, in Halifax, a number of the officers apparently made no bones about who they preferred when it came to a choice between de Gaulle and Pétain. So I'm sure you will understand HMG's concern, especially if it comes to having some monstrosity out of the pages of Jules Verne rampaging around France's Caribbean colonies flying the flag for Vichy. What would our American cousins say? And that is why we would like to have some forewarning about what's going on down there . . . and we are relying on you, God help us . . . to help us out.'

'I see, Sir,' said Harry, with that sinking feeling you get when you're being roped into someone else's caper that you'd rather not know about.

'I'm sure you do, young Harry,' said Fleming, with Harry thinking, *cheeky, patronising bastard.* 'Just one more item on the agenda,' Fleming continued. 'Just out of curiosity, will you be discussing our little chat with Captain Syvret by any chance?'

Harry considered him. 'I hadn't thought about it, Sir. Am I being ordered not to?' All ingenuous.

Fleming sighed and rolled his eyes at the ceiling. 'Would it make any difference?'

Thank God he was back at sea, was all Harry could think to himself, out of the bloody road. It was funny how all that water between you and the drag of the land let you park what you didn't want to deal with. Like the contents of the sack of letters that had caught up with him. And one letter in particular; from Shirley Lamont, short as it was. But out here, with the Hampton Roads and Virginia Beach a bare dozen miles or so over the western horizon, half a world away from home, all he had to deal with right now was Stalin, suddenly on the conning tower, rubbing against his legs, up for fresh air; his eager, upturned face demanding a chucking under the chin, and probably a lift for a better view of the wide ocean and America. Harry briefly wondered what Fleming would have thought of *Radegonde's* Skipper having a dog called Stalin, but then decided he probably knew the dog's name already.

Chapter Fourteen

The sheer volume of shipping along the US east coast impressed Harry; tankers from the Gulf going north, general cargo going south, all of it sailing independently. With the United States resolutely neutral, what need was there here for convoys or escorts, or a blacked-out coastline. There were no U-boats to thwart in these waters. It did, however, require a studious watch to be kept, especially through the hours of darkness as the horizon danced with navigation lights, and even the odd Christmas-tree display thrown out by passing cruise liners heading, like them, for the Caribbean.

It was a pure, sweet run south, across an ocean so calm that Captain Syvret ordered a rota allowing crewmen – who sometimes never saw daylight from one end of a patrol to the other – up on deck to spend two hours at a stretch lounging on the warmed wooden deck planks, smoking and sunning themselves.

Also, as a tactic it would go a long way to allaying the suspicions of any patrolling US Navy PBY. A deck full of crew wouldn't suggest a potential target ready to dive in a hurry, and might prevent them getting too excited at coming across a foreign submarine on the surface. It meant they might remain calm and stop to read the Morse code being frantically flashed at them from *Radegonde*'s bridge, and tune into the radio explanation of who they were dealing with.

The one Treasury class US Coastguard cutter they passed didn't even bother to close with them, so famous had the Free French submarine's silhouette become on the coast by the time they reached the latitudes of Florida.

It was down on these latitudes, on the morning of 23 June, that Leading Signalman Lucie, on radio watch, picked up from a Miami station the surprising news of Germany's invasion of the Soviet Union. That night, at dinner, the subject came up for debate. It was momentous news, but when *Radegonde's* officers sat down to dine, Harry had something else on his mind.

There had been other news that day: a signal from the Admiralty to Allied ships in the western Atlantic. This time it had been Cantor who had read it off for Harry to decode. The Free French submarine *Durandal* had sailed from New York's Brooklyn Navy Yard on 16 June, without telling her British Naval Liaison team. And since then, there had been no routine radio contact. She was supposed to have returned to Halifax, but having slipped her moorings while her attached Royal Navy Lieutenant and the two signallers who manned her radios were still tucked up in their hotel rooms, a good many people were now trying to surmise where she was headed instead. Repeated attempts over the previous week to raise *Durandal* on the usual naval frequencies had been unsuccessful and all units were alerted to keep a radio and visual lookout for her. Harry surmised that no one would be in any doubt now that her loyalty to Free France, de Gaulle and the Allied cause, had lapsed. Who her Captain was intending to sign up with next was the question. Was she heading back to Vichy, or would her Captain simply hand his command over to the Kriegsmarine?

Harry was certain the routine radio traffic Lucie and Cantor were now receiving from Carlton Gardens for *Radegonde*, to be decoded by Captain Syvret only, must have contained similar alerts. But he wondered what other details those signals might contain.

Meanwhile, back in the wardroom, the wider aspects of the war were being debated over several grilled dorado, caught that afternoon off *Radegonde*'s aft deck using homemade trawling lines. The fish was exquisite, Harry remembered thinking, as Poulenc and Bassano sagely agreed that with the Russians now on side in the war against Hitler, victory was assured. Thierry was doubtful; a highly mobile Wehrmacht moving fast on Moscow would obviously succeed where Napoleon had failed. Captain Syvret was uncharacteristically reticent, so Le Breuil baited him.

'The pact, Captain, Sir,' he said. 'Was Stalin just playing for time, do you think? Pretending to be chummy in order to build up his forces so he could slam the trap shut? Luring Hitler on, eh, Sir? You communists, you're damn cunning, Sir, aren't you? We never believed you were really pals with Hitler, did we lads?'

But Le Breuil had gone too far. Syvret had stared hard at him, cold hostility radiating from his flat face, until all conversation round the table had burbled to a stop, and they ended up eating in silence.

Harry had gone up to check on the radio watch and was chatting to Cantor when Captain Syvret had gone past them in the kiosk on his way up to the bridge. Harry followed him into the balmy, star-blasted night, taking his cigarettes and coffee mug full of red wine up with him.

Syvret was leaning in Harry's usual spot at the back of the conning tower, behind the periscope stands, well away from the lookouts and Faujanet, who had the watch. A long, dancing and sparkling wake stretched behind them straight and true, in iridescent greens and blues from the accumulation of billions of small plankton that glowed and shimmered in the darkness with a light they could see reflected in each other's faces.

Harry and Syvret had become much closer since Halifax, after Harry's meeting at Admiralty House and his little chat with Fleming. Harry had gone looking for Syvret and had found him in the dockyard hut, closeted with the work schedules and the blueprints. He told Syvret everything that had been said both during the official meeting and his subsequent conversation with Fleming in the hotel. Syvret had heard him out, and when Harry had finished, he asked, 'Aren't you betraying secrets by telling me that?'

Syvret's reaction, the casualness of it, had given Harry pause for thought. Enough that he had later confided his concerns to Bassano, the friend of drunken runs ashore and discussions of English literature, to see if he could shed any light.

'What did you say?' Bassano had asked.

'I said, if I had to choose between betraying my country and betraying my friend, I hope I should have the guts to betray my country,' Harry had replied.

'E.M. Forster,' said Bassano, with his customary sage nodding. 'Did he get the quote?'

'I've no idea,' Harry had said, a bit exasperated that Bassano wasn't getting the point. 'I just wanted him to know that I felt we were both on the same side, and obviously in the same boat, and that it was only right he knew what was going on.'

'Hmm,' Bassano had said. 'Don't much care for Forster as a writer, but good quote though.'

Bassano obviously had not wanted to discuss his Captain, but Harry could see from the wrinkle on his brow, he was equally puzzled. What did Syvret have on his mind that was so distracting?

Harry hadn't told Captain Syvret, or Bassano, about everything Fleming had said; about what he claimed he knew about Syvret's indiscreet past, or what Fleming had been telling him about his own past, and about his father. Especially about his father, since he didn't know what to think about Fleming calling his father, the holder of a

Military Medal, a conshie; it had touched a nerve. There was history involved. A lot of it.

For as long as Harry could remember there had always been a cloud over his father's role in the Great War. Nobody talked about it. Nobody. It was one of those family things that was always steered away from, that neither time nor distance ever seemed to tire; ever eager to start gnawing away at your guts again if you dropped your guard. Harry hadn't known whether to be angry or frightened, or both.

But discussing his family skeletons hadn't been why he had approached Bassano. Harry had been serious about them all being in the same boat. They might be in different navies, but Gil Syvret was his Skipper as much as Bassano's. The way Harry saw it, he had been ordered to serve aboard *Radegonde* by the Royal Navy, and that meant that, while at sea, Lieutenant de Vaisseau Syvret was his Captain. Harry had received no orders to the contrary from any naval authority since being appointed and that meant while he remained a member of *Radegonde*'s ship's company, Captain Syvret had every right to expect, indeed demand, his complete loyalty and obedience. Nothing that had been said during his meeting at Admiralty House had changed any of that. And as for that lounge lizard Fleming, whoever the hell he was, well just because he knew a hell of a lot about Captain Syvret, and about Free French internal intrigue, and, more importantly, about Harry, that didn't mean he was in Harry's chain of command; or had any right whatsoever to issue him orders of any kind. And, anyway, Harry hadn't liked him.

No, it was all because he liked his Captain, and he wanted him to know that stuff was going on behind his back, that people were pulling his strings. Harry hadn't a clue how or why, but it simply felt important to let Captain Syvret know. And now Harry was worried because Captain Syvret hadn't seemed interested or concerned; hadn't even seemed, on the face of it, to be particularly grateful, or even to care whether Harry had done a right thing or a wrong thing. And that was why he was telling Bassano about it.

Bassano let him fret it out for while, before saying, 'I wouldn't dwell on it. You've told him. The Captain probably knows there's "stuff" as you put it, going on behind the curtains. String-pulling. Probably the only way you'd have shocked him would've been to tell him it wasn't. He's a fly old bird. He'll be all right.'

So Harry forgot about it, but he couldn't help but notice that once they were back at sea, the Captain's attitude towards Harry had become markedly more friendly; confiding, even, to the point where they now frequently met here, leaning over the aft conning tower rail for an evening smoke after dinner.

'Why does everybody seem to think you're a communist?' asked Harry eventually, studiously not looking at Syvret.

Syvret turned to face Harry, and said, very deliberately, 'Can I ask you a question first?' But he didn't wait for an answer. 'Why is it when you ask me that, you make it sound as if you were asking me if I have syphilis?'

'Sorry, Sir. I didn't mean to sound disrespectful. I'm just curious, I suppose,' said Harry, looking back at him.

'About whether I'm syphilitic?'

Harry laughed, then composed himself. 'Sorry, Sir. You know I didn't . . .'

'I know, I know,' said Syvret, waving a hand dismissively. 'Am I a communist.' He said it as if it was statement rather than a question. 'You want to know if I am a communist. To tell you the truth, I don't know anymore. Am I? Was I ever, even? Well, there was a time when I thought the idea of communism was very intriguing, I suppose; when I was your age, or even younger. Growing up in a country that had just won a war, except it didn't look like it. A notion abroad that there might be a better way. I suppose I thought there was something a bit noble about it. But, then, so was medieval chivalry, and we both know what a damn con that was.'

The notion of someone actually being a proper communist was still something quite exotic to Harry; especially a continental communist. Yes, he had known some odd undergraduates with very public ideas about politics; and during the Spanish Civil War a lot of shipyard workers had demonstrated, and some of them actually went and got on ships to go and fight. But the students were all hot air, and the workers were too far beyond Harry's world to be quite real. But hearing Syvret talk about communism, for the first time Harry felt he was in the presence of a considered life. Syvret was from a culture where ideas like communism and fascism were treated as real possibilities, and not just flights of fancy too extreme to be polite, let alone seriously contemplated.

Harry had always thought himself well read in world affairs; he poured over the newspapers and even attended the odd public lecture; he had followed his country's inevitable slide into war and he knew who the bogeymen were. In short, he knew why he was fighting; why Britain and her Commonwealth, and the Free French were fighting, and now the Soviet Union. But when he talked with Syvret, he felt he was talking with a more penetrating intellect, who saw more deeply into the cataclysm that was engulfing the world. There was a silence as they considered the dazzling light show cast up by the submarine's wake, then, as if apropos of nothing, Syvret started talking again.

'Engels maintained that the future of man was either socialism, communism, whatever you want to call it, or barbarism,' Syvret said. 'But it appears now we have a third alternative being touted. Vigorously touted, you might even say. Utopia.'

Harry looked puzzled. 'The ideal world?'

'Yes. A perfect world.' Syvret smiled. 'How else would you describe Hitler's vision for Germany, and for the rest of us for that matter? His ideal? His perfect world? Have you read *Mein Kampf?* But Syvret did not wait for an answer. 'Of course you haven't. You are a right-thinking, well-educated, middle-class, British young man. You would never even consider reading something so vulgar; infecting your mind with such drivel. It would never occur to you, at least I hope it wouldn't. It occurred to me to read it, though. And it's all in there; his vision for perfection, triumphant. Which is all very well, but beggars the question, what happens to the imperfect in a perfect world? When your prime minister Mr Churchill says the world faces being engulfed by a new dark age, I don't think he is speaking figuratively. This is not an old-fashioned war like all the others we've ever known. This one isn't about the politics or the injustice of the Great War settlement or the balance of power in Europe or a fight for trade or empire. Or even class.

'So when you ask me if I am a communist, I don't think I can see how your question can be relevant. But if you were to ask me why I fight. Why I think this war is just and right? That's different. I know the answer to that, and it isn't complicated at all. I want what everyone else wants. To live in a world where I can go to bed and sleep safe and well, get up in the morning and go to work for a living wage, and where no one can drag me off for no good reason without my neighbours shouting, "Hey! Hold on, you!" Where I can think my own thoughts and say so. And where, if I fall, there'll be someone to pick me up. What ism would you call that? Simplistic, yes, I'd agree. But this war is all far too real for nuances, Harry. We're up against a Utopia here; a vision of perfection; a place darker than hell. You can't oppose that with ideas or arguments. The only thing that will work against that inhuman monster is the prompt application of maximum violence. That's why I fight. How about you, Harry? Is that why you fight too?'

'Well, if it wasn't,' said Harry, 'it bloody well is now.'

Chapter Fifteen

Martinique was exactly where it should have been, at fourteen degrees, forty minutes north, sixty-nine degrees west; a rugged, mountainous green jewel set in a turquoise sea, with a little lace cap of wispy cloud clinging to its peaks. It was only just after ten a.m., but already it was hot and the humidity was rising on *Radegonde*'s bridge when Faujanet, who had the watch, spotted the peak of the island's 1,400-metre-high volcano, Mont Pelée, as it popped above the horizon almost perfectly on their bow.

The Windward Islands, thought Harry, gazing at the fuzzy peak in the distance; fancy I should ever get to see the Windward Islands. Although it must be said, his sense of boyish amazement was dulling a little by now. They had steamed the 2,500 miles from Halifax down to the latitudes off southern Florida through open ocean; hugging the offing, yes, but with land seldom more than a loom in daylight or the glow of reflected coastal lights at night.

After Florida, however, Captain Syvret had navigated them on an inter-island cruise, with luxuriant landfall after landfall, past a succession of verdant outcrops and silver strands: chocolate box settlements and anchorages out of paradise. They had slipped into the Bahamas chain between Eleuthera and Cat Island, and steered south-west, keeping Long Island and the Acklins to starboard before passing between Great Inagua and the Turks & Caicos and heading to raise the northern coast of Hispaniola, just west of its border between Haiti and the Dominican Republic.

From there they'd headed for the Mona Passage, the strait that separates Hispaniola from Puerto Rico and connects the Atlantic Ocean to the Caribbean Sea. Over eighty miles wide, buffeted by huge tidal flows and dotted with sand banks and three islands, yet still choked with shipping, all heading to and from the Panama Canal; one of the most vital and busy shipping lanes in the world.

Harry was convinced Syvret had chosen the Mona Passage out of contrary badness aimed directly at him; no malice intended, just to keep him on his toes. Because Harry had offered to do the navigating.

'So you're a bit of a navigator, Harry,' Syvret had replied, during their last after-dinner debate before entering the strait, when Harry had broached the subject. 'Well I think you should spell M'sieur Bassano on the chart table. He's been very busy bringing us down through the islands. He needs a break for sunbathing now too.'

And that was when Harry's main role aboard *Radegonde* had changed from lying around contemplating his navel, to practically living inside *Radegonde*'s conning tower kiosk, where he spent several hours every day between scooting up to the bridge to take chart fixes through his sextant, and then back down again to drip sweat over the chart table; but everyone else knew better. The Captain was playing with him.

'It's a sad day,' Captain Syvret would say, 'when you can't get a laugh at someone else's expense.'

When ribbed, Harry had blamed all his sweating on the sweat-box air, and it was only on the day after he'd watched the steel lattice of the Mona Island lighthouse pass by on his starboard quarter, so that it was just a matter of a direct 500-odd mile run out to

Martinique – Leeward Islands a long way to port – that Harry began to make his own jokes about Captain Syvret choosing this route; accusing him of being just a ship-spotting twitcher at heart; and didn't he get to see an awful lot of really big boats in the passage to write up in his really big spotter's book.

When he stopped to think about it, Harry felt quite sick at the level of insubordination he'd sometimes find himself lapsing into; backchat to a degree that would have been unimaginable in the Royal Navy. Yet he kept getting away with it. In fact, Syvret seemed to find it hilarious. The Captain certainly never gave the impression he felt his authority was being undermined, and nor did anyone else. On the contrary, everyone seemed to find it held a certain entertainment level. So in the end Harry just acquiesced in the knowledge he'd never really understand, or get used to, the way they did things in the Marine Nationale; but it was a habit he'd better shake off pretty damn quick when it came time to return to the old Andrew.

As they closed on Martinique, the Captain allowed a succession of crew up on to the deck. Even the soldiers were allowed to take the air and look at the passing scenery. Harry could see now that the peak they had spotted earlier dominated the north end of the island and was a sort of velvety green with foliage and bearded with jungle. The entire north end, in fact, looked pretty rugged, with deep slit ravines running down to scores of little scalloped bays, rimmed with dull, pumice grey-black volcanic sand and tiny settlements. And there were lots of Tricolours, wafting listlessly in the scrappy breeze.

By the time *Radegonde* was only a few miles off, a large bay opened ahead and as they came up it, on its north corner, a large town revealed itself, scattered up a narrow rising plateau that ended in yet another escarpment jutting out from the island's central massif.

'Fort-de-France,' Captain Syvret announced. 'Capital of Martinique and a department of France. Our destination, gentlemen.'

It was indeed a big town, and colourful too; like a giant box of Liquorice Allsorts spilled across a series of hillsides. It was dominated by a tall church steeple, as well as a promontory sticking out into the bay on which sat a seventeenth-century fort, all dull grey stone and mossy, with bluff walls that looked as if they might brush off any insult a cannon might have to offer. And above it flew a preposterously large Tricolour, practically the size of a farmer's field, and so big it made Harry laugh. He thought about saying something witty along the lines of, *Is the Captain sure this is France?* Until he saw the look on Syvret's face as he regarded him, and he shut up.

But Syvret wasn't looking at him anymore, he was watching the progress of a small steam pinnace, huffing and wheezing its way out from the fort on the promontory and definitely heading in their direction as they slid in under the loom of the town. Standing, peering at them, were two men in suits far too stuffy-looking for this weather, and an indeterminate gaggle of others in blue uniforms who looked more like gendarmes than soldiers.

Syvret turned to Harry and said, 'Mr Gilmour, please go below now, take your signallers and make yourself scarce somewhere aft of the motor room please. For the time being.'

In all his time aboard *Radegonde*, Harry had never more than stuck his head into the aft crew's quarters. Cantor and Lucie had been in there for cards, but for the voyage out this had been the domain of the Fusiliers Marins. They were no longer resident now. Harry had watched them go up through the aft hatch to be mustered on the deck boards as he, Cantor and Lucie had come squeezing in. But the place still smelled different from the rest of the boat; ranker, Harry thought, as he sat down to sulk. *Radegonde's* had always had what he'd assumed was a garlicky whiff to them, that took the edge off the usual cocktail of armpits, crotches and diesel. But these

Fusiliers Marins were just pongos in blue suits, and stank no better than they should. And he said so to Cantor and Lucie before he'd thought about it. *Hmm*, he said to himself, *I am getting slack, being so familiar.* But the two sailors laughed and agreed with him.

Cantor produced the latest crop of signals for him to decode, should he be looking for something to pass the time; and then Lucie, who'd slipped back for'ard into the motor room a moment earlier, reappeared clutching a bottle of gin that had already taken quite a few hits.

'Lucie!' said Harry in his best quarterdeck tone. 'What is that?'

'Gin, Sir,' said Lucie, admiring the bottle. 'There's not much left, but since we're here now I thought we might polish it off. Would you like a nip, Sir?'

Harry's jaw dropped, and he gawped at the older man, whose face was now gazing back at him, wreathed in a benevolent smile. Many thoughts passed through Harry's mind in that brief second. The first thought was, what in God's name was Lucie doing in possession of a bottle of spirits on board – spirits that were obviously his own, and not issued as part of his ration? And then, had he, Sub-Lieutenant Harry Gilmour now lost every last vestige of his authority over these two men, that one of them felt free to openly offer him illicit alcohol? Aboard their boat? While on an operational patrol? What was he to do? Put Lucie on a charge? Certainly, he was spoiled for choice on what he could haul him up on. But here, now? While the French were in the middle of some political negotiation? And what would Captain Syvret think? What would his own chain of command think? That he had allowed the standard of discipline of two crewmen he was responsible for to have collapsed to such a degree; and everything *that* implied about his fitness to command, to hold the King's commission. Oh, dear God!

Cantor, he reckoned, must have read the turmoil on his face and understood what was really happening.

'George, he doesn't like that vin rouge stuff they give us, Sir,' explained Cantor.

Well, said Harry to himself, *you haven't understood that much, Leading Telegraphist Cantor. And look, Lucie is already pouring tots of the damn stuff . . . and has his own little flask of angostura bitters! He must've been guzzling since they left Halifax; probably even had stashes aboard since . . . Plymouth? Before?* Harry suddenly saw him again, sprawled in that wheelbarrow being rushed back aboard before *Radegonde* left on patrol from Dundee. Other visions sprang up, of Lucie at sea; his glassy stares and slow reactions. But then, Harry recalled, never while he was on duty. Ever. A bloody good radio watchman, and a very, *very* fast – and disturbingly accurate – finger on the Aldis trigger. Dammit, Harry had seen him read Morse from a flashing Aldis lamp through horizontal rain in a full gale.

'So what d'ye think Cap'n Syvret and that Frenchy marine officer are up to upstairs, Sir?' asked an oblivious Lucie, '. . . and here's yer tot, Sir.'

As he reached out and accepted the little glass of pinkish gin, Harry was thinking now, not about how to punish this man, but his own acts of insubordination towards Captain Syvret; and how Syvret had thought them all too hilarious.

'I shudder to think, Lucie,' said Harry, realising that he had just been taught a lesson about discipline; submarine discipline. That there was a difference between being shown disrespect, and being shown he was trusted. And, anyway, wasn't Lucie entitled by right and naval tradition to a tot a day? So what if it wasn't regulation issue. The three of them knocked back their glasses.

'D'you think they'll let us ashore, Sir?' asked Cantor. 'Eh, the West Indies, George. I've never been to the West Indies.'

'I can't imagine Captain Syvret will keep us cooped up too long,' said Harry, smiling now, 'not unless there's a fight.'

'Oooh. A fight, with shootin' and all. That'd make Ens'n Thierry's boys happy,' said Lucie. 'I'd pay money to watch that.'

'Rum, Lucie?' asked Harry.

'What, Sir?'

'Rum. I'm not sure they do gin in these latitudes. You might have to go back to the local rum for replacing your stash.' said Harry, always concerned for his men's welfare.

Radegonde's diesels shut down, and Harry heard the electrical hum as they went on to motor power and slowed. Suddenly, there was a bang, and a reverberation through the boat. They all looked at each other.

'The deck gun,' said Lucie. 'We're firing at something, Sir!'

Then another bang. Was there really a fight starting after all? A big fight if the Captain was shooting off the deck gun at somebody. And then there was another bang, and another. But a rhythm was starting; it wasn't random shooting. They sat in silence until the gun had fired fifteen times, and then silence. Complete silence; no sporadic rifle fire or a machine-gun rattle in response.

'No. It's a salute,' said Harry eventually, his conclusion final. 'A fifteen-gun salute. I think that's for a Governor. Captain Syvret's paying his respects. Doesn't look like there's going to be a fight after all, Lucie. You can put your wallet away.'

'At least until we get ashore, Sir,' said Cantor.

Then they had another tot, and Harry could feel the thump of feet above, and voices. Then there was a distinct bump. They had come alongside somewhere.

⌣

A little over fourteen hours later, they were at sea again, steaming south with a magnificent sunrise emerging from the Atlantic over their port quarter, sending its low rays to glint off the bridge glass and searchlight faces of another warship, coming down on them from the north at what Harry estimated as a good fifteen to sixteen knots to *Radegonde*'s ten. She was already only a couple of miles away, advancing out of the vanishing gloom, however the angle on her was a bit too tight for Harry to make a proper identification. A destroyer, definitely, and the stiff morning breeze coming out of the sun, showed the Stars and Stripes straining out from her foremast halyards.

'Can you identify her, M'sieur Gilmour?' asked Captain Syvret, but before Harry could answer, the other warship's signalling lamp opened up with a series of staccato flashes. Harry had Lucie, binoculars stuck to his face, on the bridge beside him. The signalman began to read off the message, '. . . I am United States Warship *P . . . R . . . Pruett* . . . I wish to converse. Request you heave-to and identify yourself . . .'

International law was pretty clear-cut on who could and who couldn't stop any ship on the high seas, and the couldn'ts far outweighed the coulds. But the Americans were requesting, not ordering.

'Well, since they're being so polite,' said Syvret to the bridge in general, before turning to Harry. 'Have your signalman make, "I am Free French submarine *Radegonde*. Am heaving-to. Please approach me on my starboard quarter." There. Since it's him that wants the chat, he can do it with the sun in his eyes.' And he leaned to the voice-pipe and ordered a ten-degree turn to starboard to show the US destroyer *Radegonde*'s flank. 'And M'sieur Gilmour, ask your man in the radio kiosk to make to Halifax from *Radegonde*: "I am heaving-to to converse with US destroyer *Pruett* at its request", and give time and exact position.'

Their exact position was some fifteen miles east-north-east of the Presqu'Île de la Caravelle lighthouse, about two thirds of the way down Martinique's west coast. Harry had been wrong when he'd told Cantor and Lucie he was sure Captain Syvret would be granting leave when they reached Fort-de-France. No one had been granted leave. Indeed, only Captain Syvret and Bassano – carrying the Captain's pencil case – had gone ashore. Everyone else had had to stay aboard, by direct order of the Governor; and there were four gendarmes, with guns, posted on the jetty where they'd moored up, to discourage any dissenters.

'M'sieur le Gouverneur, Chevalier de Legion d'Honneur Tassereau has assured me he is a loyal servant of the legitimate government of France,' Syvret had confided to the wardroom after he'd returned from his visit to M'sieur le Gouverneur in his official residence. 'And since, according to M'sieur Tassereau, General de Gaulle's origins in no way can be regarded as legitimate – and yes, he personalised that assertion, using the usual epithet – that can only mean his loyalties and that of this department of France must lie with the government of Maréchal Pétain and his administration in Vichy. And if I think otherwise, then I must be a traitor and must be arrested, tried and shot. I think he wants rid of us.'

Syvret, Harry and all *Radegonde*'s officers, and even Thierry, were sitting down to a splendid dinner of goat stew courtesy of the port's traders' eagerness to make a franc, although they had stated a preference for US dollars, and the loyalties of France's Lesser Antilles colonies were the subject of that night's debate. The wine flowed, and so did the outrage. *No one does indignant like a Frenchman,* thought Harry. The list of punishments they wanted inflicted on M'sieur le Gouverneur for his Vichy stance and collaborationist sentiments would have outdone the Book of Revelations; not even the quality of his goat stew was going to save him.

The talk was fast and vernacular, and Harry gave up trying to follow it, and instead watched the indulgent smile on Captain Syvret's face fade to a strained expression that told him the Skipper was now finding these rants tedious.

'*Ecoutez moi!*' barked Syvret, but he had to shout it twice more and bang the wardroom table before he brought the wardroom to order. He'd then treated them to one of his baleful gazes, before puffing out his chest and beginning a speech that Harry would have found comic if it hadn't been for the reaction of his French shipmates.

'It is to France, above all the great civilisations, that the responsibility has fallen . . . of upholding the ideal of *humanité*,' said Syvret, all sonorous and serious. 'But if we, here, now, allow Frenchmen to fire upon Frenchmen . . . we have lost that mantle. We cannot go charging through this island, guns in our hands . . .'

And on and on he'd gone, grandiose, authoritative, until Harry had tuned out, attentive instead to the seriousness with which his French shipmates were lapping up the speech. They weren't going to storm the island like Christ come to cleanse the temple, apparently. He, Captain Syvret, had been given a name, several names; people who he'd been told would help them out in just such an eventuality. Yes, they were going back to land on Martinique, '*l'honneur* of France demands it,' Syvret had declared. Except this time they were going in through the back door.

They'd been on their way to do just that when the USS *Pruett* had come over the horizon, stalking them.

Pruett was now lolling gently on the Atlantic swell about a hundred yards off *Radegonde*'s beam, and approaching them was one of her motor whalers manned by four US sailors in their blue denim work fatigues and those silly little white sailor hats Harry had only seen in the movies.

In the whaler's stern stood two officers, head to ankle in khaki, caps on heads. Once the whaler had, in one elegant sweep, come alongside *Radegonde*'s saddle tanks and lines had been thrown and the officers had stepped aboard, the French crew could see how scarily polished were the Americans' shoes. And it was only when

Harry, leaning out of the wardroom banquette, saw the first set of feet coming down the conning tower ladder, that he too, saw the scarily polished shoes. *Now that's serious Nay-vee*, he thought, this being his first encounter with the US fleet.

'She's a *Gleaves*-class destroyer,' Harry had told Syvret, when he'd got a good look at her, as she was lowering her whaler. 'New. They only launched the first one three years ago. She's about 1,600 tons, 350 feet long, twin screws; does about thirty-eight knots flat out. And well armed. As you can see, five 5-inch guns, ten 21-inch torpedo tubes and two depth charge racks.'

'I'm going to call you Jane from now on,' Syvret had said. 'The Jane who publishes that nice book about Fighting Ships. Now go below and wait in the wardroom. We don't want to confuse them with a Royal Navy officer on the bridge before they've had a drink. Later we'll confuse them.'

And there he was, standing on the control room deckplates; Harry's first US Navy officer, a clean-cut, sportily built blond American, with a square jaw yet to sprout a whisker, wearing a cap that had never been sat on, and a uniform so starched it could support a bridge span. Bassano was there to greet him.

'Good morning, Sir.' Harry heard the American say, 'I'm Lootenant Jay-Gee Foster, of the USS *Pruett*. Glad to be aboard.'

Harry would later discover Jay-Gee wasn't actually his first name; the J. G. apparently stood for Junior Grade – same rank as Harry, a Sub-Lieutenant. The next man down was a lot older, and a full Commander; he was followed by Syvret who introduced him to Bassano.

'Commander Gene D. Bewley USN,' said Syvret. '*Pruett's* Captain.' They all made their way into the wardroom. Bewley was also fair-skinned, but instead of tanned, his face was all razor rash, pockmarks and lines of perpetual disgruntlement. Same squared-away uniform though, unlike Harry's which, when you compared them, looked as if it had done more sea time than the ancient mariner. As he passed through the bulkhead door, the first thing Commander Bewley said on seeing Harry standing up to greet them in his Royal Navy uniform was, 'What's with the Limey?'

The encounter set up the subsequent atmosphere of suspicion. Commander Bewley had no pleasantries to exchange.

'The government of the United States of America has a defined policy that covers all its dealings with European powers seeking to exert their influence in the western hemisphere,' intoned Commander Bewley in his finest Boston Yankee. 'It is called the Monroe Doctrine, after the fifth president of the United States, James Monroe, and it is a doctrine that we take mighty seriously, gennelmen.'

And so began the lesson, where Commander Bewley talked, and a patient, polite Captain Syvret, who knew all about the Monroe Doctrine – and more, because he had read de Tocqueville – listened. The thrust was the US government wasn't going to stand around and let the European powers export their damn war into Uncle Sam's backyard, and Commander Bewley was here to make sure nobody got up to any monkey business. It was bad enough having the damn Limeys sailing their merchant ships in and out of US ports, but that was all about making a buck. Just so long as they were fighting their convoy battles out in the Atlantic, who cared? But here, in the Gulf and the Caribbean, that *was* Uncle Sam's backyard. And no French warship, Free or otherwise, was gonna be allowed to drag their war over here. And where was that other damned French submarine, anyway?

He was obviously referring to *Durandal*. Harry wanted to say, *you don't mind fixing their warships, though. Was that all right, because it was making a buck?* But he didn't, and then suddenly Captain Syvret was talking, asking everyone else to leave him and Commander Bewley, as matters could proceed more smoothly if they could be left to speak freely with each other. Bassano headed back to the control room and Harry nodded to the young Lt. j.g., and led him up the conning tower ladder. The Lt. j.g. went first, and Harry followed via the galley area of the conning tower kiosk, bringing with him two mugs.

The two young officers stood aft at Harry's favourite spot, and Harry offered one of the mugs. The Lt. j.g. peered in, puzzled.

'Vin rouge,' said Harry. 'All the rage in the Marine Nationale. Cigarette?' and he proffered his open packet.

'Umm,' said the Lt. j.g.

'Oh, go on. I won't say, if you don't', and with that Harry lit both cigarettes and passed one to the young American, along with the mug of wine.

'Sorry. We have a no-alcohol code aboard US warships.' He hesitated, then relented. 'But when in Rome, eh? And yes please.' He reached for the offered cigarette. 'My name's Harcourt. Harcourt Foster. But I answer to Harry.'

Harry burst out laughing. 'My name's Harris. But I answer to Harry too.'

'How about that?' All wreathed in grins now. 'But better than Henry, huh? I'm Harcourt because that was my maternal grand-father's name. How about you? This vin rouge is no diesel juice by the way. Nice. Very nice.'

'I'm Harris because that was the island upon which I was conceived . . .'

'Yuck! Your folks liked to tell you that stuff?'

'It could've been worse. There are other islands in the Inner Hebrides, like Eigg . . . Rhum . . . Canna . . . Muck.'

'I guess you're right there. Muck!' and US Navy Harry raised his mug of vin rouge with a merry glint in his eye.

'I don't think your Skipper likes me,' said the newly rechris-tened Muck.

US Navy Harry took a drag on his cigarette like he needed it; then a slug from the mug of wine.

'He's fourth generation Boston Irish. He doesn't like the English as a matter of principle. But don't take it personally. He doesn't like any son-of-a-bitch as a matter of principle. So, how's your war going?'

Harry considered pointing out that he wasn't English, but when he thought about having to explain everything that this meant to a man from a culture that didn't know the difference, and cared even less, he couldn't be bothered. 'Nobody tells me anything,' said Harry and took a belt of his own wine.

'Seen any action?'

'A bit.'

'What's it like?'

'The minute I get a handle on it, I'll let you know.'

'You sure are a sociable fellow, Muck.'

Harry suddenly realised he was looking way out into the distance. He turned back to see Harcourt frowning at him.

'Sorry, Harcourt. Really. Sorry,' he said, fumbling his words. 'I didn't mean to be so offhand. I read somewhere we're two people divided by the same language. I think I'm being all suave and nonchalant. And you think I'm being a rude son-of-a-bitch. Sorry. She's a fine-looking ship, the USS *Pruett*.'

Harcourt smiled, accepting the apology. 'She is. A real thoroughbred.'

'So tell me, Harcourt, what is the US Navy doing chasing all over the Windward Islands, after a clapped-out French spam can that carries fewer torpedoes than you do bottles of booze?'

'Well, Harry . . .'

Ah, thought Harry, *I'm back in his good books.*

'. . . that's a very specific question to be asking an officer from another service, on such a short acquaintance. I might ask a similar question about why a clapped-out spam can has schlepped 5,000 miles across the Atlantic to play hide-and-go-seek with one of her *big* buddies, and we don't know where the hell she is.'

'That's fair enough, Harcourt. So, how should we deal with that? What if I tell you about us, and then you tell me about you?'

Chapter Sixteen

The matelots dragged *Radegonde*'s rubber dinghy right up the sand, above the wave line so that Harry and Bassano wouldn't get their good shoes wet. Harry was in his best tropical whites – shorts and all; Bassano's French Navy whites let him wear long trousers.

'You're going ashore smart,' Syvret had told them before they'd cast off. 'I don't want Dr Harbinson to mistake you for a pair of shipwrecked pirates. I want him to take you seriously.'

'Take Harry seriously? In those shorts?' said Bassano.

It was a sublime night, not long after eleven o'clock, warm with barely a catspaw of breeze, and the moonless sky a riot of stars. *Radegonde* lay out in the bay, barely half a mile away, but invisible now; even this celestial light show was not strong enough to separate her dark hull from the dark of the ocean and the sky. They were to be back at the same spot at the same time tomorrow night, with Dr Harbinson's answer, or, even better, with Dr Harbinson himself.

Try as he might, poor Harry couldn't quell his excitement; standing on a beach in the Windward Islands!

'Harry!' hissed Bassano, disappearing into the gloomy shadow of the trees. 'Hurry up! What's wrong with you, man!'

Harry hurried up. They were on la Plage de la Pointe Marin, an immaculate white strand guarding the entrance to a long, narrow bay that opened to their left. To their right was a tiny settlement – Sainte-Anne – a collection of shacks and a few bungalow-type wooden houses with extensive verandas. They had looked at them through *Radegonde*'s periscope this afternoon, and even identified the house they were looking for. Sainte-Anne was only a short stroll down the beach to their right, with half a dozen wooden fishing boats hauled up on the sand in between, and rows of frames for drying fish and nets.

Harry heard the matelots run the dinghy back into the sea and then the only sound was the lapping waves. This was the south-west tip of the island so there was no surf to speak of. Everything so far had gone to plan, the dinghy couldn't have dropped them closer if they'd rowed them up to the front door. The two men plodded up the sand and on to a dirt track through the scrub.

Only one light showed in the settlement and it looked like it was coming from the house they were looking for. Not even a dog barked. They walked on, peering into the gloom of the slapboard and shanty dwellings, surrounded in shadows of domestic stuff: buckets and stools, woodpiles and all the other paraphernalia of island life that didn't have to live indoors. The starlight was enough to navigate the path by, so Bassano kept the torch by his side. Neither man was armed. 'Please,' Captain Syvret had sighed when Bassano had asked about guns, and rolled his eyes when it became apparent Bassano had actually expected an answer.

Both men stopped. They could hear singing. They moved on a bit further. A manly baritone was coming strongly out of the night, controlled, enunciating with great feeling. After a few more strides it became apparent it was coming from the house they sought. They advanced to the sound of the as yet to be identified aria. Then the voice stopped; not just a pause, or for a breath; but as if abruptly interrupted.

They were at the corner of the house now, the one they had identified through the periscope, and they could see slats of light in reflected strips laid across the packed dirt in front of the stairs up to the veranda. As they turned, they could see the light was coming from behind a row of closed shutters. The light revealed the veranda to be a scene of squalor: a burst suitcase and a burst sofa; two old stoves, with snapped-off rusted stumps where claw legs should have been, their pipes attached to thin air; a rocking chair with one arm missing; and piles of indeterminate refuse. The two men mounted the steps, and Bassano reached out to knock on the door just as the man started singing again. Harry instantly recognised the tune; and not from a place he'd liked to remember.

'*Now the Pope, he had a pimple on his bum; and it nipped, nipped, nipped so sore . . .*' boomed the voice.

Bassano, who had been about to knock, frowned at Harry and simply thrust the shutter door open.

'. . . *and it was on the twelfth*', tailing off in adagissimo, '*that he hung hisself*', and then up again in crescendo, '*with the sash my father wore! Bum-dy dum!* Who the fuck are you?'

'Are you Dr William Harbinson?' asked Harry.

'Huh? What? What the . . .?' garbled the singer. It was obvious now why his voice had so suddenly fallen silent a moment ago; he'd been taking a hefty belt from the huge mug of rum that he gripped in his fist.

'Take your time, M'sieur. After this the questions get tougher,' said Bassano, advancing into the room so that he and Harry now flanked the man sprawled on the large Chesterfield chair.

'He's Irish,' Syvret had informed Harry, as they'd all sat discussing Syvret's plan for 'opening the back door' to Martinique. Better to sneak on to the island than have the Fusiliers Marins storming the town, shooting everybody, he'd been explaining. Harry had stated, with some authority, that the man being Irish would just as likely mean he hated the British Empire as much as he reputedly hated the regime in Fort-de-France. He might not welcome a Royal Navy officer as cordially as Syvret was banking on.

'You speak English,' said Syvret. 'He speaks English. As a mother tongue. You're going because I do not want any misunderstandings. And as you are a member of your Majestic Navy he'll be in no doubt that you definitely represent the opposition to Vichy. And, since when did you pick up this habit of arguing over your orders, Sub-Lieutenant Gilmour? You are picking up some ideas from us that do not suit you. Or me. I think I preferred you when you marched about as if you had something large up your bottom, like every other rosbif.'

However, as any native of the British Isles could have told Captain Syvret, there are two Irelands: one independent, Catholic and staunchly republican, and the other not. And as was now all too apparent, Dr William Harbinson hailed from the other one, the northern one. Loyal to the Crown. Maybe Harry was going to get a cordial reception after all.

Dr Harbinson was a wreck; his face grey and collapsed beneath a deep tan, and clumped stubble that was more mange than beard. He was dressed all in grubby white linen, anciently crumpled; the trousers sagged over thin hips, while the tails of a collarless dress shirt that had not seen a collar or a tie in a long time, billowed over the waistband. Huge bony feet stuck out, bare, from frayed turn-ups, but his shoulders showed they had once been broad, and his chest once deep. If you looked closer, which Harry was not sure he wanted to do, you could see that maybe, once upon a time, Dr Harbinson had probably been a handsome man.

A conversation of sorts was begun. Bassano went to look for the components for coffee making.

'Yer off a fookin' submarine!' formed much of what Dr Harbinson had to contribute, but eventually, excruciatingly, credentials were established, and the reason for Harry and Bassano's call made clear. Bassano's coffee helped; a lot. They managed to confirm no other living creature shared the bungalow with Dr Harbinson, although Bassano, on his trip to find a kitchen, did find one surprise which he chose to withhold from Harry, for the time being.

Guides were what they wanted. People who could be relied upon to get Thierry and his mob from here to Fort-de-France to arrest M'sieur le Gouverneur and his henchmen in their beds, and have Captain Syvret's backside on the seat of power before the island of Martinique woke up.

Dr Harbinson mulled and thought and scratched his mange; and as he did so, and the coffee flowed, he became more sober and the harsh barks and expletives of broad Belfast moderated into a more educated voice.

Guides could be arranged, he'd conceded. But when asked how popular M'sieur le Gouverneur Tassereau and his sidekicks actually were among the populace and whether they might rise in support, he lapsed.

'That fookin' pious, sanctimonious prick! Papist bastard! I'll give him God's representative! Gawd's anointed! The power of France is vested in me, he says! Vested in his fookin' arse!'

So, the answer was no; M'sieur le Gouverneur and his sidekicks were not popular. Why? Well, all trade had ceased, for a start. Since France had fallen and the war been lost, all the coming and going between Martinique and the British and the Dutch islands had been banned. The American tramp steamers and cruise liners, the schooners and luggers from Venezuela, Cuba, Haiti and the Dominican Republic, even Brazil; all stopped by order of the Vichy regime. No contact with anyone allowed. No luxuries, no tourists, no money. Everybody living off fish and plantains; no meat or grain or vegetables. And all the sugar piling up. At least there was no shortage of rum. In short, since they were asking, everybody was hungry, drunk and very unhappy.

'So there's no need to start trying to explain about any bloody politics,' said Harbinson. 'Fer fook's sake don't do that. It's not complicated. All you have to do if anyone asks is just tell them you're here to let the Americans back; and every brown-eyed little temptress on the island will be demandin' to have yer love child,' was Dr Harbinson's final verdict on their venture. 'Oh, and if you don't mind doing yer old friend William here a favour while yer at it . . . tell them it was me that organised it, will ye.'

The sun came up, and two boys – mere slips of lads, barefoot in skivvies and singlets – came padding down the track from the settlement, carrying fish. Dr Harbinson got up to meet them on the stoop, and as he went out, Bassano indicated they should go further inside the house.

With the light flooding in, Harry could see the interior was all faded colonial Victorian: brass oil-lamp fittings on panelled walls, wood floors with rugs that had lost their pattern, dark wood furniture, and piles of newspapers. Neglect was everywhere: on the peeling paint and the cobwebs and the moth-eaten fabric of the punkah, suspended from the shallow angle of the roof above the beams, whose cords had long-since frayed.

The whole house was like that, until Bassano led Harry into the corner room. Given that Harbinson was the local GP, the fact that it was a surgery shouldn't have been much of a surprise. The sheer pristine perfection of it, however, was. The room was painted a bright white, with pale blue posts and beams, and a wooden floor sanded through to the grain of the pale wood and varnished to a high polish. There was a desk with a chair, and a patient's chair in one corner, and in the other a tall, glass-fronted cabinet stacked with medicines, dressings and instruments, a screen and a high examining table, all of obvious European origin, constructed from mahogany and gleaming, shining leather.

A huge fan hung from the centre of the room, and the electric cable that led from it disappeared through the wooden panels high on the wall. Harry leaned out of the shutters and saw that it was connected to a motor vehicle battery nestled amid the rubbish on the veranda.

Dr Harbinson's degrees hung in wooden frames from the wall by the door so that patients entering or leaving had a clear view. He held his doctorate from the University of Glasgow's Faculty of Medicine, and was qualified to practise as a ship's surgeon, if the certificates were to be believed. They certainly looked authentic.

'I used to sail with the Elders and Fyffes Line,' said Dr Harbinson, who had followed them through the house and was now standing in his surgery with them. 'I keep my underpants in the big chest in my bedroom, if you want to check there next.'

They drank coffee while Dr Harbinson fried the fish with thin slivers of sweet potato and herbs that Harry didn't recognise. Then they ate. The food improved the doctor's mood and he decided he'd start talking to them again. He'd sent forth his gallopers, he told them. The gallopers turned out to be island children, mostly boys aged nine or ten, young teenagers too, who did favours for him, running errands, carrying messages, helping out in any way they could, his gimcrack network of dissent across the island. They did it because their families could never hope to afford to be treated by Dr Harbinson in the conventional way. But treated they all were, as Harry would later discover. And because their pride dictated they repay him in some way, this was how the locals met their bills. The fish and sweet potatoes arrived as part of the same arrangement.

As they ate, messages were being delivered all over the island, Harbinson said; rendezvous were arranged and routes to all the key villas and police outposts planned. How would tomorrow night do? Because that's when they were all going off to capture Fort-de-France.

Harry looked at Bassano; was that what Captain Syvret had planned? Harry didn't know. Nor, he suspected, did Bassano.

'Is that for security reasons?' asked Harry. 'Is that why you want us to move so soon? In case people know we're here and word gets back to Fort-de-France?'

Harbinson gave him a yellowing, toothy grin and nodded behind him to beyond the veranda. When Harry looked round a crowd had gathered; a sea of black faces, and some creole: shy toddlers on mothers' hips, old men and women, some youngsters too; all in bright-coloured clothes, some barefoot some in sandals, smiling. And there were more coming down the path from the settlement to join the ones already there, peering in at the two strange sailors having breakfast with M'sieur le Docteur. Harry waved and everybody laughed and waved back.

'It's better we go sooner rather than later,' said Harbinson.

Harry looked at the gathering crowd. He'd never seen a black person in the flesh before; the odd lascar sailor in Glasgow, a Chinaman or two, but never a black person. He fought a terrible urge to stare; they all looked just so . . . exotic. What would Shirley make of all this? He shut that train of thought down immediately, and turned back to Harbinson.

'How did you end up here, Dr Harbinson?' asked Harry. 'You're a long way from Belfast.'

'I've often wondered that myself,' said Harbinson, producing a bottle of rum from a case under the table. 'Try asking me why, instead.'

Harry shrugged. 'Why did you . . .?'

Harbinson interrupted. 'It's a long way from Belfast,' he said. 'Rum, gentlemen?'

Chapter Seventeen

Everyone was on the beach by early the following afternoon. Thierry and his merry band were there in their dress uniforms; a shore party of sailors in immaculate tropical kit; Cantor in his whites carrying a satchel full of the necessary signalling equipment; Faujanet and Syvret. Harbinson had found Syvret's plan that they should move only under the cover of darkness hilarious.

'What? Like you don't think everybody knows you're here already?' Harbinson had asked, incredulous, once he'd got his breath back. 'Not that it matters. Who's going to tell the gendarmes anyway? Oh, I know! All the people who hate to have roast suckling pigs to eat, and vegetables and rice, and beer to drink; and who can't bear the touch of a US dollar on their fingers. I can see the queues now, at every gendarme post, banging on the door to denounce us.' Harbinson had looked away, shaking his head, muttering, 'Let's just get going, eh? Jeees-us Christ, it's enough to make you want to throw shite at yer grannie.'

The weapons containers had been wrestled out of the mine racks by brute force, supplied by a clambering mob of settlement fishermen delivered to *Radegonde* lying out in the bay on a veritable flotilla of open fishing boats; all gaudily daubed fifteen- to twenty-footers,

---

some of which had been lashed together to support the weight of the containers as they shuttled them from the submarine to the high-water mark. Everything was being unpacked and stacked; and the slabs of tinned haricot beans and peas and singe – the French Navy's equivalent of spam – were already being passed out to wide-eyed, grateful settlement women. And wads of francs were going to the fishermen, as per Harbinson's helpful hint.

Captain Syvret had inquired as to how best to appeal to the community. If he wanted local support would it be best to use moral arguments, or the prospect of a nice dinner of grub they hadn't tasted in over a year, and cash?

Harbinson had replied, 'Just pay them.' Because they shouldn't waste time on sharing a meal, but press on the very minute the last pack was filled and shouldered. It was only a little under thirty kilometres as the seagull flies from Sainte-Anne to Fort-de-France, but over fifty-five kilometres if you followed the rudimentary highways. No one was in a hurry to denounce them, but word would eventually get back to the authorities, so the sooner they got moving, the better.

Harbinson advised they followed the road for most of the journey. It would be a long march, if they were going by foot, but there were a couple of locations where they could pick up motor transport. They came on the first location early in the evening, with the sun still up, and the air humid and buzzy with insects.

They'd been marching in two columns, one either side of the road. Everybody was sweaty, gritty and irritable as they came over a slight rise and into the view of a clutch of buildings around a road junction. There were a couple of indeterminate shacks, and what must have been a petrol station, with a single rusty pump sporting a smeared glass diamond shape on top with the oil company's logo on it, all scratched and unreadable. Every building was overgrown with weeds, except the one facing the junction's T.

There was a beautiful little cottage; a turquoise blue with white shutters, and a flagpole protruding above its glassed-in portico. The pole sported a Tricolour and beneath it a sign proclaiming *Gendarmerie* in recently applied black paint. There was a neatly kept sward of grass in front, and to the side was what must have been a vegetable patch. Kneeling between the neat rows was a white man, obviously doing the weeding. And although he was stripped to the waist, as they marched closer, they could all tell he was a gendarme from the red stripe down his dusty trouser leg. Harry wasn't sure whether he heard the crump of their feet, or something had caught the corner of his eye, but he suddenly sat up, surprised; he squinted at them, and from the way his shoulders slumped, Harry thought it looked like he sighed. And then, without further ado, he bent back down again and resumed his work.

'Bonsoir, M'sieur,' said Syvret in the lead, as he came up on the weeding gendarme. Without looking up, the man called instead to Harbinson, marching two men behind, 'Are these your friends, William, or are they bringing you to me to lock up?'

'It's you who's going to get locked up, Baptiste,' Harbinson called back. 'That day has finally dawned!'

The gendarme looked up, his tanned, tired face gave away no secrets. He was a little overweight, head shaved to a dark stubble, and he looked about, what? Mid-thirties or even middle-aged, Harry couldn't tell. He gave Syvret a baleful look. 'Do you have to?'

In the end they didn't, and Baptiste returned to his weeding, untroubled by the fact that they took his pistol – it was, he swore, the only weapon he knew of in a ten-kilometre radius – and liberated his black Citroën Traction Avant.

'You can have them back once we've finished,' said Captain Syvret.

Baptiste shrugged; they belonged to the Government of France, whoever that was these days; he didn't care. 'Bonsoir!' he said as

193

Bassano, Harbinson and two Fusiliers Marins drove off in the Avant, on a mission to find more transport, with four Jerry cans lashed up and sticking out of the boot.

The cans had come courtesy of three mechanics who'd been asleep in the petrol station when they'd arrived, and who'd eventually decided to interrupt their afternoon nap that had considerably overrun to come out and see what was happening. They'd led Syvret round the back and showed him their 1939 Citroën TUB van. He was welcome to it, but no he couldn't take it away as there was no petrol in it, or in the pump, courtesy of Tassereau's policy of isolation. '*Merci beaucoup*, Monsieur le Gouverneur,' spat one of them at the very mention of his name. The invasion force had sat down to wait.

The next day, Harry was walking near the front of the main column, as they trudged down a descending path that hugged the walls of a huge semi-jungled gorge. Their local guide, Jean-Paul, called it jungle, but it wasn't real jungle; it wasn't one of those Borneo-style or Amazon Basin hellholes so beloved of *National Geographic* photo-essays that had given a young Harry nightmares; but it was pretty damn amazing nonetheless.

Although it was mid-afternoon, the tree canopy enclosed a permanent twilight. The trees themselves were huge, plummy things whose names and genus Harry had no idea of; gnarled and ancient and festooned with liana, with roots like twisted fists gripping the sides of the gorge. The ground was choked with ferns and low shrubs that made Harry think of snakes, and everywhere were fallen mangoes, hundreds of them, some new, others rotting. The air was steamy and sweet with their smell. And there were birds, none of which Harry recognised, all of them noisy.

Having joined the Royal Navy, Harry had never envisaged one day he would be *marching* off to war, but here he was. Trudging along wearing drill trousers, a striped matelot's vest and boots that were too big for him, with his whites and his blanco shoes stuffed into the gas-mask bag Cantor had brought him.

They'd waited all night for Syvret and Harbinson to return with two more vans and all the petrol they could find, and then had driven off at first light to a road end, where this column was dropped off to execute their role in Captain Syvret's grand plan. They were to make their way to the back of M'sieur le Gouverneur's villa before sunrise. And as they plunged deeper into the gorge, the rest of the force was ferried to their jumping-off points elsewhere around the town.

'Explain to me again, Sir, why I am here, and not back aboard *Radegonde*, liaising,' Harry had asked.

'You're the representative of the British Empire, Sub-Lieutenant Gilmour,' Syvret had replied, with arch patience. 'And you're here to assure M'sieur le Gouverneur that it is Free France that is the internationally recognised, and therefore legitimate, government, not Papa Pétain's gang of Boche bum-kissers. And when he sees you, all got up in that fetching little white confection your navy calls a uniform, it'll be like he's being confronted by his Majestic Britannic-ness himself, and he'll rupture himself genuflecting. Now shut up and start thinking martial thoughts, there's a good boy.'

Harry had been laughing to himself since they'd set out yesterday. It was all a comic opera by Gilbert and Sullivan; the whole shambolic farce, made even more farcical by the sombre and affected gravity exuded by these men of destiny *manqué*. War is hell, he was thinking, getting ready to stifle another bout of giggles, when something arced through the air from above and one of the Fusilier Marins yelled, 'Grenade!' and shoved Harbinson sprawling into the undergrowth. Harry dived with no regard as to how hard the ground was going to be when he hit it. He had the impression of all the men behind him going down too. There was a splatting sound, and a rustle of ruffled ferns; then nothing. No bang. No screaming. A dud? Then Harbinson started up, 'Jesus H. Fookin' Kerr-rist! What the fookin' . . .'

Etc. Etc. thought Harry, as the Irishman's tirade continued unabated for several seconds, until Syvret shouted in English, 'Will you shut up!'

They had been walking in a ragged row down the path, with Harbinson leading. 'You won't need a guide on this one,' he'd assured Syvret. 'I know every way in, out and roundabout that papist bastard's bawdy house. I've made it my business to know. Because come the day . . . come the fookin' day!'

There had been one of the six Fusiliers Marins behind him, then Syvret, Harry, Cantor and then the remaining soldiers. Now they were all on the ground. Harry was too shocked and winded to be frightened. It didn't seem so Gilbert and Sullivan now.

'Can anyone see anything?' called Syvret, and as Harry stuck his head up, he was just in time to see another small, round object in the air, and it looked like it was heading right at him. He only had time to suck in a breath to yell before it sailed over his head and crashed into the foliage less than half a dozen feet to his right. He was even sure he felt its impact on the ground, as his whole side involuntarily cringed and shrunk away from where the damn thing had landed. A yell rose in his throat, but got no further; even his windpipe was cringing and he was too choked even to scream. But there was no blast. A bird screamed, so loud and so close, he almost lost control of his bladder, and he realised he was shaking uncontrollably. He rose to his knees, tensed to spring away and dive to a safer spot, and as he came up, he was in time to see several other little round bombs already in the air, incoming.

And in that moment he saw them, way up in the canopy; three diminutive figures perched in the upper branches, twenty feet, maybe a bit more, above, gazing down on their victims with a simian, bland detachment: monkeys. Monkeys throwing mangoes.

As the official envoy of a foreign power, Harry wasn't armed. If he had been, he would have shot them, out of rage and shame and embarrassment. He wasn't the only one thinking along those lines, but Syvret, practically in tears laughing, was striding up the line, waving down all the raised weapons.

———————

The dawn was still just a hint in the sky when they emerged from the trees and walked down to M'sieur le Gouverneur's residence. It was a white stucco, two-storey plantation house, encircled by verandas on each floor, and with a red-tiled roof and a forest of chimney pots on each gable. In front was a huge drive, to the far side, partially obscured, were stables, and to the back, tennis courts.

As the party skirted the out-buildings, they could see the lights were on; the staff were up already to prepare for the coming day. Harry thought it was a testament to the loyalty M'sieur le Gouverneur did not inspire that none of the servants peering out of the windows at them seemed particularly fussed that an armed party had just descended on their master's home; certainly, none of them looked like they were going to raise the alarm.

Syvret led the entire troop into the house, where they made themselves at home in a huge dining room. Open French doors looked out on to a veranda and down the hill towards the town and harbour. All except Harry, who had been detained in the scullery area by a young black woman.

When Harry, Syvret and Harbinson had first walked into the kitchen, Syvret had paused to get his bearings in the house, and to ask of the old cook where M'sieur le Gouverneur's quarters were. That's when a girl had emerged from the laundry area and immediately attached herself to Harry. She was in her late teens, maybe a little older, Harry guessed, very dark skinned, with a fluid, moving tangle of black curls; she was built and moved like a gazelle. Huge almond-shaped brown eyes drank him in, and her flat, high-cheeked face radiated a smile like a million kilowatts. She curled round Harry, entwining one of his arms in hers so that her tiny high breasts and the round of her tight belly pressed against the thinness of a dazzlingly red shift, secured at the waist with an old Boy Scouts' belt.

'*Parles-tu français, M'sieur?*' she'd whispered in a girl's voice, as she had frankly appraised him.

Harry had been momentarily stunned. He shouldn't have been. For what he didn't know yet, in fact he probably never really would, was that because of all that French cooking filling him out, and a sun-kissed ocean cruise behind him that had turned his skin a luxurious tan, and with his hair grown out, all French Navy fashion, so that you could see its natural wave, he had become an extremely good-looking young man. That gangly, pallid youth living under the immanent threat of spots had long gone. What Harry did know, however, was that the use of 'tu' in the French language was as pretty a come-on as any chap could wish for, especially when it was being used by some fetching popsie who didn't even know your name.

The cook had prepared coffee for the party and carried it through to the dining room, while the girl, who said her name was Lydia, had rifled through Harry's gas-mask pack and produced his uniform whites. 'Tut, tut,' she had said and immediately began to sponge and press them, while rarely diverting her huge, liquid eyes from him, or turning down her toothy, beaming smile. She had even shoved him into the laundry and began undressing him when she'd finished with the whites. Harry had thought about fighting her off, but since everyone else had disappeared, he had decided this was not the time for false modesty. He could hear others from the landing party talking elsewhere in the house. The noise of them padding about. So far there had not been a single challenge; there had been no raised voices; and nobody seemed particularly alarmed. And no one seemed to have missed him. It was all just too unreal. And no one, *ever*, had looked after him like Lydia was looking after him. Ever. What the hell.

When she had him all togged up again, and looking fit for an Admiral's inspection, she stood back, admired her handiwork briefly and then moved in for a very unambiguous kiss.

Harry had let her lead him then, through the house to where the others were gathered, so that he was already there by the time M'sieur le Gouverneur eventually descended in his silk brocade dressing gown, ranting colourfully at the failure of his attendants to attend him; his morning toilette was quite ruined, and where was his effing coffee anyway. They were all waiting for him in the dining room.

Harry, dragged back from dreaming his own dream of this island paradise, thought the Governor took it quite well, at first. But after the exchange of pleasantries, and after Harry had been paraded in his uniform, matters became somewhat heated between M'sieur le Gouverneur and Captain Syvret.

The temperature cranked up another notch when Madame, M'sieur le Gouverneur's wife, came down, equally, if not more, irritated by this inexplicable and wholly indefensible lack of pampering she'd been subjected to. She didn't take this intrusion well at all. After a cool appraisal of the room, she promptly decided she would become hysterical and let everyone else deal with it. There was a lot of fast, flamboyant French talked, and a lot of gutter French too.

Unable to follow most of it, Harry excused himself and led Lydia off, wandering through the house, absently wondering if he might stumble on a quiet corner for a lengthier tryst with his new admirer.

It was a very vulgar, and very rich house; one that could not possibly have been sustained on a government stipend no matter how lavish a grateful nation might have felt for all of M'sieur le Gouverneur's efforts on their behalf. The likelihood that M'sieur le Gouverneur was corrupt did not surprise Harry. Pretty soon, he and Lydia had found just the secluded spot.

Not long after, Syvret had the Gouverneur and his noisy wife locked in a basement pantry. Then the phone began to ring. The first of a series of calls that soon made it apparent that the landing force's coup de main had achieved a complete, if somewhat anti-climactic, success.

The three government officials – one of the two magistrates and the two gendarme officers who Harbinson had identified as being the likeliest candidates to object – had all been apprehended by the Fusiliers Marins – they had all been in the throes of various sexual indiscretions and had been in no position to offer any resistance.

The other magistrate, a man of advancing years, had been sound asleep in bed with his equally aged and corpulent wife. According to the Fusilier Marins on the end of the phone, the old bastard hadn't seemed at all surprised when his manservant had announced their arrival, and once he'd been assured he and his wife would still be having their morning coffee, he was indeed quite eager to cooperate.

As for the rest of the apparatus of island government, it had met Thierry's force with a collective Gallic shrug. Not a shot had been fired, nor a blow landed; and when Syvret had sat down to convene a post mortem on the operation, it was realised that the only opposition they had encountered had been from the mango-hurling monkeys.

'Island life,' Syvret had observed philosophically. 'You can over-turn the government and no one bothers, eh? I could get used to living like that.'

By mid-afternoon, Syvret had everyone in his party gather in the residence's huge reception room which was cooled by its three external walls made up of French windows, each framed by gathered silken drapes of blue, and picked out in golden fleur-de-lis, as well as by fans ranked across the length of its ceiling. Big, warm slabs of sunlight filled the space.

Maître Gilet, the elderly, coffee-loving magistrate and his argosy of a wife, had also been summoned and he was told he was to act as a one-man judiciary to Captain Syvret's new role as a one-man executive. The apprehended members of the island's administration stood around looking very disgruntled, at the centre of a loose corral of Fusiliers Marins. Their fates would be decided by the new civil administration, whenever it arrived, Captain Syvret informed them. In the meantime, they would be held under lock and key in the fort.

Madame Tassereau greeted this news by becoming hysterical again, but everybody had heard it all before and just looked bored. When she swooned, Thierry advised her coolly that she could either get up and walk out with the rest, or be dragged. A sizeable crowd of servants and locals were already outside hoping to see just such a sight, he assured her. She got up and walked with the rest, dispensing gypsyesque curses at all and sundry as she went.

With the culprits gone, toasts were drunk using the finest vintage champagnes from Tassereau's cellar. Harry watched it all with growing impatience. He wanted to get back to *Radegonde*. There were signals to be sent; a duty he had been neglecting on the grounds that there had not been much to report. Now there was. But he was being kept from it by the Frenchmen all elaborately congratulating themselves in bumpers of foaming wine. Also, the sooner he reported, the sooner he could be back to renew his acquaintance with Lydia.

As he twiddled his thumbs, he couldn't help but be amused as he watched Harbinson off to the side, trying to do deals with the staff to ship a few extra bottles back to his bungalow. It all seemed just so undisciplined and slap-dash and not at all how he imagined you took control of a . . . a . . . a what? A country? A colony? Were they here as usurpers or victors, or was this just a police action to reimpose legitimate rule? Surely they had to tell somebody. And then Captain Syvret was before him, beaming.

'More champagne, Harry?'

'Thank you, Sir,' said Harry, returning the smile, holding out his empty glass and thinking to himself, *oh fuck it! Why the hell not? I'm not in charge.*

Chapter Eighteen

Harry was with Harbinson, leaning over a parapet on the fort's harbour side, looking down on the harbour, watching a paint-scabbed museum-piece of a steamer creep up towards Fort-de-France's wharves. The tub – for a veritable tub she was – must have been about 4,000 tons by Harry's best guess; a couple of hundred feet long, with her bridge and two accommodation decks in the middle and a towering, greenish coloured natural draught smokestack with a red band round it which was belching oily smoke that only rose so high before it hung and then puddled out all over the harbour sky like spilt watercolour paint. Her hull was grey, her superstructure white, and both were crazy-paved with erupting rust. She flew a huge Stars and Stripes from a stubby little mast atop her sun-and-wind-bleached slatted, wooden wheelhouse. She was the *Pascagoula*, a Caribbean cargo-passenger tramp, out of San Juan, Puerto Rico, with nowhere better to be than here. The only thing that puzzled Harry was how she managed to get here so soon.

The question only served to underline his growing feeling that the seeming random events of the past several days had, in fact, all been part of the same meticulous plan that no one had bothered to tell him anything about. But then, why should he, the lowest form of marine life ever, be kept up to date on the intricacies of grand strategy? Who cared if the likes of him wanted to be kept in the know? Just shut up and get on with it.

Harry had written his signals, showed them to Syvret, who nodded as usual and, as usual, suggested no changes; then Harry had encoded them and transmitted. Syvret had written, encoded and transmitted his own signals without showing them to Harry. But then why should he? What was French diplomacy to do with Harry, a lowly RNVR Sub-Lieutenant? So why did Fleming's terse acknowledgement to Harry's signal demand to know what Syvret was telling Free French HQ in Carlton Gardens? What did that sleek rat expect Harry to do? Rifle the Captain's sock drawer for the French code books and spend hours secreted in the heads decoding the Captain's dispatch? Surreptitiously?

Always assuming it was Fleming who was receiving and replying. Harry had no real idea who he was reporting to. He'd sent his Navy report to Halifax, up the chain of command, as was expected of him; a repeat of *Radegonde*'s log, basically: course, speed, events – the usual. And he'd received his acknowledgment, as expected. His duty was done. But the other shower, Fleming's lot, whoever the hell they were, wanted more, and they always got shirty if it wasn't enough; and it was never enough.

Days had passed. Then a US Navy PB2Y Coronado flying boat had arrived in Fort-de-France out of the blue, carrying the new French civilian administration. Harry had watched it lumber overhead, its four roaring piston engines throwing out plumes of exhaust smoke and the most tremendous racket. It was like one of those new-fangled, huge American railroad diesel locos, but with wings; like the ones he used to see in *National Geographic*, along with the jungle photo-essays and, of course, the bare-breasted African tribeswomen. *And now look*, he'd said to himself, smugly, as he watched the huge flying boat angle down to land in the harbour, *You've now seen all three for real.*

Only when the spray had finally settled from the Coronado's touchdown, did he actually get his one and only sighting of the new civilian administration: three distant, indistinct stick figures in identical white tropical suits, standing, vacant-looking, as they were carried towards the town on the back of the asthmatic steam pinnace that Harry had first seen carrying M'sieur le Gouverneur's representative out to meet *Radegonde*, all that long time ago.

Ident. new civ. admin. members – stop – report agenda political prog. soonest – stop, had been Fleming's reply to that particular item of news.

Arsehole, Harry said to himself. He was feeling unappreciated, bored, grumpy and irrelevant.

'Charming,' said Harbinson, looking at him askance. Apparently Harry had said it aloud.

Harry was too hot to realise or care. He could feel his shirt sticking to his back, and trickles of sweat in his hairline. He adjusted his cap and rubbed his eyes, which felt strained through perpetually having to squint against the glare from the water below.

'Not you,' he snapped.

'Now you're surely not referring to that fine gentleman Captain over there,' said Harbinson, waving at the American tramp steamer, 'who's been kind enough to navigate his equally fine big tub full of lamb and pork belly and every kind of beer and bourbon . . . not to mention petrol for my nice new government-surplus Citroën that I have recently liberated from Fascist control . . . all the way to this here harbour . . . just for me and my future peace of mind . . . as an arsehole, Harry?'

Harry turned and looked at the wreck of Harbinson's slouched frame propped against the hot stonework of the parapet. After a while, Harbinson could tell Harry wasn't in a jollying mood.

'Whit about ye, Harry?' he said.

'What about me?' said Harry. 'What about you? What are you really doing here? What's all this about? You, here on this island. Drunk. Running little private armies one minute, doing laying on of hands for the natives the next. Like you're Robin Hood and Jesus all rolled into one—'

'You're cruisin' fer a bruisin', sonny,' interrupted Harbinson, turning away, his face flat as an iron. 'I'd chuck it while I was ahead if I was youse.'

But what did Harry care? He had an assignation ashore, and a nice big brass bed in which to conduct it. And he wasn't the only one bent on enjoying himself. Most of the crew had been billeted in the town and Fort-de-France had proved a welcoming port of call for the boys off the *Radegonde* – well, most of them. Stalin, for one, wasn't so sure.

Coming and going from the boat, you frequently noticed him, standing on his hind legs, propped against the aft guard rail of the conning tower, which was where, almost from the moment *Radegonde* had secured alongside, Stalin had stood guard for the boat, never once even attempting to go ashore, forever glowering along the quayside. For the first time for many of her crew, they had heard him bark. No suspicious longshoreman or shuffling dockside trader or dockyard cat escaped his notice. But there was never any attempt at hot pursuit. This was Stalin's first real exotic port, and he didn't like it. He was lord of what he knew, and he was going to stick with that, and defend it against all comers.

What Stalin didn't get to see in the old town of Fort-de-France was a warren of three- and four-storey houses, with long, shuttered upper windows and iron fretwork balconies, their wood and stone all painted in pastel blues, yellows, pinks and greens; all peeling in various degrees of genteel neglect. Trees shaded most of the wider streets where seas of people – black, creole, white – milled and traded. Or just sat about watching the world go by in their loose-fitting white linen trousers and patterned skirts with light and airy shirts and blouses, some men in hats, some women in scarves. Harry had been watching them from his window, and now he was lying on his bed, in the little pension up from the docks he shared with *Radegonde*'s officers, and, more often than not, Lydia, listening to the hum of streets drifting in through the open shutters.

The streets had thronged since the *Pascagoula* had come in, with people busy trading for goods not on her cargo manifest, and enjoying the newly stocked shops. Lydia was out there now, likely in the thick of it. Harry, on the other hand, was feeling ruminative; the sailor far from home and the people he'd left behind. Thinking about Shirley, really, and not completely understanding what he was thinking, or feeling.

The door burst open, and in the doorway stood Lydia, all bright-eyed with excitement; breathless even.

'*Vite! Vite!* Harree!' She was saying in her heavily accented French. Quick! Quick! '*Venez voir! Venez voir!*' Come and see, come and see!

He went out with her, into the blazing afternoon heat, and was sopping wet in the humidity before they'd gone a dozen yards, even though it was impossible to hurry in the busy streets. They reached the Rue de la Liberté and went down it – the big park, La Savane, on their left – to the little *place* on the shorefront, and when they emerged from the small crowd gathering there, no explanation was needed as to the cause of Lydia's excitement. There she was, lying about a quarter of a mile out from Fort St Louis, bows pointed into the port area, her 12-inch gun levelled for firing over open sights; the huge Tricolour above her bridge flapping listlessly in the land breeze. There was only one boat it could be: the *Durandal*.

She was huge, almost 400 feet, Harry estimated, and painted in two tones of grey, like some sedate roadster. Her long, low hull was adorned by a huge cylinder for a superstructure. Forward, it ended in a scalloped bulb, with the fat slug of its gun projecting. The gun itself had a strange, scab-like device at the end of the barrel. Obviously some kind of watertight and automatic tompion to keep the sea out when submerged. It was open now, and at this distance, the way it hung looked like a lump of frozen discharge.

Abaft the gun was the bridge; a small thing by comparison, like the cab of a Roman chariot, with two periscope stands, one carrying her flag. Harry could see a lot of figures on the bridge and a lot of bustle. Down a step, and a long tube extended out, its watertight hatch open to what looked like rails running half the length of the aft casing; there was a little crane with another clutch of figures, using it to hoist out some kind of motor boat. The *Pascagoula* was still in the port area, so was *Radegonde*, snug alongside, engines shut down and nearly all her crew ashore. Harry had seen enough. He needed to find Captain Syvret.

Harry, in his best whites, stood with Faujanet behind Captain Syvret, Poulenc and the little magistrate – whose name turned out to be Hippolyte Dix. The three civilian administrators, who had been somehow miraculously transported from London via the US Navy flying boat, were nowhere to be seen. This was awkward because *Durandal*'s Captain, who was about to arrive in a state of some pomp and circumstance, had demanded their presence; and he had the 12-inch gun.

While they waited, Harry leaned forward and, whispering in Syvret's ear, asked just exactly what was going on.

'Well,' said Syvret, 'overcome by your government's generosity in paying for the Brooklyn Navy Yard to fix his boat, Captain Boudron de Vatry has obviously discovered that his heart really lies with Vichy, and so he has sailed down here to ensure that France's colonies do not fall into the hands of any traitorous Free French rabble. That's us, by the way. And that's why he wants us all, including our newly arrived Carlton Gardens political cadre, here on the jetty waiting for him so as he doesn't have to go to the bother of rounding us up before he shoots us.'

'The fiend,' said Harry in a voice dripping with sarcasm. Somehow he couldn't take the arrival of this renegade tub with its overgrown pop-gun seriously. He'd didn't know it then, but he'd learn to think differently. 'I take it you're going to set Enseigne Thierry and his thugs on him,' he added.

Syvret didn't answer. He was watching a tiny monoplane seaplane that had been unfolded from the bowels of the *Durandal* some hours earlier begin its take-off run across the waters of the bay. It lifted and climbed away, coming over their heads, *vvvvv*-ing away like a sewing machine on a power surge. The giant submarine's motor launch continued its approach, a matelot in the bow clutching his boathook.

Captain Boudron de Vatry was about to make his landing.

His arrival had been presaged by fevered Aldis lamp activity all morning, during which demands were made to Syvret and nearly all ignored.

Eventually Syvret had succumbed and dispatched a reply. He agreed that de Vatry could come ashore to pay his respects. No mention was made about de Vatry's demands for the island's surrender. Instructions were flashed as to which jetty *Durandal*'s motor launch should come alongside. The steps where it was to land were conveniently located between *Radegonde* and the *Pascagoula*.

Harry watched as the motor launch drew near. He could still see only the matelot on the bow and presumed the *Durandal* delegation were all in the launch's deck cabin – giving their paperwork a final check, perhaps, or having a nice cup of coffee, or a brandy to stiffen their sinews. In fact, he was quite taken by the entire notion of a motor launch being carried on a submarine, a motor launch with a cabin; imagine ever seeing that?

The matelot made his salute with the boathook and the launch swept up to the steps with an impressive precision. Crew emerged and brought their own lines to secure her. Once fast against the jetty, *Durandal*'s delegation emerged too, led by Captain de Vatry, who was wearing a sword. Harry tried to imagine the luxury the Captain must live in that allowed him room to stow a ceremonial sword among his kit on a submarine. Syvret ordered the five Fusiliers Marins he'd been allowed by Thierry to attention in salute. They smartly stamped their feet and presented arms as de Vatry mounted the steps, followed by two other officers.

'I am Capitaine de Vaisseau Bourdon de Vatry,' he said, presenting himself directly to Syvret. 'Commanding Officer of the Marine Nationale submarine battlecruiser *Durandal*. Whom do I have the pleasure of addressing?'

'Slick' was the word that leapt to Harry's mind. But the words 'utter shit' swiftly followed. Neat, clipped, pressed and polished smooth to a narcissistic perfection, the clean-shaven de Vatry stood to attention in a leisurely fashion. His uniform looked as though it had been newly whitewashed, and his gold braid looked like real gold. Syvret introduced himself and saluted. There was a mild quiver of de Vatry's nostrils; as if he had detected something slightly malodorous but was too polite to say, and then he clicked his heels and looked around him, taking in the Fusiliers Marins, Poulenc, at whom he nodded, and Harry in his RN uniform, whom he sized as if for a coffin. Dix, he ignored.

'Where is M'sieur Tassereau?' he asked, without even bothering to look at Syvret.

'Under arrest, Sir,' replied Syvret.

'Who ordered that?'

'The island's authorities.'

'In the absence of M'sieur Tassereau, I think you'll find I am the island's authorities.'

'The civil authorities have instructed me to ascertain your intentions, Captain,' said Syvret, ignoring him. 'But first, allow me to introduce the representative of His Britannic Majesty's government . . .' turning to Harry.

'No,' said de Vatry, at last deigning to look at Syvret. 'Is there somewhere we can go and talk privately?'

And off they went, followed by their daisy chain of flunkies. All except Harry, who had no intention of being snubbed again by Capitaine de Vaisseau Bourdon de Vatry. He walked to the edge of the jetty, leaned over and nodded a smile down at *Durandal*'s motor-launch crew, who had sat out the encounter, bobbing on the harbour swell, moored alongside mere feet away. They all looked totally pissed off, and they returned his gesture with a surly sneer.

'Cigarette?' Harry offered. 'Lucky Strikes. American.'

Bought off the crew of the *Pascagoula*, he could have added, but he didn't have to; the grins said, yes please. They must have exhausted their stocks bought while in the Brooklyn Navy Yard. So Harry threw a packet down, and a lighter, and sat on the steps.

'So what's a set of nice girls like you, doing in a place like this?' he said in his near perfect French, with a huge smile on his face; just one sailor talking to another.

Syvret looked at his watch again; it was the closest Harry had ever seen him to becoming nervous. The two of them were up on the parapet of Fort Saint Louis watching *Durandal* rise and fall on a long swell, about a mile out from them now; her bows, and with them the barrel of her 12-inch – or should Harry say, her

304.8mm – gun, pointing towards the town behind the cathedral. It was two minutes to ten, the morning after *Durandal* had first appeared, and at ten a.m. sharp, the submarine was going to commence bombarding Fort-de-France, and was going to continue doing so until the island's so-called Free French administration had surrendered, along with *Radegonde* and her mutinous crew; and M'sieur le Gouverneur, his wife and all the other political prisoners had all been released. Those had been Capitaine de Vaisseau Bourdon de Vatry's final words and conditions. Until they were met, the island would also be held under close blockade, with no vessel being allowed to arrive or depart.

The Skipper of the *Pascagoula* had gone directly to the Hotel des Poste and booked a telephone call via the undersea cable to the new US Navy base on Antigua; one of the bases Churchill had so thoughtfully donated to them only last year in return for fifty ancient four-stacker Great War destroyers that the US Navy no longer needed and the Royal Navy did to augment its woefully inadequate convoy escort forces.

'Help!' was what the operator reported the Skipper had yelled down the phone when he'd got through; yelling it very loudly, apparently. Harry, meanwhile, had radioed Halifax, and Fleming. So now everybody knew, *but will the cavalry get here in time*, thought Harry.

'Political prisoners,' said Syvret. 'That's how he described that collection of ninnies. Good grief! What one of them has a political thought in their body? Tassereau's only screaming blue murder because he's had the till drawer slammed on his fingers, and Madame, because suddenly there is no one to wipe her bum for her!' He stopped to look at his watch again. 'Thirty-five seconds.'

The little Besson seaplane was swooping and zooming over the town doing a reprise of its impression of a Singer sewing machine. Harry stared up at it from under the metal rim of his *poilu* helmet – Syvret was wearing one too. They all were; the civil administrators had ordered them handed out as part of the island's preparations for this newly arrived war.

Most of the town's population, however, had evacuated themselves up the hill out of the way and Harbinson had set up a mini makeshift infirmary way back at Baptiste the gendarme's post, to treat anyone who might twist their neck straining to see the action. And Thierry had been all action too: 'I have stationed my force to cover key positions around the town,' he had assured Captain Syvret. Where exactly those positions were, or how he intended to 'protect' them from a 12-inch gun, Harry hadn't a clue. *Radegonde*, under the command of Poulenc, had meanwhile cast off, motored into the middle of the port's main basin, and dived. She was now sitting somewhere on the bottom of the harbour, hopefully safe from any flying debris the immanent shelling might throw her way.

Harry saw the flash, seconds before the noise . . .

BUDUD-DDUMMM!

. . . and the shock wave rolled over them.

'Well, he wasn't joking, our Capitaine de Vatry,' said Harry.

'He didn't strike me as the joking kind,' said Captain Syvret, as they both looked behind into the town. Above them came the sound of tearing cloth, then the ground shook and another shockwave hit them like a punch, they felt pressure in their ears, and their eyeballs distort; and from the town, slightly to the right of centre, a huge bouquet of smoke and debris rose up like a speeded-up cine film of a blossoming plant; Harry even recognised a telegraph pole in the middle of it, sailing through the air like a tossed caber.

Syvret sighed. 'Now what does he fucking imagine he's going to achieve doing that? Stupid, stupid bastard', and then he turned and shouted out over the water to where the *Durandal* lay, far too far away to hear him, 'Those are people's houses, you arsehole!'

Another three shells were fired at the town, with rather long pauses between each shot. Harry wasn't sure whether the pauses

213

were to allow the townspeople and the civil administration to meditate on the error of their ways, or whether *Durandal*'s gunnery wasn't that good. Or maybe they actually felt a little guilty, firing on a French town; being Frenchmen themselves.

One thing Harry did observe, though, was the tremendous pounding the submarine was inflicting on itself, just by firing that bloody great gun. Looking through a pair of borrowed binoculars, it was as if her whole hull seemed to judder to the fearsome recoil, and he wondered, big though she was, whether *Durandal*'s hull was a strong enough platform for a gun of that calibre. She looked as if she was shaking rivets loose left, right and centre every time the bloody thing went off.

It was mid-afternoon when something changed aboard the big boat. Syvret spotted it first. 'Oh-ho,' was all he said, peering through the binoculars. 'Something's up.'

The big submarine had just finished manoeuvring, turning her gun on the port area, before firing again. A big warehouse had been demolished with the next round; Harry had watched its roof timbers pirouette in all directions, including into the basin, and he had hoped *Radegonde*'s pressure hull hadn't been speared by a stray plank. He looked back to *Durandal*, and to his amazement, the sub was now under helm, and looked to be heading back out to sea. Something else seemed to be happening with her. The little Besson seaplane spotter had noticed it too; it was banking steeply, its little engine straining away, and diving directly at the giant sub.

'What did you say about those *Durandal*s you talked to from the motor boat?' asked Syvret, still looking through the binoculars.

'Well, they hated me and everything Royal Navy, for a start,' said Harry, 'and they didn't mind smoking my cigarettes to prove it!'

'No, no. About them being pissed off and wanting to go home.'

Harry shrugged, remembering, but wondering about the relevance. 'As far as they were concerned, the war was over; Jerry had won. They hated the communists on principle; and the English on principle *and* because they were war criminals too, who'd slaughtered their mates at Mers el-Kebir. But, as Jerry was going to beat them, that didn't matter so much. And as for themselves, they were buggered if they were going to carry on fighting for some deranged French army officer who thought he was Joan of Arc grown a pair of bollocks . . . *especially* if it meant taking orders from the English. And they hated their officers, because they were all jumped-up bastards who were liable to get them all killed for the honour of France, whatever the fuck that is these days . . .'

Syvret put the binoculars down and gave him one of his looks. 'I get the picture,' said Syvret.

Harry shut up, then after a moment, '. . . and they just wanted to go home and forget all about it.'

'Well, I wonder if they've just decided to do exactly that,' said Syvret, handing Harry the binoculars.

Harry trained them on *Durandal*; the spray of water coming from her flanks wasn't because she was turning hard. She was venting her ballast tanks. It wasn't happening very fast, which was what had deceived Harry when he hadn't been looking through the binoculars, but, yes, she was definitely diving. And the little Besson seaplane was buzzing around so much, Harry definitely had the impression it was mightily pissed off about that.

'Well, fancy that,' said Harry.

'I fancy if you train your glasses twenty degrees to starboard,' said Syvret, 'you're going to see the reason why.'

Harry did as he was bidden, and there, sharp in the lenses, maybe three, four miles away, coming down the coast was the USS *Pruett*, a huge battle ensign flying from her mainmast.

215

Chapter Nineteen

It was night and Harry was sitting with Bassano and Faujanet outside a street café opposite La Savane park. Three glasses and a bottle of brandy newly arrived on the *Pascagoula* sat before them. Dr Harbinson came walking up the street from the direction of the *place* and the shore, his crumpled linen suit clearly revealing its disreputable state in the light of the full moon.

'Ah've jist seen the funniest thing,' said Harbinson, taking a seat without being invited. 'Your man, Enseigne Thierry, trying to interrogate that wee floatplane pilot, and being told to eff off.'

Durandal had dived without waiting to recover her little Besson seaplane or its pilot, despite the tiny aircraft spending the afternoon flying around spotting for *Durandal*'s gunners. The pilot had eventually had to put down outside the harbour, been rescued by fishermen, and, when landed on one of the jetties, immediately set upon by a handful of Thierry's Fusiliers Marins.

Not getting any reaction, he tried another tack.

'That daft Yank is still charging up and down out there,' he said.

Bassano waved for another glass, and Harbinson accepted his measure without even a thank you.

'The *Pruett*?' said Harry in English. 'He's making sure our recent visitor stays down, or leaves.'

Faujanet was making eyes at a table of creole girls, Bassano was staring into the trees.

Harbinson squinted at him, not understanding.

Harry smiled. 'Because there is a submarine about, a surface warship like the *Pruett* can't just drop anchor or potter about. She's moving and zig-zagging to make herself a more difficult target for a torpedo. And because she's doing it all over the offing out there, she's also making it impossible for *Durandal* to surface anywhere near Fort-de-France. And since *Durandal* will need to surface, because sooner or later the air is going to get bad down there, that means she'll have to bugger off somewhere over the horizon to do it – or *Pruett* will see her and, well, intercept? Do whatever it is she intends to do to *Durandal*. Throw hot dogs at her? I don't know. Do you? Anyway, whatever she's doing, it's the right thing.'

'I hear the civil administrators want our old governor and his chums off the island,' said Harbinson, pointedly ignoring Harry's lengthy exposition. 'They want to send them back to de Gaulle, for smacked botties.'

Harry had a sinking feeling; surely they weren't going to be put aboard *Radegonde*. He flashed a questioning look at Bassano, who merely shrugged. 'I don't know anything about that,' said Harry.

'They're going to stick them on that Yank rust bucket,' added Harbinson, 'and pack them off to the Bahamas and get us perfidious Albions to bang them up for the duration, and then the General can get around to doing what he's going to do with them after. Which won't be nice. You can bet on that.'

Harry breathed again.

'It's just what I heard, mind,' concluded Harbinson, then he scrutinised the company for clues of confirmation. Harry stared back. It was one of those moments when you just knew stuff was going on; stuff you knew nothing about, and weren't meant to. He'd felt it before, when his last proper boat, HMS *Trebuchet* had returned from that escapade off the Soviet Union, and God knows it wasn't the first time he'd felt it on this patrol. He was too busy thinking about it to notice Lydia until she had plonked herself on his lap, and removed his cap to place it on her own rich mane.

'Hullo,' said Harry. 'Where have you just turned up from?'

She started sticking her finger in his ear, and giggled.

'I think she wants a drink,' observed Harbinson, dryly.

'From the docks,' said Lydia, drinking Harry in with her huge almond eyes. 'They've just finished loading the gold. Everybody was down there to watch. It's very exciting. Being *sooo* close to all that *gooold*!'

Lydia's drink arrived; her usual tumbler full of cloudy spirit that smelled of aniseed.

'What gold?' asked Harry, astonished, looking to Bassano; who was now suddenly interested in the conversation.

'The pirate gold, of course,' said Harbinson. Harry turned to look at him now. He'd tried to put a joking sneer in his voice, but his expression was boilerplate flat and hard; and utterly devoid of humour.

'The gold the *Émile Bertin* brought—' said Lydia.

'The French light cruiser *Émile Bertin*?' interrupted Harry.

Lydia scowled slightly; 'light cruiser' meant nothing to her, she only knew about the gold. 'Tons and tons and tons,' she said. 'They kept it at Fort Desaix.' She gestured up into the hills behind them. 'Up on Morne Garnier.'

'Oh, aye,' sneered Harbinson again, tapping his forehead this time, and gesturing to Lydia and her drink. 'You know what they say? Absinthe makes the mind go wander.'

But nobody laughed. Harry slid the lithe girl off his lap, and stood. 'Fancy a walk down the docks, Henri?' he said to Bassano, and he pulled a startled Faujanet to his feet, leaving him just enough time to blow a kiss at the creole girls before they set off.

They were in time to see the stern lights of the *Pascagoula* head out of the port's main basin. A crowd of people were dispersing, mostly dock workers, but a few people from the town too, who'd been there to wave off the rusty tramp steamer and its crew of their new best friends. Three big floodlights drenched the area in a sulphurous light so that the only evidence here of the full moon was its reflection dancing on the water. Two large cranes cast a latticework of shadow along the jetty where the tramp had been moored, and standing by a gangway in their shade was a small knot of figures. Harry recognised Syvret immediately; and among a half dozen Fusiliers Marins was Thierry too. Harry had a lot of questions and he was still young enough to imagine he might receive answers.

'Aha!' said Syvret, walking towards them, and heading off any such questions. 'My officers. I don't have to send someone to look for you. We're sailing at first light.'

Harry went back to look for Lydia to say goodbye, feeling ill at ease at how little guilt he felt at their liaison, and how abruptly it was about to end, for he was still young enough too, to be so conceited as to take it for granted that their summer dalliance had meant something more to her than it had to him. He didn't find her, and given what was about to transpire it was just as well. It certainly saved him a lot of embarrassment.

He did find Harbinson, however, sitting at the same table, consoling himself with the remains of their brandy.

'So, did you find old le corsair Beardy Noir's gold then?' said Harbinson, pouring a glass for Harry.

'It sailed away,' said Harry, 'on the *Pascagoula*.'

'So they've given it to the Yanks, eh? Never thought they'd do that. But what do I know? Wheel in a cog, me.'

'Is that why you're here?' asked Harry.

Harbinson let out a harsh, rasping laugh, then stared hard at his brandy. 'I've always been here, ye daft wee shite,' he said eventually, totally without rancour. Nothing was said for some minutes, then Harbinson began to talk.

'Tassereau,' he said. 'It was how he treated the darkies that got to me. Poor darkies, eh? They always get the shitty end of the stick. I know that. I know how the world works out here. I'm no' daft. But that bastard? That bastard turned it in to an art form. He. Did. Not. Give. A. Fuck. Up in that residence, with that harpy of a wife of his, and all his bum-lickers. Anybody can be corrupt, but he was taking fucking liberties even at that. So when that Timothy Tight-Arse turned up claiming to be a commercial traveller in desiccating machinery, and wanted to know if I'd be prepared to do my wee bit for King and Country, I said, if it involves fucking up that bastard Tassereau, fucking right I do.'

'Who is Timothy Tight-Arse?' asked Harry, and Harbinson gave a convincing description of Fleming, London's man in Washington DC.

'So what was all this about gold?' Harry asked, embarking on another tack and naming the man he knew they were both talking about. 'Is that what Fleming asked you about? What were you to do? Steal it? Keep an eye on it? Whose gold is it, anyway? How much of it is there?'

Harbinson cast him a contemptuous look. 'Cap'n Blackbeard's,' he said. Then after another drink, added: 'It was French government reserves. So said Timothy. They'd sent it here to keep it out of the Jerries' mitts. Some here, some to Canada. So he said. I got the impression HMG weren't too happy about it coming here though. Which was why Fleming was so interested in what was happening to it. And me still being one of His Majesty's subjects, he wanted me to help him out. Shows what he knew.'

'I don't follow,' said Harry.

'I've always been a pain in the arse, Mr Gilmour,' Harbinson said. 'So how smart would you call it to ask the local troublemaker, known to the police, as your secret snitch?'

'I see,' said Harry. 'Instead of you watching them, they were already watching you.'

'Aye.' Harbinson considered this for a moment. 'Although when I think about it . . . they were always expecting me to be running about, fomenting. So when I kept on at it, nobody was that surprised. So maybe he was that smart after all.'

'So what were you doing?' asked Harry.

Harbinson guffawed. 'Shoutin' and bawlin', basically. Pointing fingers and sayin' "see youse!" In case Tassereau thought nobody was looking. Ah'm a hero of the revolution, me.' And he reached out to clink glasses. 'You know every time we do that, we kill a sailor,' he added, back to his old evil self.

'Are the Yanks here because of the gold too?' asked Harry.

Harbinson started laughing, a raspy, gurgly sound. 'A don't know. Ah've no been reading the intelligence updates they send me, Western Union.'

'A Yank officer told me it was because they were worried in case Vichy might have let Jerry turn it into a U-boat base,' said Harry, ignoring the sarcasm. 'You know what they're like with their Monroe doctrine. Permission *not* granted to fight your war over here in our hemisphere.'

'Na. It's the gold. The Yanks knew it was here,' said Harbinson. 'Our Timothy told me that much. It was supposed to have arrived here in secret. But you can't keep a secret on an island. So they knew. And once they knew, they'd have got themselves involved all right. You don't know what they're like, but I do. They've been my neighbours since I was last sober. Can't see shite but they want a bite of it. And now they've got it. Better them than Jerry, or Tassereau, or his pals. Anyway, one thing we can both be absolutely sure of; we'll never know the half of what's gone on, or why.'

Harry said, 'Too bloody true. Well I better collect Cantor and Lucie, whatever state he's in, and get back to the boat.' He stood to shake Harbinson's hand, and then added a little sheepishly, 'Look, if you see Lydia . . .'

'Wait,' said Harbinson, fumbling in his trouser pocket. 'Talking about Lydia, I have something for you.'

Harry sat again as Harbinson produced a small bundle of folded paper sachets, muttering to himself, 'Lucky for you the *Pascagoula* had a whole packing case.'

Harry could see they contained powders. 'What's this?'

'It's about Lydia,' said Harbinson counting them out and handing them to Harry. 'A matter of some delicacy, as they say.'

'What do you mean?'

'How can I put this . . .?' sighed Harbinson, with a licentious glint in his eye. 'She's a girl with a lot of love to give, Harry. And the heartbreaking truth I have to tell you is, she didn't save it all for you. If you'll pardon the turn of phrase. You're going to need these, if not right now, then certainly in the next few days. One in the morning and one at night.'

Chapter Twenty

Harry was on *Radegonde*'s bridge. Faujanet had the watch, but Captain Syvret was up too, glumly regarding another squall front approaching from the south-west. It was the third they'd encountered since just before midday. He'd read the weather forecast broadcast by the US Navy on Antigua that morning just after they'd sailed, and knew what was coming along behind it. Even without the forecast, the long, deep swell building from west-sou'-west would have told him. It was July, after all, and the season was getting going; although really big blows didn't usually originate in the Caribbean Basin at this time of year. Likely it would just be a tropical storm if they were lucky; a hurricane if they were not. But as the beast still hadn't lathered itself up enough yet to merit the name, they could always hope.

Also, he wasn't talking to Harry.

Harry had been quizzing him about the gold; about how much he knew about it; about whether 'liberating' Martinique, or getting *their* hands on the gold had been their mission all along. And now that the Yanks had it, had they succeeded or failed? Captain Syvret was not a natural dissembler, and it hadn't taken him long to get exasperated, and then irritated, with his Royal Navy Liaison Officer.

'In the first place,' he'd finally snapped, 'it's got fuck all to do with you; and in the second place . . . it's got fuck all to do with you in the first place!'

This was a bad sign. Captain Syvret, Harry was forced to note, rarely swore. Also, while he might not have been quite polite, he was entirely accurate. It was nothing to do with Harry. So Harry had shut up. And that was where they were now, standing nonchalantly on either side of an uncomfortable silence, looking in opposite directions. The two matelots on lookout up on the bridge affected not to notice, but smirked at each other every time they took their ten-second binocular break, between their sweeps of the horizon. Faujanet was oblivious, and, being Faujanet was probably lost in some vague carnal reverie.

Syvret called down the voice-pipe to alert them he'd be bringing *Radegonde* under helm in a moment; ordering her a few points to port to take the squall on the bow to save her being rolled all over the place and the lunch preparations sent flying.

The sun had been well up when they'd finally put to sea from Fort-de-France. The crew were all on board, but the Fusiliers Marins were staying behind, manning their new post.

There had been signal traffic during the night; Free French signal traffic, in Free French code, so Harry had no idea what *Radegonde's* orders were. Cantor might have taken the Morse down, but it was Captain Syvret who had decoded it using his own books, and right now, he wasn't sharing.

The USS *Pruett* was hove-to, a few hundred yards off the harbour, by the time they were underway, which suggested that *Durandal* must be long gone. The US destroyer had hailed *Radegonde* to close with her for a chat. *Durandal* had indeed left the area. The US Navy Coronado flying boat out of Antigua had spotted her on the surface about fifteen miles south-south-east of Marie-Galante Island, a tiny outcrop between Martinique and the island of Dominica. She had been heading out into the Atlantic, but the big four-engined flying boat's presence had sent her down, like she had a guilty conscience, apparently; at least that's what *Pruett's* officer of the watch had told them.

He had news of the *Pascagoula* too; she was well on her way now, he said, heading for the Mona Passage and then off north to Nassau in the Bahamas to off-load her cargo and passengers. Harry knew she'd been loaded with sugar and bananas; no one mentioned gold.

As for the *Pruett*, she'd be sticking around for a while to make sure *Durandal* didn't double-back to cause any more trouble; at least until some Free French surface units turned up to deter her permanently.

Cantor had confirmed *Pascagoula's* movements; he'd been listening to her sparks, 'gibbering on like a budgie on an overdose of Trill'– all of it *en clair* – with his head office, it sounded like. The passengers were not shaping up to be popular, apparently! But the sparks had gone quiet ages ago.

From his last look at her course on the chart, Harry had reckoned *Radegonde* too was heading to pass between Martinique and Dominica, and then out into the Atlantic, when she wasn't turning the other way to prevent the squalls catching her beam-on. And here came the next one, racing now, preceded by a wall of rain and black cloud; the first spits of it already stinging Harry's face as he braced himself behind the periscope stands for the first buffets.

Harry would be a liar if he said he didn't find the violence of these damned storms completely exhilarating; that they filled him with a sort of child-like glee. The violence was untrammelled; *Radegonde* shuddered beneath his feet as she lurched downward into a precipitous hole in the water, and the air – indeed, the whole firmament – seemed suddenly to be filled with flying water and roar, as if the elements were trying to flatten the very steel fabric of *Radegonde's* construction as if it were spring wheat.

Harry was trying to see more, to experience more of the phenomenon, but the truth was, he was instantly totally engrossed in hanging on for dear life, with even his pressed shut eyelids being battered by the flying spray. He had no idea how long the assault lasted, and then it was gone. Lifted like a curtain so that all that was left was the water sluicing from the conning tower deck and off the hull's casing.

Harry, and everyone else on the bridge, were as wet as if they had been under water. They all had a look round to make sure they were all there, and to share the nervous laughter of the just reprieved. Captain Syvret unplugged the bridge voice-pipe and ordered the boat back on to her mean course, and, as she turned, the port lookout made the call.

'Objects in the water, fine on the port bow!'

Syvret ordered the turn stopped, and they veered away to have a look-see. Harry didn't have binoculars with him, but Faujanet, who was fixed on whatever it was, began giving a running commentary.

'It looks like a lifeboat,' he said, 'but it's very, very low in the water . . .'

And as they rose up on the long swell he got a better look: 'and other . . . debris. Can't make out . . .'

Harry, squinting, could see that the debris spread for some distance; splintered angles of wood, and other stuff he couldn't quite identify, like a lot of multi-coloured bobbing bundles. Cargo?

'It *is* a lifeboat!' called Faujanet, '. . . but it's right down to its gunnels . . . it's practically sunk. And there! There's a bit of another one. It's the bow. Sticking up vertical. Way over there to the right.' Then he stopped describing and was so silent, Captain Syvret put his binoculars to his eyes. The two men fixed on the stuff strewn across the swell, not saying anything, until Harry felt his eyes begin to hurt from screwing them up against the sun's glare. Syvret broke the moment, going to the voice-pipe and ordering a deck party up

with boathooks and a scrambling net. Then he went back to looking again.

Although the sun was back in the sky, Harry was conscious his
clothes weren't drying. The air was so humid, it felt muddy, and the
orb of the sun was clung with a huge wind gall. He suddenly felt a
sick dread in the pit of his stomach.

'What do you see, Sir?' he asked Captain Syvret.

'Bodies.'

What do you do? How are you supposed to react, to feel, as
ordinary blokes going about your business, and then suddenly, you
are confronted with an atrocity? In wartime, some might argue,
it's different. You wear your country's uniform, and sail under its
flag. And you engage the enemy. There are fights; full-scale battles;
chance encounters. People die either way – your friends, shipmates;
the enemy dies too. You have victories, defeats; sometimes it's even
hard to tell the difference. But that's what happens. It's war.

Then you encounter something like this. They're ordinary sailors, merchant sailors, not fighting sailors; men with homes to go to
when they're ashore; sons, brothers, fathers. Men who get their pay
remitted, so that the people who need them, depend on them, love
them, can buy their groceries and pay the rent. And here they are,
bobbing in the middle of the sea. While their loved ones safe ashore
are going about their daily business believing they are going about
theirs: hauling on ropes, greasing an engine part, laying a course for
the Mona Passage. But they're not; they're here, in the sea. And who
would know, if you hadn't found them? Floating, bullet-punctured
on a scum of bunker oil and flotsam, their lifeboats shot to pieces.
Lifeboats. Do you hear me? Think about that word; what it means.
Their *lifeboats*. Shot to pieces.

Radegonde wasn't going to recover any bodies, Captain Syvret
was specific about that. She did not have the space to hygienically
store them. But she would look for survivors. The deck party on the

casing, with boathooks, dragged the floating bodies close, but any examination was perfunctory; had to be. They did not have the time to haul each one aboard and check for pulse or breath. Why they did not have the time, Captain Syvret chose not to make clear right then. A lifebelt confirmed what everyone already knew; the ship's name was painted on the cork, SS *Pascagoula*.

Cantor, meanwhile, was given a series of signals instructions. Harry supervising, they radioed their find to Halifax in code for onward transmission to the US Navy. The news would find its way to Antigua, as would their request for any sightings of *Durandal* to be relayed back, through Halifax, to *Radegonde*; in code. Captain Syvret, apparently, did not want *Durandal* to think that *Radegonde* might be interested in her movements; and Harry was sure he didn't have to wonder why.

'We'll leave it to Antigua to arrange for the recovery of the bodies,' said Captain Syvret to a curious Harry on his way to begin transmission, but the Captain chose not to enlighten him any further. They were almost finished when Harry was hurriedly summoned back on to the bridge. 'And the Captain says to bring your hat,' said the matelot.

When Harry got back up into the cloying, unmoving heat, Syvret was looking down on to the forecasing, just by the gun. A group of matelots had the semi-submerged bow section of a lifeboat up-turned, and half hauled on to the saddle tanks. He could see clearly how a tattoo of machine-gun bullets had separated the bow from the rest of the lifeboat's hull. A figure in blue denim overalls was sprawled on *Radegonde*'s deck planking and one of the senior rates was stuffing wound dressing into a rip in a dark matted stain that covered the sailor's whole hip. Harry absently noted that all the matelots down on the casing had removed their red pom-pom hats. They were in a pile by the gun mount.

'Put your cap on,' said Captain Syvret, 'so as he'll see you're Royal Navy.'

As our new guest has just had a rather unpleasant experience at the hands of the French, thought Harry. *What a considerate man you are, Captain*, was what he was thinking, but didn't say.

When Harry got there, the sailor was fish-belly white and his eyes were rolling. Before Harry knelt, de Maligou, the Maître principal, stood beside him to talk in his ear. Harry could see the Frenchman's own lighter overalls were smeared with the wounded sailor's blood. 'He'd wedged himself up in the lifeboat's covered fo'c'sle when the shooting started,' said the stony-faced senior rate, 'but they put a few bullets in it anyway, just in case. His hip is shattered, and half his lights are hanging out under his overalls. He isn't going to make it.'

Syvret looked down on the tableau, his face as stony as his Maître principal's; it was like watching a man's last rites, and he thought young Gilmour, the tender way he cradled the man, could pass muster as a padre if he fancied a change of career. Syvret then leaned to open the control room voice-pipe and ordered a course change; there was nothing more they could do here, and it was time they attended to the other matter now outstanding.

After it was all over, Harry found his Skipper at the wardroom table with a series of charts and an atlas spread out before him. Despite the heat, he had a huge mug of coffee too, that Harry had smelled from the next compartment.

'Half of it's brandy,' said Syvret without looking up. 'Want one? You probably need one as much as I do.'

Harry sat down, but said nothing. Syvret leaned forward into the passage and called, 'Another one of these!' Then he looked over at Harry and said, 'How is the poor bastard?'

'Dead.'

'Well,' said Syvret, looking back at the weather report he'd just received, 'seeing as I am your Captain, a report would be good.'

Harry recovered himself; he was really getting too lax aboard this boat. 'Sorry, Sir.' He paused. 'It was a bit garbled, as you can imagine, but the gist is *Durandal* surfaced on them not long after first light, fired across their bows and ordered them to heave-to and prepare to be boarded. Any attempt to use their radio, and they'd be blown out of the water. With the big gun pointing at them, they did what they were told. The boarding party went aboard, and began to search the ship. Everything came to an abrupt halt when they met Tassereau's entourage. They were immediately transferred to *Durandal* and then the *Pascagoula*'s crew were ordered to get into the lifeboats and stand off. Again they complied. Boom! Boom! And the *Pascagoula* was turned into steel confetti. Then they turned their machine guns on the *Pascagoula*'s boats. His boat disintegrated, he got hit, there was a very loud noise – the *Durandal* diving I presume – and then God knows how long after, we arrived. The end.'

'And that was it?' said Syvret.

'All of it,' Harry replied. 'No mention of any cargo being transferred.'

Syvret frowned at him.

'Cargo,' repeated Harry. 'No cargo. There was no gold on *Pascagoula*, was there?'

'No. I never said there was,' said Syvret, and when that failed to stop Harry staring at him, he continued in a tired voice, 'It's still in Fort Desaix. I was ordered not to discuss it; and now I have. Happy? And there is no point in continuing to look at me like that. How the hell am I supposed to know what our political masters do, or what deals they make? Maybe they think now we're all friends together, it'll just be safer there. Maybe de Gaulle threatened the Americans . . . demanded the Statue of Liberty back. Or he told the British he'd put arsenic in Vera Lynn's Ovaltine. If you know, do please tell me.'

Harry remembered being back aboard HMS *Trebuchet* – his old *Bucket* – sitting in that dank, cold wardroom while they all discussed the finer points of Anglo-Soviet relations, as if they could second guess the inner workings of Whitehall and the Kremlin; trying to work out whether they should attack German transports in Soviet waters. He had been struck then by the sheer pathetic ludicrousness of their presumption that they could divine their masters' intentions. And here he was again; where the path of the ordinary fighting sailor gets all mixed up with the convoluted imperatives of politics and grand strategy – and no prizes for guessing who gets fucked up at the end of it all. What was it about submarines that sooner or later you ended up here? The only answer to that was to stop worrying about it and just get on and do your duty.

'If there was no gold, why did *Durandal* have to kill them all?' Harry asked. He couldn't help himself despite what he'd decided – to stop worrying about it and just get on and do his duty. 'And even if there had been gold, and they'd got it, would they have needed to kill them all? For the sake of a couple of hours start when they have the whole Atlantic to hide in?'

'Spite?' said Syvret, shrugging. 'I've crossed paths with that bastard Boudron de Vatry before. He isn't what you'd call an honourable man.'

Harry's brandy-laced coffee arrived and he took a big belt; Syvret had been right, he did need it. 'What happens now, Sir?' he said, wiping his chin.

Syvret's jaw set, so that his teeth were still clenched when he spoke. 'He's mine,' he said, quietly.

Chapter Twenty-one

The weather system curling up from the coast of Honduras had formed days before, from along the trailing ends of an unseasonal cold front that had descended from Canada down through the central United States and then hit the warmer waters of, first, the Gulf of Mexico, and then the western Caribbean Basin. The system had run into thunderstorms in the Basin, which had acted as an internal escalator, seamlessly transporting heat and moisture up into the growing storm's core, kick-starting a cyclonic turning of the winds in the upper levels of the atmosphere, allowing what was now becoming an incipient tropical cyclone to grow and develop.

It was now advancing west-nor'-west on a hundred-nautical-mile front and was less than thirty-six hours behind them as they headed out across the Atlantic along the same track. The long swell and the warm, syrupy air preceding the storm already held them in a firm grasp.

A chart of the eastern Atlantic, off the Windward Islands, was spread over the wardroom table, along with a stack of all the US Navy weather forecasts transcribed by Cantor over the past twenty-four hours; an atlas lay open at the pages showing the full mid-Atlantic reach, and on it in red pencil was a great circle line following the curve of the globe all the way from Martinique to Casablanca in French Morocco. Syvret was presiding, and all of *Radegonde's* officers were there too, apart from Poulenc who had the watch. Even Maître principal de Maligou and Beyfus, the engineering Premier maître, were there, perched on stools in the passageway. The wardroom's little deckhead light gave the scene an air of some Jacobean conspiracy, except no one was drinking; with the fiddles gone to make room for the chart, the long, monotonous rise and fall of the boat would have sooner or later rolled any tumbler or bottle off the ends. Harry was aware that Stalin was curled up under Syvret's feet, busy being very still.

'I've sailed these waters before,' said Syvret, 'and so has the Maître principal, and from what we're seeing here', he patted the pile of forecasts, 'we both agree our friend does not look like she's going to grow up to be a hurricane; at least not before she hits us.'

'It's too early in the season,' agreed a grim-faced de Maligou, 'and from the wrong direction.'

'But we're still going to be in for one hell of a blow,' Syvret added. 'Tropical storms are not ladies to be trifled with.'

Syvret leaned into the chart where he'd already roughly pencilled in the track of the storm, and drew a dotted line, south of Martinique and up out into the Atlantic and north in a huge curve.

'She'll go where she wants, but that is my best estimate for the path this young lady will take,' said Syvret. 'She'll advance at about thirteen and fourteen knots, but her cyclonic winds – they blow anti-clockwise – could be anything from thirty-five to sixty knots, gusting much higher; and as for the sea state, we can expect waves of at least four metres. I am not planning to avoid it; I am planning to use it.'

Harry had noticed, when he'd sat down, that something was wrong; something in the air. And it wasn't just the lack of drink, either. Because whatever it was had just ratcheted up a notch. And that's when it hit him; the reason. He wanted to slap his head. Of course! What else could it have been? He hadn't said as much yet, but Syvret was planning to chase *Durandal*, and when he found her, he was planning to sink her. And everybody knew exactly what that meant: Frenchmen killing Frenchmen. And these Frenchmen weren't happy with that. *Durandal* might have been responsible for killing that mongrel crew on *Pascagoula* – the Americans, Jamaicans, Mexicans and Costa Ricans. Yes, it had been an atrocity. But atrocity or no atrocity, by going after *Durandal* they were talking about the lives of fellow French sailors here, and who made Captain Syvret their judge and jury? And who said the *Durandal*'s sailors were *all* guilty? They were men just like them. *Radegonde*'s officers, and the senior rates who were there to represent her crew; they didn't like the idea at all.

'As it turns north I intend to get us into the western hemisphere of the storm,' continued Syvret, seemingly oblivious. 'If we get there ahead of its eye we can get out of it ahead of *Durandal*. Because of the winds blowing counter-clockwise, if you end up in the eastern half, the actual speed of the storm system as it advances gets added to the cyclonic wind speeds in the system itself. But once you're on the western side, it's different; the system's track speed acts against the cyclonic speed, and you can lose up to thirty knots of blow. The sea state will also be less and that means we can move faster. It also means we are better able to dive, and to surface.'

Even Harry knew the dangers of submerging or surfacing in heavy weather; the near impossibility of maintaining trim, the likelihood you'll uncover vents when you don't intend to, or have your blowing tanks smothered by seas. Then there was the matter of metacentric height. Harry had seen the diagrams and the equations in books and thought he'd understood them then. But sitting here, at sea, with the Captain talking about navigating in hurricane winds, it all went blank. All he could remember was that it was all

234

about calculating the stability of a vessel and the relationship to its centre of gravity, and if you got it wrong, you capsized. And that loss of control was just a raging wave crest or plunging trough away.

'And since *Durandal* doesn't know we're here,' added Syvret, 'then we have every chance of getting ahead of her before she emerges from the storm. Because I think we all know where she'll be headed. I don't think there's any doubt. She's running home to papa, just like all bad girls do. Back to Casablanca. Into the arms of Admiral Darlan and ready, like the rest of the Vichy fleet, to be handed over to Hitler. Well, I don't think so.'

His speech was met with glum faces, and a silence and disinterest Harry had never seen before. While the Captain was all gestures and enthusiasm, everyone else round the table just sat; each one with an expression like a mongoose watching a cobra. Which was about where Captain Syvret finally cottoned on to the fact he had a problem.

'Harry,' he said affably, not looking at him, 'please ask the First Lieutenant to come down here. And Harry, would you mind taking over the watch for a bit.' It wasn't a question.

'Aye aye, Sir,' said Harry, and was glad to be gone.

Radegonde was on a heading that was essentially the great circle route to Casablanca, following a 3,500-mile curve across the face of the globe at a steady twelve knots. Somewhere out ahead of her would be *Durandal*, following the same course, if Captain Syvret was right; but probably at only nine to ten knots. She was a bigger boat, Syvret had said by way of stating the bleeding obvious, and burned more fuel to push herself the same distance as *Radegonde*; *and* she might well have fuel worries on top of that unfortunate fact, not having topped up since leaving the Brooklyn Navy Yard. 'While we, as our American friends say, are operating on a full tank of gas,' Syvret had added.

Harry scanned ahead every time they rose on a wave crest, searching the far horizon line across a huge expanse of rising sea. He didn't notice Bassano had come on to the bridge until he was standing beside him. Bassano should have asked permission of the officer of the watch, but one look told Harry his friend was more than a little distracted.

'Captain Syvret's sure *Durandal*'s heading for Casablanca?' Harry eventually asked, to break the silence. The three young matelots on watch with Harry, binoculars stuck to their faces, did not flinch from their duty, but even out of the corner of his eye, Harry could've sworn their ears were twitching to catch every word of what was about to be said.

'*Jean Bart*'s there,' said Bassano, not really engaged.

Harry interrupted him. 'The new, fast battleship?' he said.

Bassano nodded. 'And three or four light cruisers. Destroyers. Other stuff. To get into Toulon or Oran, *Durandal* would have to sneak past Gibraltar. The Atlantic ports are all in Jerry hands. So it's a good bet.'

Another pause.

'He keeps insisting Admiral Darlan's going to hand the whole lot to Hitler,' Bassano eventually resumed, still staring out into the rolling troughs. 'But we don't know that. It's not what Darlan's saying. He's saying it's all about the treaty. Compiègne the second; where Hitler made sure we surrendered in the same railway carriage where we made the Boche surrender after the Great War; just to rub it in.' Bassano sighed. 'We keep to the treaty, Jerry keeps out of Vichy. The treaty says we don't hand over our fleet to Churchill. We break the treaty and Jerry doesn't stay out of Vichy.' And then there was a long pause.

Harry didn't interrupt this time, to state another 'bleedin' obvious' – that Hitler didn't have a very good track record on keeping treaties.

'The Captain believes Darlan's pro-Nazi; and so is Boudron de Vatry,' Bassano finally broke his own silence. 'But he isn't . . . Darlan isn't; he's just playing politics like he always does. I wouldn't like to speak for Boudron, though. And none of it's helped by the fact that the Captain doesn't like either of them. So now he's on a mission.'

'And the crew don't like it?' said Harry.

For the first time Bassano looked at him, and Harry could see the fear in his eyes.

'You can see that?'

Harry didn't reply.

'I suppose it's obvious,' said Bassano. 'The crew don't give a stuff about treaties, or Admiral Darlan, or that Boudron is a murderer and maybe even a fascist, and that he has shamed the Marine Nationale; but the crew won't kill French sailors.'

'And what does Captain Syvret say?' asked Harry.

'That the *Radegonde* isn't a commune. And they will obey orders.' Bassano rubbed his face in his hands. 'So here we are, playing nursery games with a nearly hurricane, and a surly crew. I don't know these waters, but I've seen a nearly typhoon, trying to beat it into Cam Ranh Bay. It scared the shit out of me. All to hunt a quarry that if we catch it, we could end up with a mutiny.'

———

Captain Syvret was busy with his diagrams; marking the path of the tropical storm. From the latest weather report it had clipped the south end of Martinique several hours previously, with its eye passing up to thirty miles off shore. Even so the sustained wind speed had hit over sixty knots, with five-metre wave troughs, but the storm front had shrunk a little, to something a bit less than seventy miles; and it was already beginning to curve north, closing in on them.

Already *Radegonde* was bouncing on a sea that was beginning to become more confused as the outer fringes of the storm advanced and was no longer pushing the sea, but starting to churn it. Syvret ordered *Radegonde* trimmed down to decks awash. By partially flooding her tanks, just a little, he was lowering her centre of gravity. For, in many ways, a submarine, even on the surface, is one of the most seaworthy boats to brave a storm in; sealed as she is against wind and wave. She might bounce around a bit, and things could get very uncomfortable for those on watch on the bridge, but she could never be overwhelmed. And if things got too bad, you could always dive; but if you left that too late, getting down could be tricky. Coming up could be even trickier, and you never knew how long it would take a storm to pass as you consumed battery amps and sat about while your air turned foul; the gigantic waves making it difficult to tell whether you were still underwater or on the surface, ready to roll back down into the deep. No; riding it out on the surface, you'd be fine, just as long as the battery acid didn't spill and mix with bilge water and turn your boat into a chlorine gas chamber. And *Radegonde* had already had to have some battery cells repaired after action against the U-boats in the Atlantic.

Harry watched Captain Syvret sketch his plan, but not being experienced in this kind of bad weather, he didn't realise the plan was to execute a manoeuvre no mariner should ever attempt – to cross the T of a hurricane, or indeed anything approaching it, like a tropical storm. So he was curious, instead of afraid, as he should have been. No one else was at the wardroom table – no one else was talking to the Captain.

Syvret made room for Harry and smoothed out the chart.

'We're here, and this is the track of the storm,' he said, indicating an X on the expanse of ocean and a circle about the size of a two-bob piece. 'This is the likely curve of its arc as it turns north, and I aim to hit that outer ring of wind about here' – another jab with his pencil. 'Your men Lucie and Cantor are being very good about keeping me up to date as to where our friend is now. She's singing like a songbird. God knows what she's saying, but Boudron obviously thinks he's got away with it. He'll be telling papa all about it. Then it'll be just a short summer cruise across the Atlantic, and he'll be home.'

Cantor would know *Durandal's* radio operator by his fist all right; it was his talent, being able to tell one operator from another simply from the way he stroked the Morse key.

'He's in no hurry, so he'll go south about, round the bottom of the system,' continued Syvret, 'and then come back on his great circle course about here. I can't think of any reason he'll shut up now, so your radio boys will pin him as he does.' He gave Harry a quick smile, and slid a big French coin to cover the pencil outline of the storm; then he moved it following his pencilled curve. 'Now, when the storm is here, if we cut across, into the thirty-five-knot wind boundary, we'll be inside the system, with the system's cyclonic winds fine on our port bow; but the northerly track of the storm will be acting against the cyclonic wind. The two titanic blasts will be acting against each other. Yes, we'll have to slow down a little because of the sea state, but by cutting across the leading edge of the storm, we will have less distance to cover; and if we escape the system here, we'll be waiting for Boudron as he comes back on to his mean course, here' – another jab at the chart, at another X. 'Elegant, *n'est-ce pas?*'

Bassano had the watch. There were only two matelots on the bridge with Harry now, pixie-like in sou'westers, not that anyone was able to see much anymore. They were getting close to the cyclonic winds; Harry could tell by the contrary buffets that hit him when he put his head above the bridge front.

Night was coming; all around as far as the eye could see in the water-filled air, it was already dark, but the night itself was a different thing, like an obsidian lid, slowly being rolled over them from the west. The sea was confused with waves, no longer endless rolling ridge lines, but cross-hatched and colliding, throwing up crests of flying spume; and it was cold now. All the humidity had gone out of the air, and Harry was shivering in his already drenched shirt.

The matelots were secured by safety lines and Bassano, bareheaded like Harry, had to undo his to follow him to the aft end of the conning tower. The periscope stands provided little cover from the wind, which was now a semi-permanent roar, and the spray.

What happened next was a series of bawls and yells in each other's ears as Harry communicated to Bassano the Captain's intention. Bassano kept shaking his head – crossing a storm's T? He is mad! He risks the boat! He cannot know how fast or slowly the storm will advance; where he will enter it. He has only the last readings; he cannot know what it is doing now: its winds, the sea state; and even if he does get lucky, and they get through undamaged, what then? What happens when he orders the torpedoes fired? At other Frenchmen?

'He has to be stopped!' Harry yelled in Bassano's ear.

Bassano stared back at him through a plastered flop of his hair.

'I know!' yelled Harry. 'We can't. But Boudron de Vatry can.'

Bassano continued to stare, worried now.

'By not being there,' said Harry, finally.

⌣‿‿‿⌣

Harry hadn't slept more than a catnap since before *Durandal* turned up and started bombarding Fort-de-France. He was pretty sure Captain Syvret hadn't even managed that.

'How long until we intercept her, Sir?' Harry asked, peering between Syvret and Poulenc at *Radegonde*'s chart table. The Captain and his First Lieutenant were discussing their course.

Syvret shrugged. 'Hard to say. There's a lot of variables . . . maybe as much as eighty nautical miles to run . . . we're already having to reduce speed. Ten hours, maybe more. Why?'

'When did you last get your head down, Sir?' said Harry, his face suffused with concern. Even if a vestige of conspiracy had shown through, Captain Syvret was far too tired to notice.

'Harry's right, Sir,' said Poulenc, entirely innocent of Harry's motives. 'A couple of hours now; you'll feel the benefit when the time comes.'

Harry gave Syvret ten minutes in his cabin before he dragged Cantor from the comforts of the Stokers' mess. Lucie was also there, asleep in a borrowed bunk, tucked in with Stalin, and Harry couldn't help but suspect that Lucie had climbed into it drunk. How else had he stayed asleep when the dog had jumped up and burrowed in with him? There'd be a time to worry about that later. Maybe. Harry and Cantor climbed up into the empty conning tower kiosk. Above was Bassano, on watch; below, Le Breuil was in the control room, dead reckoning their waypoints on the chart.

'I want you to send a signal, *en clair*, to Halifax and to our special little mailbox,' said Harry as Cantor sat down at the radio transmitter and got himself plugged in. 'I want you to give our position and report we are hunting *Durandal*, and intend to sink her as a result of her sinking the neutral American freighter *Pascagoula*, and then murdering her crew. Then ask for a message received. Send it twice.'

Cantor replied, 'Aye Aye, Sir', as he was supposed to, but his body froze in a way that said he had a lot of questions. As he started to draft the words he'd transmit, he couldn't help himself. 'The Americans will already know by now, Sir, what happened.

241

From our earlier coded signals. You asked them to be forwarded, Sir. Remember.'

Harry put his hand lightly on Cantor's shoulder; the message was clear. Shut up. Then he relented and said, 'It's not for the Americans. It's for the French.'

'The French, Sir?'

'That Vichy station *Durandal*'s been gibbering away to,' said Harry, looking over Cantor's signal. 'Between them, they'll be able to get a fix on us, won't they? If they're not asleep, or drunk?'

'Not a fix, Sir. You really need a triangulation for that. But they'll get a box that they'll know we're in. They'll know we're here, Sir.'

'Good. Now get tapping, Lionel. And if anyone asks, deny everything. And if that doesn't work, say you were only obeying orders.'

Harry sat in the wardroom with a coffee, most of which he lost carrying it from the small pantry as the boat corkscrewed up and down waves that were now following no particular direction; churned by the storm. He wedged himself in on the banquette, and reflected on what he had done.

Radegonde was a good boat; a happy boat, and an efficient boat. They might not do things Royal Navy fashion, but they were a good crew who knew what they were about. And Gil Syvret was a good Skipper. It was a knowledge that made Harry search his conscience; and it told him he had barely a fig leaf of an excuse for what he had done. He could say he wasn't really a member of her crew, that he was an LO to another, foreign navy, and that was where his loyalty lay; he had different priorities, and sending signals updating his chain of command as to what was going on aboard his posting was one of them. But he didn't believe that, and he knew Gil Syvret wouldn't countenance it. And maybe that was why he couldn't let *Radegonde* continue on her course, or let Gil Syvret pull apart all the bonds of trust and loyalty that bound this crew and their service; just because politicians had fucked it all up and put bad men into positions where they could do bad things, and because Syvret, their Captain, couldn't let it pass. Because Syvret was bound by his ever-so noble, finely wrought moral certainty as to why he fought; as if it was his own special bloody altar.

Maybe Syvret had a point. Maybe all good men should have their own special bloody altar to serve in a chaotic, immoral world. Harry didn't know, but right now he was buggered if he was going to stand around and let Gil Syvret sacrifice himself on his; or any of his crew, or any other crew for that matter. Harry's signals would warn *Durandal* off and *Radegonde* would be left to hunt an empty ocean for a quarry long gone. Let the politicians sort out *Durandal's* atrocity. *Radegonde* still had its war to fight, and its sailors to bring home safe.

At length Harry found himself wondering who would actually court martial him for what he'd done; and what offence they would decide to call it. It would certainly be an interesting conundrum of jurisdiction. But in the end, he decided he didn't care; he'd sorted it out in his own mind. He was doing this for his friends; for their own bloody good, which he could see, even if they couldn't.

Radegonde battered on into the night, until eventually Harry guessed Captain Syvret and all his sketches and guesses must have been just about on the money as he could feel from the boat's move-ment that the sea state and the wind had actually moderated, albeit a very little. They must be in the system, butting into the counter-clockwise, cyclonic winds and waves; which were themselves being butted back by the onward advance of the storm's front. Harry won-dered how the bigger, leaky *Durandal* was faring, going round the storm, far to the south.

Sometime in the night, a commotion woke Harry from where he was wedged sleeping on the wardroom banquette. Engine room crew were running forward, or at least trying to, given the heave and roll of the boat; figures made unnatural in the red light, their silhouettes bug-like as they awkwardly clutched canvas tool sacks in one hand, while trying to steady themselves with the other. Harry lurched up to follow.

He went through the control room, and there was the Captain and Poulenc with the deckplates up, and Beyfus, the senior engine room rating, half in the hole. Torchlight was spilling up and another matelot was wrestling something from below. It took a moment for Harry to work out that they were rummaging in the forward battery space.

Radegonde carried two huge batteries to drive her electric motors while submerged. Harry knew all about batteries from his previous boats, mainly because they were so big, mean and potentially dangerous.

'You'll have seen an ordinary car battery,' the Warrant Officer Engineer aboard HMS *Trebuchet* had once observed to him. 'Six cells, each producing two point two five volts when fully charged, and generating forty-five to fifty amps.'

Harry couldn't remember *Trebuchet's* battery capacity, but *Radegonde's* two had 126 cells each and could generate over 15,000 amps in parallel. And they were big buggers; when Harry translated it to imperial measurements, each cell was about fifty-four inches high, fifteen inches deep, and twenty-one inches wide, and weighed about 1,650 pounds – that was almost 750 kilogrammes. Lumped together, her two batteries weighed in at something over 200 tons – a tenth of her total tonnage submerged. But it was not the size that posed the threat to those who depended on them.

Like a car's battery, the cells were made up of lead plates, suspended in an electrolyte solution of sulphuric acid and distilled water. As the cells were charged, the water would break down and produce hydrogen gas. That required an elaborate ventilation system to draw any hydrogen off and discharge it outside the pressure hull, because, as any schoolboy would tell you, hydrogen, if allowed to accumulate, becomes explosive and would sooner or later blow up the submarine.

And that wasn't the only hazard, or the most insidious for a crew sealed in their hull beneath the waves. All submariners feared salt water contamination of the batteries. If salt water got into the electrolyte, chlorine gas would be given off – and if it was a lot of salt water, it would be an awful lot of chlorine gas. That was why each cell was secured in a special, acid-proof glass container. A container that could sometimes crack if handled too roughly, as it might be by the continual pounding of a storm.

Harry was suddenly aware of Le Breuil at his elbow; he had been on watch in the control room when Harry had passed, but had stepped forward to see what was happening.

'Anything?' he asked. Harry looked at him blankly.

'They think some of the battery cells might have cracked,' explained Le Breuil. 'They're testing the pH.'

As he said it, Harry saw Beyfus, who was clutching a long strip of something, look up at the Captain and nod grimly. Harry didn't want to know anymore. He turned and lurched and grabbed his way back to the wardroom. There was nothing he could do.

'They've put some lime down,' said Syvret, sitting with Harry at the wardroom table later, drinking fresh orange juice from a can; no galley could remain open in these seas, and nothing hot could be served. He was drumming his fingers, not really paying attention to what he was telling Harry. 'It'll help neutralise any acid that's already escaped. Beyfus thinks he's identified all the cracked ones, so we've isolated them. I know we're not drawing that many amps just running on the surface, so what he's left us with is more than enough. Also, we've reduced speed at bit, and we'll make sure we keep her head into the seas as much as possible to reduce our roll and try and limit any further damage. I've told Beyfus to have a team of greasers nurse the bilge pumps like babies. We'll keep them going flat out, to keep the seawater levels in the bilges right down; although they've got a lot to handle since we need to keep the conning tower hatch open to keep feeding air into the diesels, and a lot of water is coming down that hatch. God, it's never ending.'

'You could rig some canvas or tarpaulin under the hatch,' offered Harry. 'Catch the big lumps, then try to bail it. I saw that done on *Trebuchet*.'

Syvret pursed his lips. 'Hmm. Not a bad idea. Every little bit helps. I'll tell the Maître principal. Who's a clever boy then . . .' and he smiled at Harry and reached over and pinched his cheek!

'Cheeky bastard!' Harry had been in danger of telling him, but Captain Syvret was gone, off to stay busy; to keep his eyes from rolling with fatigue; to keep focused on his mission. The rest of the boat was busy too; busy conning her through this bloody tempest; too busy, in fact, to let show their sullenness at being made to drive *Radegonde* towards a rendezvous that no one except the Captain wanted to keep; and that Harry hoped against hope, he had managed to sabotage.

The sun must have come up somewhere beyond the roiling cloud and rain, because apparently the bridge crew coming off watch said the sky had grown lighter. The storm continued moving north, its violence increasing as *Radegonde* rose and tumbled over the huge seas, now well down into its north-easterly hemisphere, where its northerly advance was shouldering its cyclonic winds and waves to greater strength.

Harry had been up again for a couple of hours, wedged in the control room this time, with a handful of Davis Escape Sets. Other cells had cracked in the night; there was more gas. Enough, in fact, for Captain Syvret to order Le Breuil, the torpedo officer, forward into the torpedo room with his crew. He then ordered the watertight doors at either end of the compartment above the battery space to be sealed. When the time came for *Radegonde* to fire her torpedoes,

Le Breuil and his men would be there, ready to do their duty, sealed in with their weapons and cut off from the rest of the boat, their shipmates and their Captain; reachable now only by the sound-powered telephone system. Alone, waiting for orders no one could be sure they would obey.

With what passed for daylight above, the red lights were out. Beyfus and his engine room team were spread out on the control room deckplates, struggling with tools and battery straps, waiting for the Captain to order them back into the sealed compartment. They would search for other damaged cells, to isolate them too, and to lay the last of the boat's lime in a final attempt to neutralise any further leaking acid. But they could never succeed if it meant they had to breathe the chlorine gas generated when the salt water mixed with battery acid. And the only way they could breathe anything else was to use a Davis Escape Set and its oxygen bottle. This wasn't what the sets were designed for, but they'd have to do. And since Harry was still the only man aboard who knew how to work those damn Davis Sets, that was why he was on hand to fit them on Beyfus's men; to make sure they knew how to operate them to give them clean air to breath and not air laced with chlorine, burning their eyes and nose, and their throat and lungs; burning them until the mucus drowned them.

What they really needed was calmer seas so the forward torpedo loading hatch could be wide open, and the conning tower hatch too, so the blowers could go full blast to air the boat and Beyfus's men could rig a chain hoist, lift each damaged cell out and clear of the main battery, and then drain and clean it and assess it for repair. But none of that was going to happen while they moved through the arms of a tropical storm.

It was while Harry was waiting that the shout came.

'Captain to the bridge!'

'What in God's name . . . ? Harry mouthed.

Syvret was already halfway up the ladder, neatly dodging the tarpaulin sheet bellied with water below the hatch, and the length of rubber tubing the engine room boys had rigged to suck the seawater out instead of trying to bail it.

The lookouts had to have spotted something. But what on earth would be where they were now, in a storm system? Surely no other ship would be insane enough? Surely no aircraft? Could it be wreckage? Could it be . . .?

Syvret was back down the hatch, his boots knocking the hose out of the tarpaulin trap, spewing seawater everywhere as it drained clean. He looked first at Bassano, who now had the watch in the control room, and Poulenc who should have been sleeping but was never going to be sleeping, not through this, and then at Harry.

'It's *Durandal.*' Syvret said with an almost breathless disbelief. 'I can barely make her out through all the shit that's flying about up there, but I'm sure it's her. Five, six miles. She's standing right towards us.'

Harry stood frozen as he watched Syvret reach for the sound-powered telephone. He was obviously going to tell Le Breuil to clear the torpedo tubes for firing; and then he stopped. There would be no torpedo fired from *Radegonde* in this sea. Even Captain Syvret, the man with a mission, knew that. If you fired one to run at a depth of two metres on a crest, it would run only until it exploded out of the wave and would instead go flying through mid-air; and if you fired on a trough, yes, it would run at two metres depth, but only until the next wave rose, and then it would suddenly be running at a depth of a dozen metres; and even then only if the washing machine forces of the waves themselves hadn't already tumbled its guidance gyros and sent it diving into the abyss. Nobody would be firing torpedoes. Not in seas like this.

This wasn't meant to happen. *Radegonde* was meant to have emerged from the storm system and be back astride *Durandal's* great circle course direct to Casablanca; waiting for her in calmer waters, with her torpedoes primed and ready to fire. But *Durandal* was here, in the middle of the storm, slicing through its most turbulent quadrant, coming for them.

All Harry could think was, *what have I done?*

Poulenc was away and up the hatch to the bridge. But Captain Syvret just stood, fixed to the control room deckplates, wearing an expression of immaculate incomprehension.

'Your orders, Sir?' said Bassano. Syvret just looked at him. Then he snapped out of it, all too aware that the control room crew were all witnesses and needed his response.

'Helm, steady as she goes,' he called up to the man at the wheel. 'Give me revs just for steerage way.' Other orders followed, but Harry switched off to the technical French and tried to work out in his head what was happening and what their options were. He was interrupted by Syvret grabbing his arm. 'Harry, on the bridge with you. Give the First Lieutenant another pair of eyes.'

Harry climbed out into an insipid grey light and a maelstrom of turbid, moving slate-coloured mountains, each one streaked with roiling tendrils of white spume. The air was cold and filled with tiny packets of flying water. They were going down a steep gradient, and a wall of water was advancing from the other side of the valley. He had to crick his neck back to see the crest, and hold on to prevent himself being thrown into the well of the bridge front. When he looked down, he could see Poulenc crouching there in its lee, frantically waving to him to get down. Harry obeyed, bracing his feet against the lip of the conning tower hatch combing, as he felt *Radegonde* begin to rise; and then stall. *Her bows are digging into the advancing wave*, he thought. And then he was under water; a huge mass of it had hit him, pinning him to the deck, his lungs bursting, until, just as suddenly, it was gone, sluicing away leaving him gasping as he felt *Radegonde* come up on the crest.

As he stood, a solid wall of wind hit him, coming over the starboard bow. Binoculars would have been useless in all the flying spray, the best he could do was squint, just off the line of the wind; peer into an endless succession of crests. And then, as he felt the boat beneath him begin to tilt towards its next plunge, there she was, climbing into view; the bow and then the barrel of the 12-inch gun rising up to crest her own wave. *She's closer than six miles*, was Harry's first thought; his second was that *Durandal* was under helm, turning bow on to them, and then with Harry's last glimpse of her through stinging eyes, he was certain: *Durandal's* gun was rising from its stowed position.

Harry was now staring directly into another advancing wave; the wind was gone, and the boat was running downhill fast.

Durandal had heard his transmissions all right; but she had not run. Instead, there she was, charging towards them, preparing to fire that monstrous great weapon. Syvret was suddenly beside him.

'I think she's going to fire at us, Sir,' said Harry.

Poulenc was at his shoulder, nodding in the affirmative. 'She's adjusting her heading to fire,' he said.

'He won't want to try his traverse mechanism in this sea,' said Syvret half to himself. 'It'd be like opening the front door, she'd take in so much water through that stupid turret.'

All three dropped behind the bridge front to await the next wave, and as they did, above the roar of the tempest, they heard the dull report of *Durandal's* gun. Harry was incredulous; had Boudron gone mad? He could never hope to hit them with such a wild shot . . .

'He's ranging,' said Syvret, in the moment before the next lump of water dumped itself on them, and Harry finished the thought himself; *to see where the shell landed: how much over or short, ahead or behind.* De Vatry's gunner would be more considered when aiming his next shot.

Harry and Syvret, crouching in the bridge, didn't see where the first shot landed. The water from the last wave subsided around them and Harry looked into Syvret's streaming face. What were his options now? He had to hold this course; he didn't have the luxury of heaving-off and running through a cross sea, not unless he wanted to do more damage to his batteries. He could dive, but diving would put a full load on them, and who would want to be underwater in a boat filling with chlorine gas? And fighting? That wasn't really an option either, now. No torpedo could work in this, and no gun crew could survive a minute on the submarine's casing, even if he could find volunteers to try and fire their little deck gun. And what about ramming? There was always ramming. But ramming meant murdering in cold blood Le Breuil and his men, now sealed in the forward torpedo room, trapped by the gas-filled compartment behind them; no way back into the boat for them.

Harry struggled back to his feet in time to see Poulenc disappear down the hatch. It was just Harry and the Captain now, and the two young matelot watchkeepers, lashed by their securing lines to the bridge wings; they steadied themselves for the wind as *Radegonde* clawed her way to the crest. *Durandal* was already up on hers, so they got a good look at her now. She must have been just over thirty-five degrees off *Radegonde's* starboard bow and her conning tower and periscope stands looked bashed about. It was impossible to tell whether she was trimmed down, as she needed to be to fire her gun; the sea was too confused. But the gun was raised, and even with their eyes screwed against the wind and flying water, both Harry and the Captain could see she meant to fire again. There was a puff of white smoke, snatched instantly into oblivion, and then they heard the bang.

Harry never saw that shot land in the sea either, distracted by Bassano struggling on to the bridge, holding some bulky lump of mechanism. It took him a moment to realise it was *Radegonde's*

TBT – her target bearing transmitter – the gizmo they used to aim their torpedoes for surface shots. He'd never seen it out of its box, and right then was wondering why Bassano was bothering to show him now. Because Poulenc had told him to, presumably; hope springing eternal and all that utter bollocks. Bassano wrestled the device on to its binnacle, but even he must have known it was going to be useless to them.

'That was actually quite close,' said Syvret aloud to no one in particular. It took Harry a moment to realise he'd been referring to where *Durandal*'s 12-inch shell had landed. When Harry looked back at the Captain, he seemed to be strangely detached. *Radegonde* didn't dig into the next wave, but rose on it smoothly. They all awaited the Captain's orders. But none came. *Durandal* was again on her crest when *Radegonde* breasted hers. They could see the gun fire clearly, and for the first time, the effect of the recoil on the wallowing submarine; how it seemed to shiver her and drive her down by the bows, squash her into the chasing seas. Then came the dull boom and as *Radegonde*, barely crawling forward now, her speed cut to steerage way, began her next descent, a giant candle of water appeared at her starboard beam, less than 200 yards away, and Harry heard the splinters hit the conning tower beneath him.

Syvret bawled into the control room voice-pipe; the man below must have received an earful of water along with the orders he shouted, and immediately, as *Radegonde* came off the crest, Harry felt her accelerate, but still on the same heading, still shunning the cross-seas, but still battering onward towards the edge of the cyclone.

If they kept going like this, in less than half an hour, *Durandal* would be firing over open sights; aiming her 12-inch naval gun like a sniper's rifle, directly at their guts. They dropped into the lee of the next wave, and Syvret continued staring ahead into its slab-grey front.

What was Boudron de Vatry doing? Harry kept asking himself. Why was she here and not running? What was there to gain? Was it rage at being thwarted by someone he considered a lesser man? They could see his boat had suffered damage, but what must she be like below decks, having slashed her way across the most turbulent seas and winds the system was generating? How many aboard must be injured? What state were his battery compartments in? Yet he didn't seem to care. He could be cruising to safety. So what if that fat slab of France's gold reserves had slipped through his fingers? So what if he'd realised too late that *Pascagoula* was a decoy and France's gold reserves were still in Martinique? What about all the propaganda potential he was carrying with Tassereau and his entourage aboard. Tales of coup d'état and French neutrality violated by a cavalier, aggressive – nay, imperialist – United States. Yet he was risking his command and his crew just to slake his petulance; to vent his spite.

In the relative quiet of the trough, Harry watched Syvret's unblinking profile. Then he heard Bassano say something in his ear.

'*Saint Joan*,' he said. 'Shaw's *Saint Joan*.'

Harry turned to him, disbelieving that his friend was going into one of his literary reveries at a time like this. But Bassano was grim-faced. He was making a point, not sampling literary allusions.

'The Chaplain's speech, after she's been burned,' he said, staring fixedly at the Captain. '"I did not know what I was doing. I am a hotheaded fool; and I shall be damned to all eternity", that's what he said.'

He was talking about Captain Syvret, and when Harry looked back at the Captain, he knew the truth of it. For all his own hatred and contempt for Boudron de Vatry, it was as if Captain Syvret knew now he had been guilty of the same sins, the same pride, the same reason-clouding lust for vengeance; to the point where even his crew and his boat had been offered up for sacrifice. Knew it as certainly as he knew it was now too late. And Harry knew it had not been Syvret's fatal decision that had brought them to this pass, but his own. And only he and poor Cantor knew. He'd had to interfere, hadn't he? To know better. To play God.

Fuck, fuck, fuck, fuck, he repeated to himself endlessly in his head.

The next round from *Durandal*'s gun or the round after would hit them. They were too close now to miss, despite the bouncing platform *Durandal* made for her gun layer. And in this sea, they would all die. *How absolutely bloody pathetic,* thought Harry. *After everything, this.*

They rose on their next crest, as *Durandal* was corkscrewing down the face of hers, but it was a mountainous sea that followed her; they could all see that and held their breaths. And then another wisp of smoke was snatched from the muzzle of *Durandal*'s gun, and it was as if they were left looking directly down its barrel. And then everything happened in what seemed like slow motion.

God had sent no miracle to save Saint Joan from the stake, but to save *Radegonde* He sent a big wave.

The recoil from her gun squashed *Durandal* into the wave's face again, but she was far down the face this time and it buried her bows into the trough; just as the rising, towering wave rolled under her. It caught her aft end and twisted it against her bow, buried in the confused seas ahead, and it was as if the torque of it shoved her stern out of the water, her twin propellers whining and screaming; not against water, that would give them power, but fresh air. And as the wave pushed, her stern climbed higher.

Harry saw a figure tumble from her bridge front into a sea that was now vertically below him. Up and up until her stern stood proud, upright, two thirds of her length standing out of the wave front, and the rest of her, the submerged end of her, now pointing directly down into the abyss of the Atlantic Ocean. And she hung there, until the wave enfolded her, and thrust her down; and she was gone. Nothing left; any dying bubble lost in the tumult of the storm.

Harry, Bassano and Captain Syvret and the two young watch-keepers stood rigid, their eyes fixed on the spot where a moment ago 130 French sailors had once manned a French warship. And then *Radegonde* went over the edge of her own wave, and down into her next trough, and all they were left looking at was a wall of water.

Postscript

It was a clear, blue summer's day in Liverpool. It had been morning when Captain Charles Bonalleck, Assistant Chief of Operations to Flag Officer, Submarines, got off the train at Lime Street Station. It had taken all night to get up from London, and most of the previous day just to get from Portsmouth to London. But he was here and feeling chipper with himself; he was, after all, reputed throughout the trade to be able to sleep through even a depth charging, so the overnight train journey hadn't taken that much of a toll, and his hangover wasn't that bad. He'd certainly had much worse. There was a warm sun, calling seagulls overhead, and the city centre area was getting into the full bustle of the day as he walked to the Liver Building on the corner of Chapel Street, leading down to the docks.

If you'd passed him on the street, and noticed the smile that wreathed his face, you would have said there goes a man with a clear conscience, and you would have been right; as clear as any man's who cared for nothing but himself.

Because in many ways the Bonny Boy was a changed man these days. A much soberer man. Because when you've as good as committed bloody murder because of drink – and got away with it – it tends to focus the mind wonderfully. Especially on your own survival in a hostile world. Oh, the Bonny Boy still enjoyed his drink, but not so much as he was prepared to risk his own survival anymore, there were too many debts to pay off against all who'd wronged him. And they were legion.

He was up in Liverpool, summoned here to meet his boss, the FOS, Vice Admiral Max Horton VC. Another submariner from the last war, except Max had since done considerably better for himself than Charles, the Bonny Boy, Bonalleck. Apart from in the VC department. The Bonny Boy did have his own VC. And now another DSO – to add to his previous brace from the last lot. The Distinguished Service Order was what they handed out when they'd run out of that month's quota of VCs, and he'd just been gazetted for one for the sinking of that Jerry heavy cruiser back in 1940. One of the few good news stories to come out of that whole Norwegian debacle. And, of course, he'd made sure he got the credit for it. Should have been another VC of course, but he wasn't bitter. Things had worked out quite well after that little action, considering his real role in it and what he'd done afterwards.

Max wanted the Bonny Boy here to back him up, for he was meeting his own boss, Admiral Sir Percy Noble, the Commander-in-Chief, Western Approaches; the man who ran the Atlantic convoys. The Liver Building, overlooking the Mersey shorefront, had been the C-in-C, Western Approaches' new lair since February, so obviously the old crock was keen to show it off; which was why Sir Percy had dragged Max half way up bloody England, and why Max had dragged the Bonny Boy behind him. Except, knowing Max, he'd probably commandeered a Coastal Command Anson and flown up to Speke, while he left the Bonny Boy to catch a bloody night train crammed with all manner of wartime riff-raff from pongos going on leave to travelling salesmen of ladies' foundation wear.

The Bonny Boy would have been angry if it hadn't been for one of the items on the agenda; a report he had written, grandly titled:

Proposals for the establishment of operational hunting/support groups along the north Atlantic convoy lanes and Western Approaches.

Max had liked that when he had read it; liked it so much he had spent twenty minutes lecturing the Bonny Boy on how he had been having the same thoughts himself, before going on, in exhaustive detail, to demonstrate how he, in fact, knew far more about the matter than even the Bonny Boy did. When that happened you knew you'd scored. It was always a sure sign Max liked an idea, when everyone suddenly discovered the boss had thought of it himself ages ago, but was extremely grateful to you for reminding him.

Now Max was up here to sell it to Sir Percy. And the Bonny Boy was here to 'remind' Max of the answers to any awkward questions that might need answering. *Never mind, Bonny Boy*, Captain Bonalleck said to himself, as he sipped tea in the spare office he'd been plonked in to wait. *You put that one past him, and it all adds lustre to your cluster.*

And wait he did; but he didn't mind. It gave him more time to savour the other exquisite aspect to all of this. The idea had come from that Free French sub's little battle around convoy SC27 back in the spring; written as an addendum to the action report of her Royal Navy Liaison Officer; which was thoughtful of the Royal Navy Liaison Officer as it saved the Bonny Boy from having to unpick it from the full report, which as a formal document, was not supposed to be for picking at.

And a bloody good report it had been too, but it was never going to go anywhere; not written by a Wavy Navy type. 'Thank you very much Sub-Lieutenant, just file it in the bin on your way out,' he'd parroted to himself when he'd read it. No, he'd told himself, by putting his own name to it, he'd be doing the report – the service even – a favour. It will have more traction as it climbs the rungs of command if it's written by a Captain; because you are a

Captain now. Promoted as well as decorated since that little fracas with the Jerry cruiser; you clever chappie, you.

All that, of course, was before he read down and saw who the RNVR Sub-Lieutenant was.

Sub-Lieutenant Harry Gilmour RNVR. He couldn't believe his eyes.

After that, it all became pleasure rather than business, for Sub-Lieutenant Harry Gilmour had once served under him. That was why the Bonny Boy hated him; and feared him too.

The door opened and in swept Max, firing off greetings and bonhomie. He was bareheaded, so no salutes, and he was carrying nothing except a little signal flimsy. He took a seat the way people do when they are only passing through.

Max Horton was a big, bluff man, gimlet-eyed and craggy of jaw with slicked dark hair worn close to his big round head. No nonsense was what his whole persona said, in case you hadn't heard him the first time; which was unlikely. He filled his uniform, and he looked like his sleeves had sported ranks of gold braid since birth.

'Everything with Sir Percy went splendidly,' he announced. 'Didn't need you in the end.'

That was that subject dealt with. Next.

'There is another matter', and he brandished the flimsy. 'Someone somewhere in the Min. of Inf. has decided they're finally going to release the loss of *Pelorus*.'

'Sir,' said the Bonny Boy in his finest non-committal; thinking, where was this going? All he knew was that *Pelorus*'s loss had been suppressed at the time. They never gave a reason. Maybe it was because they'd feared her loss might take the shine off him having just sunk the German heavy cruiser *Graf von Zeithen*. For, as everyone knew, the Bonny Boy had commanded *Pelorus* during that action, and he was keen to keep it that way.

'It's to do with the matter of that RNVR Sub you had aboard,' said Max, leaning back like nothing in the world could worry him now; a true Max danger signal. 'Your fourth, or was it fifth?' Watch officer, he meant. 'It was in your report. Something about him leaving his station. All very serious.'

'His name was Gilmour,' said the Bonny Boy; if anyone knew when not to dissemble, it was him. 'It was his first war patrol.'

'Ah. A new boy,' said Max. 'A new *RNVR* boy.'

'Yessir.' The Bonny Boy was too cute to let himself be led. Could Max know about the connection between Gilmour and the discussion paper? Surely not. Or, worse, could he know about what had really happened aboard *Pelorus* on the patrol?

'What are your thoughts about where we go now?'

'Sir?'

Max was now getting exasperated. 'Dammit! What are your intentions? Are you going to want to nail him for it? Good God, man! Do I have to spell it out?'

Caution, Bonny Boy, he said to himself; although how sweet that would be, to see Gilmour crushed. For Sub-Lieutenant Harry Gilmour knew everything that had happened aboard *Pelorus*'s last patrol, and why. And Charles, the Bonny Boy, Bonalleck had long dreamed of destroying him for it.

'His was a very grave dereliction of duty, Sir,' he said, testing the water. 'The sort of thing, in the trade, that makes you wonder whether you actually want to ever sail with a chap like that again. Whether you want anyone to have to sail with him.'

Max frowned, silently. Obviously that had been the wrong answer. Max continued to say nothing. The silence dragged on, but the Bonny Boy was buggered if he was going to give that little Gilmour shit even just one inch of line.

Buggered, dammit.

However, when you stopped to consider, it really was no disgrace giving way, not to Max when Max wanted his own way; whatever that way was. He always got it in the end. Always.

'Although,' the Bonny Boy said eventually, reluctantly, 'he was very young at the time, Sir. And it was, as I said, his first patrol and first action.' But what he said to himself was: *one day.*

'Quite,' said Max. 'Young, *and* raw.'

Max stared long and hard at the Bonny Boy, as if daring contradiction.

'He's been an LO since *Pelorus* was lost,' Max said eventually. 'With the Free French. And they seem to rather like him. So we must assume he's mended his ways, or just pulled the wool over their eyes. I don't care. What does concern me is that the French are proposing to give him a *Croix de Guerre* for some feat of derring-do . . . sticking his thumb in a hole on one of their vin rouge barges, probably.' Max was wrong about that. The little shit had served aboard a T-boat before he went to the French; with some distinction too. The Bonny Boy had always kept a weather eye out on young Gilmour's progress through the trade. But he didn't want to let Max know that.

'I don't care,' continued Max, 'I just don't want us to be seen trying to put him up against a wall while the French are trying to garland him in glory. It wouldn't make us look good. But as you're prepared to let bygones be bygones, then it doesn't arise.'

Max paused again, daring his man to challenge him.

When he didn't, Max said, 'Good man, Charles. I can always depend on you to do the right thing. Carry on. I've got to dash.'

Author's Note

It is true that a substantial quantity of France's gold reserves ended up on the island colony of Martinique. In May 1940, in order to save it from German occupation, the French Navy light cruiser *Émile Bertin* had sailed from Brest carrying the reserves. She eventually unloaded at Fort-de-France, where the gold ended up at the centre of a prolonged and rather convoluted intrigue involving the British, American and Free French governments. That story, thankfully, has no bearing on the tale just told.

That French submarines were fitted with a special tank to carry their vin rouge ration is also true. Anyone who wants to learn more about the life of a Royal Navy Liaison Officer serving aboard Free French submarines should read the memoirs of Sub. Lt. Ruari McLean RNVR (Rtd.), entitled *Half Seas Under*, published in 2001. It is excellent!

Acknowledgements

My thanks again to Captain Iain D. Arthur OBE RN, a former Captain (S), Devonport, who has acted as my technical adviser. Where I get it right, it's down to him. Where I've got it wrong, I wasn't listening.

About the Author

 David Black is a former Fleet Street journalist and television documentary producer. He spent much of his childhood a short walk from the Royal Navy Submarine Memorial at Lazaretto Point on the Firth of Clyde, and he grew up watching the passage of both US and Royal Navy submarines in and out of the Firth's bases at Holy Loch and Faslane. As a boy, the lives of those underwater warriors captured his imagination. When he grew up, he discovered the truth was even more epic, and so followed the inspiration for his fictional submariner, Harry Gilmour, and a series of novels about his adventures across World War Two. David Black is also the author of a non-fiction book, *Triad Takeover: A Terrifying Account of the Spread of Triad Crime in the West*. He lives in Argyll.